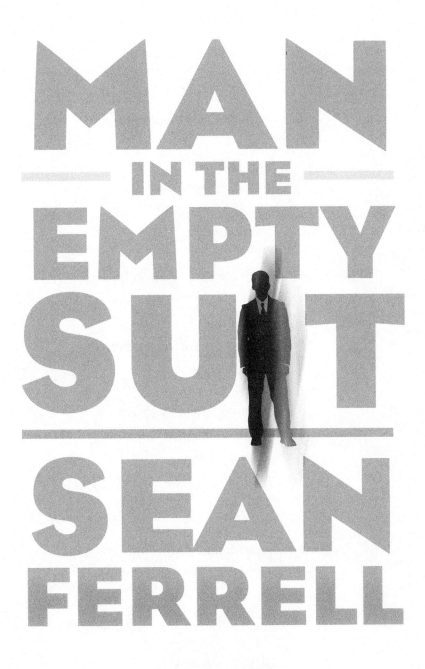

MAN
IN THE
EMPTY
SUIT

SEAN
FERRELL

SOHO

Published by
Soho Press, Inc.
853 Broadway
New York, NY 10003

Library of Congress Cataloging-in-Publication Data

Ferrell, Sean.
Man in the empty suit / Sean Ferrell.
p. cm.
ISBN 978-1-61695-125-2
eISBN 978-1-61695-126-9
1. Time travel—Fiction. 2. Identity (Psychology)—Fiction.
I. Title.
PS3606.E756M36 2013
813'.6—dc23   2012035254

Interior design by Janine Agro, Soho Press, Inc.
Interior art: 4 X 6 / iStockphoto

Printed in the United States of America

10 9 8 7 6 5 4 3 2 1

For Aidan

$$S = k.\, log\, W$$

CONVENTION RULES

1. Elders know best.

2. No guests.

3. If it broke before, let it break again.

4. Don't demand more information than an Elder is willing to give.

5. Nothing comes from nowhere: Don't expect something if you don't remember giving it.

6. No one is younger than the Inventor.

7. Stay below the third floor.

8. Try not to ruin the fun for the Youngsters.

9. Gambling makes no sense in the past tense.

10. Don't park in the same place twice.

11. Never reveal the future.

12. Act like you've been here before.

13. Don't expect anyone to be impressed.

14. Keep your promises.

15. Don't come back until you've aged a full year.

IT IS UNFORTUNATE for me that I am, by most any objective measure, a genius.

I was forced to realize just how unfortunate on my thirty-ninth birthday. As had been my custom for nineteen years, I arrived at the Boltzmann Hotel in Manhattan on April 1, 2071. One hundred years earlier, across town at New York Medical Center, lay my mother, lightning flashing outside the single window in her gray cube of a hospital room as I kicked and refused to come out. Later, in my twenty-sixth or twenty-seventh subjective year, while horribly, inevitably drunk, I paid a visit to the hospital on the night of my birth in 1971. I'd stolen an orderly's uniform and faked my way through the halls, arms filled with bedpans, until I found the maternity ward. There she'd been, my mother, younger than I could ever remember, screaming and sweating. Inside her was me, preborn me, nascent genius (by objective standards, not mine), stuck on her pelvis and grinding my head into her spine.

She never saw me. I left after placing a bedpan on the floor—the doctor had to trip on it, fall headfirst against the bathroom doorknob, and spend the rest of the night concussed and vomiting. He had to be replaced by an intern and a near-retirement nurse who knew more than all the rest of us present, who took hold of me and pulled me into the world despite all my objections. I knew this from many tellings of "The Night You Were Born." So I left the bedpan for the doctor.

That was the only year of my time-traveling life when I spent my birthday anywhere other than the Boltzmann. It was the year I stopped serving drinks to myself from behind the bar and focused instead on the drinking of them before it.

As I traveled, I counted my days. When another 365 had passed for me—subjectively, not objectively; objective time and I stopped talking years ago—I would direct the raft back to April 1, 2071. I would dock in the city at easily recalled locations—the mouth of the Holland Tunnel, the mayor's Gracie Mansion bedroom, beside the Astor Place "cube" statue, atop the Empire State Building's observation deck—and then walked directly to the Boltzmann. These places would echo with my footsteps, silence sealing in around me as the raft cooled and lost the pop and crackle of heated filaments and nearly burned-out wiring. In parking, my focus was making the raft easy to find. My celebrations were cloudier each year, and by my thirty-ninth subjective birthday, the possibility of entirely forgetting where I was parked and being stuck in the vacant city seemed very real. Sometimes I left chalk arrows on walls, signed with my age, pointing me back to where I'd left the machine. I could also follow my own footprints in the ever-present mud—a mix of the constant rain and the slow demise of the city's concrete and stone. The city in 2071 is full of good parking places. Just one subjective year earlier, when I was thirty-eight, I had parked inside what was left of Lincoln Center. It resembled a rookery, flocking with parrots, their inane chatter filling the darkness with conversations echoing Playbill notes and intermission critiques of performances ended decades earlier. Manhattan had become a parrot's island. I'd parked at Lincoln Center with Isadora Duncan in mind, a sentimental ode—I'd just left her in 1927—but upon returning to the raft, I'd found it covered in bird droppings. Lesson learned.

This time I parked in the dried-out bowl of Central Park's Pond. My machine winked in about four inches above the brown-clay mud bottom and then slid slightly lower into the septic water. I swore softly, but there was no finding a better spot. Once landed, the raft took nearly a full twenty-four hours to run again, and so parking was always cautious guesswork seasoned with a rush of panic. I powered the raft down, muttering to myself about the stupidity of choosing such a spot in a rainstorm. None of the drug dealers doing business in the bushes around me said anything. People willing to brave the storm to hang out in Central Park weren't the sort to talk about seeing a shuddering metallic platform appear in midair. I took my time covering the raft with a blue tarp and left the park, guided by familiar lightning flashes, one ear perked for parrot conversations.

I could take my time, and did, spoke loudly to myself as I walked. No one would mind. No one would hear. I'd seen few people on the streets on my first trip to that date, and I saw fewer with every visit. Buildings lurked, dark and empty. Electricity worked sporadically at best, rising and falling as if with a tidal pull. The hotel I'd made my base was abandoned, rotting and rotted, and I'd never seen a soul other than myself near it.

Exiting the park, I slipped in some mud, landing hard. I didn't mind. My coveralls were always filthy. I'd recently been on the raft for twenty-three days straight during a cool September, docked in a fir tree in the Teutoburg Forest in the first century, waiting to see Germanic tribes battle Roman soldiers. I had grown sticky with sap, camouflaged with dirt and needles. I'd nearly given up after two weeks, when a small group of Romans, sick with dysentery, filthy as rats and rank as shit, finally staggered into view and built a camp. They were slaughtered a week later, in the middle of the night by some hunters while I slept, their skulls left nailed to the nearby trees, including one directly below me. History books yet again proved how far off the mark they could be.

I found a subway entrance near Times Square and descended to the train platform. The station, lit somewhat strobingly, echoed with my steps. I was alone and cold in my nudity as I peeled away the filthy coveralls. In one pocket I found my two flasks, one for business and one for pleasure. This was time for business, and I opened it and poured water onto a rag. I cleaned my body as best I could. The water lasted only a little while, the rag slightly longer before it ended up tossed onto the tracks. I didn't feel clean, but I could pretend I looked it. Thoroughly frozen now, I rubbed my skin dry with my palms and then pulled my new clothes out of my travel bag: a suit, the Suit. At last my turn to wallow in the shit of self-adoration.

Nineteen years felt like a long time to wait to finally become yourself. Since my first visit to the hotel, my wardrobe had been a means of understanding events, framing them, and of differentiating. I recognized versions of myself based on what they wore. This me was Turtleneck, that one Ugly Tie. Yellow Sweater. Spats. Hanfu. Toga. No matter when I came from, I tried to look my best. Most impressive of all was the Suit. Simple, black, foreboding. I had longed to wear the Suit since the first time I'd seen myself in it, longed to be the type of person who had such confidence and focus, someone above the fray. Every year the entire party—all my selves—paused in respect when the Suit made the Entrance into the ballroom. All my other visits to the party were tainted. I always tried too hard to be the center of attention, even with myself. Especially with myself. But the Suit was beyond that; everyone paid attention to him without any effort on his part at all. A few times I tried to get close to him, to get a sense of when I might be him, but I had never been able to get his attention. It was as if he were attending a party to which no one else was invited.

In the meantime I'd browsed shop windows in many eras. I would know the suit when I saw it, I told myself. Patience— overrated, useless, relative—was not something I enjoyed. But the Suit was older than me, so I'd be him eventually. He'd been far older at one point, but I was gaining. As the subjective years passed and I realized that the gray in my hair began to match his, I grew to be more of a fatalist in my shopping. I would find the suit, I assumed. I didn't need to put effort into the search.

Drinking helped. During a bender through the 1960s, I woke in Chicago near Soldier Field. I found a note pinned to my sleeve reminding me that the raft was on a docked barge on Lake Michigan, due to leave at noon. In my hurry to the docks, I nearly rushed past a men's clothing store. In the window, on a headless mannequin, stood the suit. I hadn't even needed to alter it; it fit as though it had been made for me. My turn had come. This year I would be the Suit, and I would make the Entrance. I mulled over a dozen memories of watching myself make the Entrance from my earlier per-spectives—sitting around small tables in the Boltzmann ball-room drinking scotch, tequila, even—God help me, just that once—a wine spritzer, when the Suit walked in, powerful, impervious. I think the Suit may be one of the only reasons I kept returning. He promised, in a way so smart and casually expensive, that I would "make it."

Now, on the night of the Entrance, I stood on the subway platform and wondered when to arrive. I checked my watch—my own design, eight hands spinning at various speeds to show both objective and subjective time, from years to sec-onds, laid upon a face that would never be the same twice. I was actually early for the gathering, which seemed strange. In my memories the Suit arrived late, made a dramatic entrance.

I wondered how I was going to kill time, at least a few hours. Despite the suit, I was exhausted and too long drin-kless. I felt no different than I had prior to putting it on. Disappointing. I hesitated but went for my flask anyway. A toast to the suit. Two. I stopped there, since I remembered the Suit had not been drunk when he arrived. I would look sharp, polished, and focused on my way to the ballroom bar. I walked slow; the liquor had made me feel better, more relaxed. I knew how these things worked; I trusted fate would deliver me at the right moment by presenting some unexpected obstacle to delay me.

Port Authority Terminal—redundant stairs, inexplicable turns, and filthy dead ends—had a tunnel entrance to the Boltzmann. Rainwater leaked through the ceiling and ran down walls, pooled at the bottoms of stairs where so much runoff had collected over the years that stalagmite stone grew black-gray on lower steps. I broke the first rule of feeling secure in the subway: Don't look at the ceiling. I walked faster.

I reached the final turn before the entrance and paused, lurked behind girders. Shadows moved around me. Behind a garbage can. Beside a maintenance-closet door. Someone held the tattered remains of a Radio City Music Hall advertisement in front of his face as he skulked along the wall. These were other versions of myself, obviously older, as I had no memory of having hidden in those places. I made a mental note to remember to use those hideouts in my future, when I would be those paranoid, shadowy figures. Despite never seeing another soul near the hotel, I was annually embarrassed to be seen coming in, as if someone might notice the same man in an array of outmoded outfits—what amounted to a tacky historical fashion show—and wonder why his lapels were so wide or when the cape had come back in. None of me would be able to explain that.

My poster-carrying self made a break for it and charged the hotel's entrance, shedding flecks of old glue. I took this as my opportunity and stepped out from behind the girder, hands in pockets. I was the Suit, trying to be casual. I passed through the revolving door. The poster bearer, only slightly older than me, stood on the other side, brushing glue from his hands. On the dark granite floor lay his discarded Rockettes poster, beautiful legs kicking in a wrinkled heap. We nodded amiably at each other.

I gestured over my shoulder at the shadows behind girders and garbage cans. "Should we wait for a few more of them and enter together?"

"No, I don't think so. We get a little more scared every year, don't we? A little more cautious? They might be out there an hour."

I nodded. He was dressed in a simple white shirt and a knitted sweater-vest. Unimpressive, I thought, compared to my suit. He wore a short, carefully maintained beard, one some Elders wore at various lengths, and his hair was neat and recently trimmed. I regretted not getting a trim myself, though I hadn't yet made up my mind on growing the beard. I was still unsure of what it did for me, but apparently someday I would decide it was a good idea.

He looked me up and down. "I did love that suit."

"Thanks. What happens to it?" I asked, knowing he wouldn't answer. That was against the rules, too.

He half smiled. "You'd really rather not know." He climbed the stairs into the hotel's basement entrance. "Let's go."

I took one last look at the figures hiding in the shadows outside the revolving door's thick glass, then followed his clicking soles up the stairs.

The elevator was waiting for us; it would break later in the evening. It was an old, wood-paneled box with a metal cage pull door, and it looked more like a kitchen entrance than an elevator. In a couple hours, there would hang a sign on the door that read, in my handwriting, *Out of Order*. It was this sign that made the subway entrance so crowded. To be late meant a rain-soaked arrival through the lobby entrance.

We climbed in. He pressed the button and watched me take my flask from my pocket.

I tilted the top toward him and said, "Cheers." He smiled and nodded. He produced no flask of his own. "Did you forget this?" I asked, shaking the suddenly-too-empty flask to hear its contents slosh. It had been a gift to myself, liberated off the body of a Union soldier at Gettysburg.

"No, I didn't forget it. Just didn't bring it."

"Have a hit off mine, then." Mine was his. Sharing it was no different from taking two drinks. I didn't even mind the backwash. Just spit that my mouth hadn't made yet.

"No thanks. Believe it or not, I'm trying to quit."

I laughed and took a swig. "Good luck with that." He knew as well as I what some of our older selves were like. The one that was the worst—the Drunk—made such a spectacle of himself that he drew attention away from the simpler drunks, the ones who merely spilled and swore as they struggled with their zippers in the bathroom. Without the Drunk around, any of them might have looked up at the barrel's bottom. A chill ran through me as I realized that after my evening as the Suit, all I had to look forward to was thrashing about as the Drunk.

The elevator rattled as it rose. We passed the lobby, then the second floor. "Damn, what's happened?" I reached out and pressed the L button hard. "Did you hit the right button?"

He stood at the back of the elevator, behind me. His voice was quiet as he said, "I thought I did."

The hand of the dial over the door crawled clockwise past floor after decrepit floor. The Boltzmann had been old when people still walked the streets of the city, and after its abandonment it had suffered a slow degradation. The elevator buttons didn't illuminate, and to my left was a pale section of paneling where a conductor's coat had brushed for so many years that it left the wood polished and faded.

I said, "Wonder where we're headed."

"Only so many choices."

The uneven ride was pierced by irregular cable twangs and metal clangs. The sound was exciting, unnerving. My hours and days were usually filled with nothing but the hum and throb of the raft's quiet engine. Even the raucous music of a possible plummet was a nice change. As we reached the twenty-third and last floor, there were several violent shudders. I looked at my companion. He wore the calm smile of foreknowledge.

I pointed a finger at him, uncapped my flask again, and took a drink. "You could have warned me that we'd miss our floor."

"Would it have changed anything if I had? We still needed to get into the elevator. The fact that I know how the ride turns out, and the fact that you're frightened, doesn't remove that need."

"Awful self-centered of you."

"And you." He gave me the smug grin that I knew so well. It was a gift I hated to receive but gave so often.

At last the elevator shook to a stop. On the other side of the door's dark window, a few flashes of lightning streaked across a bare wall. I looked up at the dial. "We're at the penthouse."

"Let's have our look."

Thunder shook the building. "We get out?" One convention rule I never broke was number seven: Stay below the third floor.

"We do." He pulled back the gate and stepped into a dark hallway. He didn't wait for me, and the elevator door swung shut behind him, leaving me alone.

I looked at my watch. Still time to kill before my entrance to the ballroom. Following Sober into the suite was probably what delayed me, I thought. More thunder shook the elevator. I dreaded seeing the suite. None of the younger versions of myself who had visited the hotel over the years had ventured above the decayed building's second floor. There were any number of reasons not to go. The roof obviously leaked, floors were rotten, and walls and ceilings gave way without warning. Sprawling, rust-colored maps had drawn themselves on the ceiling in the entrance, the lobby, the halls. Part of the third floor ran with water an inch deep, which was why I'd made the rule prohibiting further exploration. It was dangerous.

I opened the door and followed him.

The penthouse, dark except for lightning, was littered with ghostlike shapes of furniture in sheets. I was surprised by the lack of damage to the room. My older self watched rain pelt the city, his arms crossed, by himself even though I stood behind him, and I wondered if it had really been so important that I come here with him. The moment seemed his alone. I wondered what he might be thinking. In a flash of lightning,

I spotted a mark on Sober's wrist, a tattoo. Another flash confirmed what I worried it was: a parrot, wings stretched in flight.

I had no plans to deface my body with a picture of a parrot—rats in drag. "Why do I do that?"

His eyes fell to his own wrist, and a sadness I could almost smell rolled off him. "You'll know the moment you decide to do it yourself." He looked up at me, sympathy in his eyes. It was worse than sympathy. It was pity. Pity for my ignorance. I felt a shameful burst of hatred for the superior position he held by having already been me, for his arrogance in pretending he'd victoriously claimed the high ground, for his assumption that aging is earning.

Sometimes the urge to strike myself was almost too much. I shook my head and pulled out my flask. I would refill it upon my dramatic entrance.

We haunted the penthouse for a few silent minutes, him watching the horizon, me pulling back sheets to reveal cheap furniture dolled up to look expensive.

"What are we doing here?" I asked.

"Enjoying the view, I think," he said. "We might be a few minutes late, but we already know what sorts of events to expect, right?" He looked at my suit. "You must be ready for the Big Entrance."

There was no denying it to him. I blushed in the dark.

"Don't worry. You still make it. I'm probably the reason you make it later than you thought you would."

"Oh, of course." I feigned comfort. "I wondered what would occupy me for . . . what? Another hour?" I watched lights twinkle through the drops of rain on the window.

They quivered in the wind. All identical but separate, able to coalesce at an instant of contact. I was reminded of my separate selves downstairs.

A crash of thunder hit especially close, and Sober shifted in the dark, turned away from me. "You'll excuse me for a moment. That's my cue to explore the other rooms."

As he disappeared into the dark, I watched neighborhood buildings flash in and out of sight. The city was an empty cemetery, markers over unoccupied graves. Was I really too lazy to make more trips through the recent past to see what had caused New York's abandonment? Was I really so self-centered that I could handle only this one night? I'd seen this same lightning storm many times, but never from this height. I took a deep breath, suddenly looked forward to revisiting this moment when I became Sober, and before I exhaled, I felt guilt at having despised him for simply being older.

Thunderous echoes chased one another between the buildings. Beneath them chattered a mechanical rattle. I turned my head to listen. When I realized that the rattle came from behind me, not outside, it was too late. The elevator had descended.

Back to the elevator, tripping on furniture in the dark. Unseen glass smashed against the floor, and I crunched shards under my heels. I stumbled through the dark hallway, felt along the walls until I found the door to the missing elevator. I held on to it, suddenly needing the support, and listened to the grinding descent. I felt angry. Worse, I felt mocked. To be abandoned, in some sort of joke. I'd never played practical jokes on myself before. There was no point. I played a joke either on a Youngster, making myself a past victim, or on an Elder, which was impossible because I could not trap memory.

As I wondered at Sober's reasons, the elevator cables sang. Gears slowed, then stopped. I pressed my face to the elevator window and saw the car lights three floors below me. Above me, in the elevator's main motor, rose a whine. Cables slipped, but the elevator stuck. Rather than stop, the motor groaned. The car's lights flickered. An alarm sounded somewhere above me, a jarring bell. It started, stopped, then sounded again briefly, as if stuttering.

I called down to myself. "Hello?" There was no answer. My anger rose. "Hope you're happy now." No reason to leave me here, but at least I wasn't trapped in the car with him. It occurred to me that my future self might have left me here so we wouldn't both be stuck in the elevator. He might, in fact, have been saving the Entrance. But why not tell me this would happen? Elders loved keeping secrets. One more sign of the Elders' superiority issues. I dismissed the fact that I would eventually inhabit those issues. Every single one.

I yelled, "Listen, I'll head down the stairs and get help."

Still no answer.

I looked around the hallway. My eyes had barely adjusted to the dark. Besides the penthouse entrance, there were two doors; I opened the first and reached gingerly into the absolute black depth. It was a service closet. I felt along the wall toward the other door: the stairway. Low light bounced along the walls, reflected from farther down the stairs. Hushed voices echoed and layered over one another into a chorus of whispers.

I called out. "Hello?" Something flickered at my feet. I reached down and found my own multiarmed clock, same as the one pinned to my lapel. I tried to read it in the dim light. Behind me something in the elevator motor let out a spark and an echoing report like a gunshot.

I returned to the elevator. "Hello?" I called down again. Still no answer. Below, in the shaft, the elevator lights seemed farther away. Something burned. Smoke wafted from the shaft, and the motor's whine grew louder.

"Is everything all right?" I shouted, pounding on the door. I watched the lights fall away and felt my stomach drop, as if it were I who flew upward rather than my counterpart descending.

I might have shouted a silly threat. I turned back toward the stairway. Whatever low light previously lit the stairs had disappeared. I felt forward with feet and hands and located the top step. Slipping one foot to the edge of each step, I toed my way down the stairs—twelve steps to the landing—negotiated the turn, then counted steps to the next floor. Twelve again. Twelve steps, landing, twelve, landing, and so on. By the fifth floor, I was flying down the steps in the dark, counting out loud to myself as I went. My heart raced, even though I knew I would find nothing at the bottom. This convention had dozens of my selves in attendance. The one who'd deserted me would disappear into the crowd. In the dark, all I had were phosphene trails of elevator lights that dropped away from me toward a single, brilliant point.

At the second floor, excited voices vibrated through the door. I tried the knob and found it locked. I hammered a fist against the gray metal. It opened, and bright hallway lights blinded me. Three silhouettes moved around me, spoke in my voice.

The one nearest me said, "Here you are. I don't remember it taking you so long to get down those stairs."

I shielded my eyes. "Takes a while in the dark. Had to memorize the step count."

"Twelve-landing-twelve."

This one was older than me, but not by much. Shaved head, plain white dress shirt.

"We're wasting time reminiscing." One in a canary yellow sweater glared at me. "Is the elevator here?"

"Yes, it's here." This voice was far older. I was able to see now, not well, but enough to know that ahead of me, holding on to the wall for support, was a seventy-year-old man. His hair was white and cut short. He wore a simple black suit and looked like a minister. He was, of course, me. "I'm afraid it's not good."

The other three moved away from me and looked through the elevator grate.

"Oh, God," said the one in the yellow sweater. The other two remained silent. I stayed where I was, unable to think of anything other than what I would say when Sober exited the elevator. He was taking a long time about it.

"Are you all right?" the one in the white shirt asked me.

"I need a drink," I said. I pulled out my flask and tipped it back. When I lowered it, they were all staring at me. I held it up, almost like an offering, but none of them took it.

I asked, "What the hell is everyone staring at?"

Yellow, a whiff of that same pity that Sober had around him, said, "You haven't seen this yet."

I didn't want to see. I walked toward him.

On the elevator floor lay Sober. His eyes were open, legs

crumpled beneath him and his arms awkwardly twisted. A gash ran across his right temple.

I covered my mouth and felt a jolt run up my spine. I needed to sit down. More important, I needed more drink. Murmurs from the others:

"Oh, God."

"Open the grate."

"It's stuck."

The one in the white shirt, head shaved and irregular stubble across his chin, pulled a screwdriver from his pocket and worked at the gate's latch. His eyes looked dulled, as if he could take in only so much and that limit had been reached long ago.

Seventy held out a hand. "He's dead. We all remember too well."

"That's not possible."

The old man's rheumy eyes watered at me. "Welcome to the secret club of the convention, boy. Now you know. This is where you die."

The hall shrank to a circle of light only as big as a watch face, and I went deaf for a moment. The others waited.

"How can he be dead?"

Seventy cleared his throat, shifted his cane from hand to hand. "That's the problem. How. We don't—"

"Don't say you don't know. I'll just come back early and watch the corners, the penthouse. We were in the penthouse."

Screwdriver finally popped the latch. "We know where you were. We've watched it. He gets in the elevator, alone and alive."

Yellow, still leaning on the wall, eyes ricocheting back and forth, barely withheld a laugh. "You watched it? When? I never watched anything."

"Since past you, obviously." Seventy studied my face. "We've tried watching the elevator, the penthouse. Each time he just climbs in, no problems. It's down here we find him dead. Short of getting into the elevator with him, we don't know what to do, and if we do that. . . ."

I nodded. I'd learned the hard way about the uselessness of interrupting past events.

I said, "So you all . . . all the Elders. . . ."

Seventy nodded. "Everyone older than you knows. And we're all fucking stumped."

Screwdriver started to lift the Body. "And it's up to you."

"What?" I decided I hadn't heard him right.

Seventy waved a hand. "Put that body down. We haven't shown him everything yet." He smiled sadly at me. "Listen. It's on you now. You've got to look into this."

"Why me?"

"Because he's your next visit here. We haven't been able to figure this out. And if you don't. . . ."

We all looked down at the Body. His beard looked more unruly than I recalled, and his face was dirtier than I could imagine myself becoming. He looked haggard and used up in a way that he hadn't when he'd been Sober.

Seventy nodded. "We'll help. But this is, at a certain point. . . ."

"My problem." I nodded back.

Screwdriver said to Seventy, "Do you want to show him?"

Yellow scowled. "Show him what?"

Seventy nodded. "Yeah, go ahead."

As Yellow and I waited in confusion, Screwdriver knelt beside the Body and pulled back his shirt. A deep purple-black bruise beneath his ribs stared at me. Wide splatters of blackish blood dried around it.

"What's that?" I asked.

Seventy yawned. "Hematoma. He may have fallen or been pushed. Beaten. Returned to the elevator, somehow, while it descended. The gash on his temple is a ruse. Someone tried to play us for fools."

I pointed at the bruise but didn't know what to say about it. It seemed to grow as I looked at it. My hand dropped. "One of us is trying to fool us?"

Seventy nodded. "Either we're fools for thinking they meant to trick us or he, whoever he is, is for thinking it would work."

Yellow said, "That doesn't make any sense."

"Yes it does," Screwdriver said, standing again, hands in pockets and eyes on the Body. "But it will take you about six months to realize it."

Yellow's eyes sparked, then clouded over. "You would know." This was the ultimate Youngster putdown, often taking the place of an ill-advised "fuck you."

Screwdriver grinned hollowly. "Show some respect." His eyes never left the Body.

We stood in a loose ring near the elevator door and watched the Body as if he might sit up and tell us what had happened. His expensive vest looked more wrinkled than I'd remembered, his clothes more ill-fitting than dapper. He seemed poorly dressed, in fact. The single light of the elevator began to spark and blink. I heard water trickle from somewhere above the car, probably from a leak at the top of the shaft. Decay blossoms without our efforts. The electrical short emitted an insect buzz and a smoky copper smell. Seventy and Screwdriver looked at me and smiled. I tried hard not to show emotion at the convention—both Elders and Youngsters interpreted emotion as weakness—but these two smiled without hesitation, and I feared and admired it.

Seventy, eyes hectic in the strobing light, said, "I don't envy your pursuit. If you fail, I'll never know, as I just won't be. But you'll know, because you'll end up lying here in this filthy elevator."

I REMEMBER BREAKING my nose. I'd come to the party a few weeks early, not yet thirty-seven but needing to wipe the late Tang dynasty from memory. I wandered the Boltzmann that year in a misty haze I'd carried from ninth-century China, where I'd been having a ruinous affair with a poet. I could still smell Chang'an on my silk robes, still hear the chatter of its full streets, merchants and servants debating the value of porcelain and grain.

Things hadn't ended well. I sought refuge in a crowd of myself. Of course, I found none, no compassion, no support. So I wandered the hotel, not eating, drinking too much, and ignoring the stares of Elders and Youngsters alike.

I should have known that nothing good would come of arriving to the party ahead of time. By early in the evening, I was sick. Youngsters chanted as I vomited in a toilet. I swore at them in Middle Chinese. As I left the lobby restroom, inebriation still unable to chase away the sound of the Wei River rushing through my head, I tripped over ceramic plates piled imprudently outside the men's room. I fell forward, smashed my face into a nearby table, and broke my nose. Blood everywhere. I lay down as Elders brought towels and ice. They'd been prepared for my fall but not prepared to stop it.

"Don't worry about this," yelled one, crooked Elder voice from the hall. "I can barely remember it." Then laughter. A loud, braying, drunk laugh.

A subjective year later, I found myself waiting in line at the men's room. Chang'an was finally fading. Ahead of me several Elders in their fifties talked quietly among themselves. They looked over their shoulders at me, as if I were trying to listen in, which I was, and as if I had no right to know of what they spoke, which I may not have. That's beside the point. The point is they were acting strange, and conspiratorial, as all the Elders did. From my thirty-eight-year-old perspective, anyone older than forty seemed to be an oddball paranoiac. So I stood behind the gaggle of unhinged fifty-year-olds and watched them sweat bourbon and rye and scoop rice pilaf off of the cheap ceramic plates with their hands. Apparently, at some point in my forties, I would decide to eschew manners.

After fifteen minutes and a muted chant of "flush it, flush it," drunk Youngsters cleared out of the men's room. (As I grew older, I realized how much alcohol the Youngsters consumed and how little of their time at the party I really remembered.) One of the three Pilaf Brothers nudged the other two and pointed to the bathroom door. They gathered half-finished plates of pilaf, piled them together, and placed them on the floor by the door. They then began to skulk away, not even having used the restroom. I realized when I was. In a moment my previous self would exit the restroom and break his nose because the Pilaf Brothers had intentionally left their plates there.

I was left staring at the plates, and at a problem. I had made very deliberate choices while planning this gathering. Much thought had gone into avoiding outside interference, accidental self-interference, catering issues. One of my personal rules was "If it broke before, let it break again." I didn't double back upon myself outside the party for the same reason: Complications arise from chasing solutions. If I was meant to trip over the plates, I would. If I didn't, who knew how it might change things? This created a laid-back attitude among all my selves. None of us were really "in charge" and, for the most part, furniture, utensils, plates, glasses, and the old hotel itself were all abused with impunity. The sack of Carthage, which I'd seen during my travels, had been eerily similar.

My fate rested amid the almond-flavored rice. But breaking my nose had hurt. Really badly. And more than that, the lack of compassion I'd felt at the time had stung deep. I stood inches from the plates that in a moment would cause me great pain. If only I moved them—not far, a half foot would do. What could be the negative consequences? I wondered. How could an unbroken nose be a problem? It hadn't affected my travels. I hadn't done anything "because" of my nose, nor had I lost out on anything because of it. It had stopped hurting after ten days, and by the time I was baking bread in the 1960s in a finicky oven in a London flat with sad and lovely Sylvia, I could actually smell the bread. I now had a slight bump in my nose, but more than anything else what remained of the incident was the knowledge that I had deliberately caused myself the unnecessary pain and hadn't cared enough to save myself from it.

I could fix it, I decided. I moved the plates back from the doorway with my foot. They left a trail of grease, and I once again questioned my menu choices. I waited. Just as I wondered why I never used the ladies' room—there weren't any other guests, after all—my thirty-seven-year-old self stepped from the men's room and walked past the plates. His left foot tapped one, tipping cold rice pilaf onto the threadbare Persian carpet.

The accident avoided, I reached up to touch my nose.

Behind me the braying laugh began again and a voice shouted out, "I told you I could barely remember it." We all turned toward the voice. An Elder, past forty and very drunk, stood near a turn in the hallway, a wild look in his eye. The Drunk. His clothes—wet, black, filthy—clung to him. Another Elder with a shaved head and a white shirt held him up. The Drunk pulled at the other's hand, for support or in an effort to get away. Perhaps even he wasn't sure which.

For a moment I couldn't understand his comment. Then I remembered the same mocking shout when my nose had been broken. I'd just stopped my accident from occurring, and the Drunk had responded to his own joke. How could he refer to something that had no longer happened? I thought of the incident, of my moving of the plates.

"How can you know that?" I called to him. He pulled himself free of the other Elder and rounded the corner. I caught up with him in the ballroom as he tried to disappear into the crowd. I grabbed his shoulder. "How can you know?"

He looked at me with watering eyes and tapped his filthy temple. "It's as clear as day."

I thought again of the accident and remembered the fall, the striking of the table, the blinding pain, and suddenly choking on my blood. I felt my nose, the now-familiar bump that the break had left behind. I'd changed nothing for me. I'd changed it for my younger self, who would now remember only striking something with his foot, turning to see rice on the floor, and wondering why I stood beside the plates with a silly grin on my face.

The Drunk laughed. "Not so easy, is it? Marrying two things that both can't be."

I nodded. "How's this possible?"

"You'll figure it out." His smile faded. "Or not." He stood before me like a post in the ground, steady and solid. He wasn't as drunk as I'd first thought. I, however, could use a drink. He said, "If you try to 'fix' anything in your past, you'll be like the guy who tries to fuck himself in the ass. It would feel great if it didn't hurt like a son of a bitch. You want to be sure of what happens; don't monkey around." He laughed at this and turned away. I remember I watched him disappear into the crowd.

HOW MANY BATTLES can you watch before the men rushing across the field remind you more of the grass that will grow there than of the men who will die there? How many important documents can you witness the signature of before all you see is the dust the paper becomes, the fate of faded ink, the ignorance of their forebears' suffering that future generations hold on to? My interests turned inward.

THE BODY'S RUIN haunted me. I walked the halls of the hotel with only one thing in mind: The main bar had a supply of twelve-year-old scotch. I checked my watch. Most of the scotch would be gone in about an hour. I hurried my pace. I pocketed the watch, then realized that it wasn't mine. Mine was on my lapel. This other had to be Sober's. A shudder ran through me. I couldn't take it out again to examine.

I turned a corner and found the hallway crowded beyond passage with myself. The congestion was a source of irritation in every convention memory. The hall felt as if it were shrinking. Against the tide I struggled toward the door no more than thirty feet away. Complaints from Youngsters rose out of the crowd as I knocked plates from hands, stepped on toes, and generally pissed everyone off. I swore to myself that I would never come this way again, and looking around me at the young faces, I realized I would keep that promise. So much youth. Why so many? I wondered. When had I returned so often? I tried to think back to last year but couldn't remember clearly whether there had been this many Youngsters. Party memories were a tinkling of ice in glasses, spilled liquor, fighting over the last scoop of pilaf. But I was almost certain I hadn't come to the convention that often. Something was off. Had I crossed myself too many times? Had I done something during a blackout? What had changed? Along the back of my mind snuck images of the Body, crumpled at the bottom of the elevator car. Could what had happened in the elevator be related to why no one in this hallway was older than me? Impossible. A coincidence of geography. Elsewhere in the building were Seventy, Screwdriver, and Yellow, all older than me. Others would be here, had to be—I'd only not seen them yet. Right then I needed to see some Elders, even though I hated what they told me of myself. The flab, the laziness, the lack of upkeep—the proof of life. I needed to see them, and I needed to collect my thoughts, find a place to breathe and figure out my next step. That meant the ballroom bar.

At the ballroom entrance, I found a wall of Youngsters fixated on the details of one's trip through Roman orgies—lies, I knew, not that knowing the truth made the telling of tales any less titillating. I fought through the mass, managed one final boost by launching myself from someone's calf. This brought back memories of the mysterious charley horse I had carried for the rest of the night during my twenty-third year. Though the apology wouldn't be remembered, I offered one over my shoulder and opened the ballroom doors.

In the ballroom half the chandeliers were burned out. The

uneven power supply turned the remaining bulbs orange and cast an ill light over the room. No one had switched on the music yet. On the dance floor, Youngsters ran in sloppy circles, throwing pretzels and ice cubes at one another. I avoided them and walked across the carpeted area in purposeful strides. No one here younger than me knew about the elevator. Even now Yellow and Screwdriver were putting OUT OF ORDER signs on the subway level. Latecomers would be making rain-soaked entrances from this moment on.

I reached the bar, an ugly scene. When I was a Youngster, the idea of tending bar had held some romantic appeal. For the three years before I turned twenty-four, I worked behind the bar, each of me pouring one for the customers, one for ourselves. Over the years, as I grew to appreciate the customer's perspective more, I realized what an annoyance the three brats behind the bar were, always snookered well before midnight. Those three years led to the evening's early lack of twelve-year-old scotch. Those three years also set a pretty heavy pattern in place, which is why so many of the Youngsters were beyond intolerable. Alcohol is a wonderful way to make a repeated evening seem fresh—details get lost in the fuzz, and the anticipated becomes a surprise. As a result I was less than clear on events from most Youngsters' perspectives, especially as the evening wore on.

I found a clear spot along the bar well away from anyone else. The Bar Brats were arguing about women from earlier epochs, and I knocked on the bar to get their attention. They all wore the same tuxedo, one obtained by the eldest of them and passed backward so that the youngest was the filthiest. He made his way down to me, his hand feeling along the inner edge of the bar, already with a good head start to a blistering hangover. I gave him my order.

His head tipped like that of a bird looking for worms. "Didn't I just give you one?"

Of course he had. He'd given me all sorts of drinks hours, minutes, moments ago.

I said, "No. You must have me confused with me. Get me something old."

"Something old?"

"Something aged." I studied the grain of the bar, thinking only of the elevator's rushing plunge. "I want to get drunk and enjoy it."

He shuffled off. "Really. I can't believe how all you old guys sound so much alike."

I couldn't recall how much of this was a joke and how much genuine inebriated confusion. The black haze in my memory was thick. Normally I would have tried to make a joke of it, reminded him that we were all "relatives," which I would have found doubly funny, from both his and my perspective, but at the moment I couldn't think of anything other than my drink. Before he returned with it, someone joined me at the bar.

"Nice suit, by the way."

Yellow sat beside me, chewing on his lips like he wanted to keep them from speaking. Before I could think to ask what he wanted, he pointed behind me. Over my shoulder at least a dozen younger selves sat around two tables, heads together, eyes on me. I recalled some particulars I'd whispered about the Suit around those tables. I'd made an impression like a superspy or a private eye on his way to meet a femme fatale. Distracted, I'd made the Entrance and hadn't even enjoyed it.

The Bar Brats gave Yellow ingratiating, professional smiles. Yellow shooed them off. "Remember, whatever you do, don't talk in front of Youngsters. They've got ears like bats and lips that wouldn't stay sealed even if you welded them shut."

"I remember."

He curled toward me, his voice hissed and hurried. Anyone paying attention would see he was bent low with secrets. "This is difficult for you, for us."

"You think?" I ran my finger around the rim of my glass until it sang. I didn't much care for Yellow. He was a bit too good at conspiring.

He said, "How can we still be here? It's very disturbing."

"You would know," I said curtly.

"Ah, yes. In other words, 'Go fuck yourself.'"

Yellow was agitated. I thought it seemed like he didn't want to be there, as if he were waiting for the next event, which he knew was more interesting or important.

I said, "Did you have something you wanted to tell me?"

He was staring past me, lost in thought. After a moment his eyes floated back toward mine. "What?"

I finished my drink too quickly and called the Brats for another. The three Youngsters tripped over one another to reach me, as if I had ever, or would ever, tip them for their services. One held the glass, another threw the ice, and the last poured. Some of the whiskey even reached the glass. I thanked them, and they chased one another to the other end of the bar, where they made a show of wiping glasses with a rag. I remembered that they would be whispering to one another about future sexual exploits they had misoverheard.

Yellow leaned in again. "I know some things don't need

to be said, but I'll say them anyway. All right? First, yes, he's dead." His eyes, locked on mine, didn't move or blink. "Second, yes, everyone older than you knows."

I sat upright and looked over my shoulder again. Beside two tables filled with chattering-bird youth were four other tables surrounded by ten chairs each, many filled with older selves either eating or talking. A low rumble of conversation echoed from the ceiling. I spotted faces turned toward me. I was being watched. Everyone older than me had recalled that I was having this conversation and had looked up to see how it was going or to relive the moment. Some deeply lined faces nodded at me. One nearly white-haired old man in a Pilgrim doublet and felt hat raised a hand with a thumbs-up for encouragement.

I turned back to Yellow and my drink, suddenly chilled. "What are they expecting me to do?"

Yellow ignored the question. He said, "How's your nose?"

"What?"

It must have been a line of thought I'd formed in my head years later. "Your nose. Broke it two years ago. Or did you?"

I rubbed the side of my nose, which had not but yet had been broken. I'd stopped the event, but the bump said otherwise.

I said, "Another paradox."

"Yes. You will die. In . . . what was he? Six months older than you? A year? Yet you obviously don't die, as you continue to come to this little wingding for years and years."

"Why keep coming? My God. How do I survive?"

"I can't say."

"Why the hell not?"

The Brats were polishing the bar suspiciously close to us. A reflective spot shone in the low light where one rubbed a rag in a lazy circle. The other two hovered over his shoulder, tried and failed to look interested in the cleaning. Both Yellow and I stopped talking and watched the Brats. When they realized we were onto them, all three coughed into fists and retreated.

I lowered my voice and repeated my question. "If I'm supposed to die but you know how to survive, why the hell not tell me?"

"Because I don't know. None of us do." He looked at my drink, almost reverent. "There's a large black spot, like a cloud, in our heads. I don't remember much of this party from the next few years."

"Why?"

Yellow stared past me, no pity in his eyes now, only disgust and judgment. "It's sitting beside me."

The answer sat on the stool on Yellow's other side. The Drunk. His odor was immense, a mix of alcohol and urine. He was one you didn't look at or talk to. He was given wide berth in the halls. The Drunk was avoided, misremembered, blamed. I looked at him closely for the first time in years and drew in a sharp breath, which I instantly regretted for the vapors rising from him. Several things I noticed surprised me. His clothes were the same suit I was wearing, redesigned by filth. Under his beard and grime, he wasn't as old as I'd always thought. He was young, barely older than me. Perhaps only a year or two older.

"God." I realized what Yellow was leading me to.

"Yes."

"He's the survivor?"

"And he doesn't remember a fucking thing. He's useless."

"So what happened? What creates the paradox?"

"Believe me, that's the major topic of discussion among everyone older than you. That and sex, the fucking perverts."

No stranger to self-judgment—especially regarding sex, particularly when engaged in the act, coupled or solo—I couldn't recall such strong admonition. I chanced a glance at Yellow's downturned mouth. "Does that lovely sweater come with a vow of celibacy?"

I'm sure he wanted to protest, but instead he waited for me to hold up a hand and mutter an apology. I offered it without feeling any genuine remorse, and both of us knew it.

Around the room the age clusters were very pronounced, as if a form of segregation were taking place. Everyone older than me drifted toward one side of the room, away from the door, near the empty stage where a single turntable played music—The Fifth Dimension, mostly. Elders took turns flipping the albums over when they reached the end. When I was in my twenties, the Elders had seemed decrepit, barely there and reeking of their inability to digest the food or drink properly, their clothes more and more worn, more repetitive. I'd avoided them, uncertain at what point I would cross that line into not caring how I presented myself, at what point not combing my hair or arriving in slept-in clothes became preferable to making even the smallest effort. Now, as I sat with Yellow, I was struck by how familiar—how comfortable—they had become.

At the other end clustered younger selves, who as of this moment all struck me as childish, even those in their thirties. Every table was covered with too many glasses of alcohol.

My life's drinking phases were plainly visible: There was my beer table, my fruity-mixed-drink stage. The table nearest me, around which some mid-thirty-year-olds sat, illustrated my current crutch. Straight liquor on the rocks. Glasses of diluted alcohol in shades of golden brown.

Yellow leaned closer to me. "Notice anything?"

It was easy to see now. Impossible to miss, really, and I wondered how it hadn't occurred to me before. Most everyone older than me was sober. There were a few drinks on a few tables here and there, but they could just as easily have been soda as anything hard. "There's very little conversation."

"Actually, there's quite a lot. But it's all the same. Constant speculation. Constant attempts to put the pieces together."

That there were so many Elders hinted at my potential success, but the tired, watery eyes, the skin patched with age spots, the bent backs and dry coughs that echoed my memories of my grandfather—these delivered a sense of inevitable failure. Regardless of outcome, my future was the chatter of birds in a graveyard, the worry of men mourning themselves, a conversation about their pursuits and failures, the sad and sadly sober discussion of my mortality. If there hadn't been one in my hand, I would have needed a drink. "What have we got so far?"

"Nothing other than that it's up to you."

"How many dozens of us, and that's all we've figured out?"

"You're the last one before it happens. When you come back next year, that's it. You're on one side of the event. We're on the other. We can speculate, but other than that. . . ."

"But surely you can tell me—"

"We've all discussed this quite a bit. I'm afraid we're going to have to follow our memories' lead and not let you know what we discussed. It might tip things."

My fingers tapped the bar. His, too, in the same impatient rhythm.

I said, "That fucking stinks." What a time for me to suddenly gain some backbone about my own rules. "So when it really matters, when death is on the line, you decide to stick your thumb in your mouth and suck?" A pack of teens howled past, one bumping into me. I reached behind me and pulled a sign off my back. Crude letters spelled LOSER. I crumpled it and tossed it on the bar. "Is it just me?" I asked. "Or were they younger than the Inventor?" It worried me.

Yellow looked after the group with the same concern I felt. "I don't know." I could tell he would be following up. "When it matters most is when rules need to be enforced most." Yellow looked at me with a straight face for a second and then laughed. "I know. Sounds trite."

I shook my head. "So where do I start?"

"Seventy told me to pass on one piece of advice. Keep an eye on that door."

His thumb jerked toward a door near the bar, one of the kitchen entrances. I tugged at my drink as Yellow shuffled out of his seat and patted me on the back. "Good luck."

"Yeah. Thanks." He was no help. "So I just sit here and stare at the door?"

He started walking toward the stage. The record was skipping, and with increasing panic the Fifth Dimension repeated a promise to fly up and away in a balloon. As I watched Yellow fiddle with the record player, the Drunk took his opportunity to slide one seat closer. By the time I realized he was moving in, it was too late. He had me. His silence and blank stare made me assume he was in the midst of a tremendous blackout. Once he was closer, his eyes regained some focus. He brought a very full glass with him and placed a hand over the mouth, then laid his head down on his hand, as if it were a pillow. I pretended not to see him.

"Not enough women at this thing."

I couldn't help but laugh. "I guess that's the truth."

The Drunk smiled up at me. "You have no idea what's coming."

"Do you?"

"I don't know." His eyes darkened, sobered for just a moment, and then they closed. When they reopened, they rolled as before. He pointed at the bottle of twelve-year-old whiskey, which was just within reach. "You'll want to refill the flask."

I took hold of the bottle. "You would know."

He chuckled at that. I was surprised at my own revulsion toward him. He was, of course, me. But I'd always stayed away from him, as if he were contagious. Even just the previous year when I'd spoken to him in the hall, it had taken effort. This puzzled me now. I could see through the beard, the dirt. It was my face.

I carefully poured scotch from bottle to flask. It sounded like someone urinating into a cup.

He closed his eyes. "Wake me when she gets here."

"What? Who?"

At that moment the door beside the bar opened, and in walked a woman. She was tall and pale, a tight red dress hugging her figure and revealing just enough of a tattoo that wound down her left arm—interlocking parrots, nesting, staring, raising their wings. They looked so alive I could practically hear their voices. Brown hair fell around the woman's face in large curls; green eyes ignored the room. I spilled whiskey over my hand and onto the bar.

The Brats scampered toward me. "Liquor spill, liquor spill." One of them shouted, "Lick her spiel," to the amusement of no one.

I put the bottle down and leaned back as the Brats swiped white towels. One knocked into the bottle, which almost toppled over. With deft ability another caught it against his wrist and righted it. They mopped up the spill and squeezed out the towels into tumblers.

I held my flask before me; whiskey dripped onto my suit, and I stared at the woman. Unsure of how I could have missed her during all my previous visits to the hotel, I watched the way she flowed around the tables. She was as incongruous as a flame in an ice cube. Around me packs of teens chased one another with cups of water and utensils. Card games sprouted here and there among the twenty-somethings. Their favorite was a memory game where a younger self sits with a deck, flips up one card after another as Elders try to recall the order. Everyone younger than me was occupied with self-amusement. It suddenly seemed like so much masturbation.

One of the Youngsters behind the bar held out a folded paper to me, soaked with whiskey, ink bleeding through. "Is this yours?"

I took it and read the message through the wet cover, words typed with a dying ribbon: *"If it's dark, I'm gone."*

"No," I said, and dropped it to the bar to float on the spilled liquor.

"Must be mine," muttered the Drunk, who fished it out of the tiny puddle and pocketed the note without bothering to read it, a desperate awkwardness in his grasp.

He was focused on the woman, and silent, as were all those older than me. I realized then that Elders had stationed themselves so that they could vicariously relive the vision. Smiles were sprinkled around the tables, and all conversation had ceased.

Seventy followed her into the room. His hand snaked under her tattooed arm and around her waist, comfortable, if somewhat arthritic, and he steered her to a septuagenarian-occupied table in the corner behind the bar. I wondered if I might have hired a nurse. Perhaps not a bad precaution.

The Drunk closed his eyes and sighed as if ready for sleep. "Check out the nose."

"What? Yes, it's very attractive."

"Not hers. Yours. Don't forget to check it out." He took his glass, a swirling mess of brownish gold and ice with a piece of napkin in it, splashed some at his mouth, and then stepped sloppily from his chair. "I gotta run. It's about to happen, and I want to see how it all goes if I don't do something about it."

I'd reclaimed my revulsion of him. He made no sense. Yellow was right. He was useless. After he'd stepped away from the bar, I looked for the woman. She sat at a table with two others, Seventy and one slightly younger, who watched her with wet eyes. She said something inaudible and reached out to stroke his arm. I did, in fact, look at her nose. It sat on her face in just the right place and at just the right angle. She turned back to Seventy. He leaned in close to her, and she gripped his wrist. At first I thought she was tickling his arm but finally realized they were looking at the place on his wrist where Sober had revealed a tattoo. The woman's eyes were dark and wet, and they seemed near tears. She nodded, he patted her arm, and then he pulled his cuff over what they'd been examining with such tender fingers.

When I could look away, I spotted the Drunk's glass, napkin bits floating inside. His mumbled exit replayed in my head. Drink lifted almost to my mouth, I froze. I was about to break and not break my nose outside the restroom. That must have been what he'd referred to. I rushed to cross the ballroom to the exit near the restrooms. I stopped halfway, turned in place, and wondered if I was really about to leave a room with a stunning woman I'd never seen before just so I could witness myself do something stupid. At a nearby table, an Elder in a double-breasted tailcoat with wide cuffs and a matching high collar of velvet, looking like a French aristocrat in a low-lit brothel, winked at me and said, "Don't worry, I'll watch her for you."

I knew he would.

Through the crowd beyond the doorway, I could see the Pilaf Brothers and the Nose Savior waiting in the line to the men's room. I stopped and watched. Pilaf Brothers, first one, then all three, turned to look at me and laughed, eyes full of serious recognition. I'd never noticed that all three of them wore slightly similar ponchos, like gauchos, one clearly still dusty from some South American trail, and I wondered if they rode around as some kind of trio. They put the plates down. They weren't casual. This wasn't pleasant. They were burdened by necessity, a gravity to what they did. The air quivered with it. Rice sprinkled the carpet like fleeing maggots.

They walked away, glanced at me over their shoulders, muttered Spanish floating through the air, and I watched now as my slightly younger self debated over the plates. All it would take was the subtle kick. Eyes locked on the sliced almonds on the floor. He was about to do it. For an instant I thought I ought to stop him. My nose would break again, but I would recall the act of stopping what had once happened. In essence I would have three true and parallel memories, and I could barely handle the two I had at the moment. I needed to debate this with someone. Where was the Drunk? All the other Elders were leaving me on my own, but he had been willing to give advice. Repulsive and helpful was better than nothing.

The Savior moved the plate aside. An instant later Nose, wrapped in his red-and-black hanfu, stepped from the bathroom and tripped lightly at the edge of the rug. He wasn't helped by his wooden sandals. Nose turned and looked over his shoulder. Savior watched him; recognition dawned that he'd spared only the break but not the memory of the pain. I watched his memory twin as he recalled both breaking and not breaking his nose.

At the other end of the hall, a cackle and a shout. "I told you I could barely remember it." The Drunk. I tried to see him through the swarming Youngsters, could make out only his back as he charged away through the crowd. He'd wanted me here. Something needed to be discovered. He wasn't simply giving tips, he worked toward a goal. Another game run by another Elder. I stepped forward. The Drunk had suggested I look at the nose. I took hold of Nose's shoulders.

"Pardon me?" He pulled back a moment, as if I weren't holding my own face, as if there were something untoward in holding oneself against a wall and grasping for a body part. His skin was slick with sweat, and he smelled like the toilet he'd just thrown up in. His eyes showed he'd been crying. I didn't recall that, ignored the reasons he might have cried and the reasons I would have forgotten.

"Let me see your nose a moment."

"Get your hands off me."

"I don't want to overstate things, but this could mean life or death."

He stopped moving, his head at an unnatural angle, a fly in a web, turning turning turning to keep my hands from a solid hold on his cheeks. "Who for?"

"You, eventually." The words came out smoothly, doubled by a new paradox I was forming. I was too aware that I hadn't done this before, too aware that Nose was supposed to be in the ballroom by now, holding a drink and laughing. My investigation was obviously going to be crossing earlier paths. I resigned myself to the fact that I'd be messing with my own head to a large degree. I'd have to learn to live with it. "Me, more immediately."

"What's happened?"

"You don't need details. Let me see your nose."

He held still in the awkward pose. I became distracted by the parrot pattern in the trim of his robe. I'd forgotten that detail. An inside joke between me and me. Behind me Savior watched, uncertain now whether he might have destroyed some major timeline as a result of moving the dish. He hadn't chased after the Drunk as I had when I'd been him. Another change.

I looked up Nose's nose. I examined both sides. "It's not broken."

"Why should it be?"

I turned in time to see Savior disappear into the bathroom, hand over his pale face. I rushed past the line after him, ignoring complaints and epithets.

Every stall, urinal, and sink was occupied, as was almost every inch of floor space. I didn't recall the bathrooms being so full, but of course I had begun avoiding the first-floor restrooms after my thirtieth year, probably just because of this. Youngsters stood shoulder to shoulder, some with drinks. The room smelled of urine and alcohol. A group of obviously young teens stood near the last stall, watching in awe as the over-twenty crowd drank and guffawed at unfunny inside jokes. Other than a lack of music, it was a club scene. Again I worried about why and how teens were there. More immediately, though, I had to reach Savior, who'd managed to sequester himself in the last stall. I followed him, stepped on my own feet several times, heard curses in dead languages I'd forgotten I had learned, and bumped into one elderly version of myself, paunched and pale, who patted my shoulder.

"Good luck. It's worth it, I think," he told me.

I gave a false smile and a nod. "You would know." I shoved my shoulder against the door, and the latch popped under my weight.

"What the hell? Get out of here."

I stood over Savior as my memory spiraled along a different path. When I'd been his age, I hadn't run to the bathroom. I'd followed the Drunk, headed to the bar, gotten a drink, even spent a moment talking to Nose. I could recall that this hadn't happened, even though the act was already done.

I pointed a finger at Savior, more accusingly than I'd intended. "Look, you didn't mean to do anything wrong. And you didn't. You just wanted to spare yourself a little pain."

"That's right. I just—"

"But it doesn't work. You've changed things. You'll start calling it a memory paradox soon enough." As I mentioned them, I ran through a list in my head of the things I'd seen so far that were different from my own memories. "It's like the kids being here."

"They shouldn't be here?"

"Did you come here as a kid?"

"Shit."

"Someone must have given them a ride, and they're here, and that's it."

"What if we—"

"Don't even think about trying to stop yourself from doing what you just did."

"Further complications?"

"Exactly."

"Shit." It was his mantra.

"Let me see your nose," I said.

"All right."

He was too stunned even to wonder why. I looked it over, and my own mind began to stir. I hadn't found what I'd expected. His nose was unbroken.

He watched my eyes as my hands fell to my sides. "Is it all right?"

"I don't know why, but yes."

"What's wrong with that? It's why I moved the plate."

"I know, but it didn't work for me."

"How come?"

I didn't know. "Shit," I said.

I stepped out of the stall. Youngsters toe-deep in urine tried to act nonchalant, failed, almost tripped in their attempts to follow me to a mirror. I leaned over the sink and examined my own nose. There, along the right side, was the bump and slight twist. Barely visible, but there. I felt it with both hands. My nose had been broken. When I'd been Savior's age and moved the plate, I hadn't spared myself anything. But this Savior had. Somehow he had been spared the break.

The mirror filled with my faces looking over my shoulder, puzzled or smiling, depending on where they fell ahead or behind me on the line of my life. Elders seemed to have arrived like tourists. Questions and admonitions to be quiet flowed around me. I kept my head tilted back and looked at the bridge of my once-broken nose.

One Elder—easily in his sixties, powdered wig and knee-high stockings speaking volumes of an ill-conceived trip through the eighteenth century—joined me at the sink. "Really far out, huh?"

I walked away from the sink. Savior called for me to stop, but I ignored him. Let the Dandy fill him in, or not. I needed to find Seventy.

I STRUGGLED TO get out of the bathroom. Youngsters called after me, demanding answers. Elders called good luck. Echoes of "You would know" bounced off the tiles.

I returned to the ballroom. The woman was gone. The table in the corner where she'd sat was vacant except for four dying drinks. One was a tall, milky tumbler that smelled of coffee. A Brown Russian? My lactose intolerance burbled at the thought. This had been her drink. The other three were watery whiskeys, which I poured together and drained in quick gulps. Coin-shaped ice pieces caught in my throat.

When the whiskey was gone, I took stock of the party. Tables were surrounded by me, in various stages of drink. Food was disappearing quickly. I finally noticed the acidic taste in my mouth; I hadn't eaten. A fist of hunger wrapped around my stomach.

I made my way to the buffet tables outside the ballroom. I

was nearly too late. Sterno warmed empty, sauce-crusted trays, and the hall stifled with chemical fumes and heat. I filled a plate with what remained of the tray of overcooked Swedish meatballs and found a basket of breadsticks near an overturned soup station. I couldn't recall getting to the food later than this. I made a mental note not to do so again and promised myself that next year I would hide a fork underneath the first table. I repeated the promise to myself several times. Occasionally this worked. Repeated promises sometimes stuck, and I sometimes kept them. I'd once managed to hide a half bottle of vodka in an empty planter for the Youngster who'd dreamed of finding one there. Still repeating my promise to leave myself utensils, I placed my food on the floor and crawled under the tablecloth.

Apparently my future self had remembered my wish and been benevolent. There was a serving bowl, rather large, and for a quick instant I hoped I'd had the foresight to put a roll under there, too. Pleased with myself, I lifted the bowl. Beside the fork and knife that I had hoped for lay a black revolver with a wooden handle, its barrel hole large enough to have an echo.

Crouched there in the dark with my utensils and firearm, I resolved never to emerge from underneath the tablecloth. I reached out blindly and felt for my plate but found someone's foot instead. Just beyond the tablecloth's hem stood a pair of highly polished shoes. They were handsome, much better than what I was currently wearing with my expensive suit. I recognized them as the pair I'd worn out last year.

Without meaning to I said, "Nice shoes."

"Thanks." The clatter of china. The other knelt down and

handed me my plate of coal-lump Swedish meatballs. It was Savior. "How goes it?"

"Fine," I lied. I put the bowl back over the gun.

"What are you doing under there?"

I shrugged. "You know. Getting away. It can be"—I waved nonspecifically—"out there, you know."

He nodded as if he understood. I was tipsy and could tell from his blurred eyes that he was, too. Had I done this back then? Had I found myself under a table? Even tipsy I think I would have remembered it. What changes were spiraling away from that unbroken nose?

"The whole nose incident," he said. "What was that all about?"

I shrugged again, as if to say, *How should I know?* or to imply that he should already know. I couldn't make him any more confused than I was myself. I wanted to say, *I have a gun.* Instead I said, "Look, I just want to eat these meatballs and be done with it." I lifted the fork from the floor and tried to spear one. Impervious to tines, the meatballs spun away, ricocheting around the plate.

"If there's something major happening, I can help."

"I know you mean well," I lied. We both knew that Savior was only in it for himself. He had created a huge paradox simply to avoid a broken nose, which I still had. I'd been selfish. He was selfish. Had been and was, the ends of my maturity spectrum, and I was probably lying to myself about where on that spectrum I fell now. So depressing it was funny. I smiled. "Nothing you can do because there's nothing *to* do. Everything's fine. I just . . . well, it's rather busy up there." I pointed toward the underside of the table.

Savior looked at me, his eyes inscrutable. "You would know."

I winced internally. "Yes, I guess I would. Perhaps I'll see you at the bar. I'll buy you a drink."

He nodded and stood. I was left with only his shoes. I felt a little pride in having picked them out. I'd always thought of myself as hastily put together—part of the reason I'd been so proud of the suit I now wore—but those shoes, they were the real deal.

He tapped one foot against a table leg. "See you at the bar, then. Enjoy the meatballs."

"Thanks."

I watched him disappear through a gap in the tablecloth, then pulled it back into place. The grayish orange light somehow seemed brighter filtered through the white tablecloth, which glowed as if charged. I lifted the serving dish.

The revolver still terrified me. The wooden handle, polished and clear of fingerprints—though I knew whose fingerprints ought to have been there—called for my palm. The black snub nose caught the low light and yawned at me. It wasn't as large as I first imagined but seemed larger than it needed to be. I picked it up, surprised by the serious weight of it, and turned it over in my hand. Fully loaded. Smell of oil.

I searched around me, wondering why I hadn't provided a note for myself. If I'd had time to plant a gun, I'd certainly had time to write a short message: *Here's a gun. You need to shoot X. Good hunting.* My mind bounced over the myriad options for who my target might be. I was already going to die in less than a year—what more could I be expected to do? I'd already created an even larger paradox with my nasal examination—all the swarming younger selves who'd witnessed my effort to get to Savior and Nose would have altered memories. And Savior himself, he was on a path I couldn't begin to predict. What had I done to him? I wondered about where he'd gone after leaving me here, under the table, and could recall only the entrance to the ballroom, staring through the open door and seeing a herd of children streak past, screams echoing in the great room. Paradoxes still unfolded, my actions too large to have a single, predictable effect. Reflections in a splashing puddle. I'd made my past fluid, kept a stable history from reaching me. Perhaps the gun was a promise from a fluid future. The Youngsters didn't have my nose. Did the Dandy? He was my Elder; he should have my nose, but I hadn't checked. Was I now outside their timeline? Perhaps I'd cut myself loose from what I had done and what I was to have done. And was the Body connected to the others anymore? Did he share my broken nose? I didn't care to follow the line that might connect me to him. Easier to imagine myself cut free from everyone here. Like an untethered boat, drifting on innumerable river currents.

I shoved the gun into my jacket pocket, smoothed it against my side, and shoveled Swedish meatballs into my mouth. Images of the Body haunted me. I would have to find it and search for the connection. I didn't want to.

When I crawled out from under the table, Yellow was looking for me, his face hard and red. "There you are."

"You don't remember my little hideaway?"

"You've got lots of little hideaways, you know. Have you been drinking?"

"Only to calm myself."

Yellow walked off, and I followed. If he truly didn't remember eating the meatballs under the table, he must not remember the gun either. I said, "You know, it seems like I'm a bit untethered."

"Untethered. Yes. Good word for it."

"You recall the sensation, then?"

He straightened, as if trying to make himself taller than me. "Of course. You've done something major to our past." I don't think I imagined the blame in his voice, and he refused to look at me.

We walked along the hall, away from the ballroom. "Given this some thought, I see."

"Yes," he said, condescending sneer flashing at me, and then, after a pause, "and I've been chatting with Seventy." I was starting to hate his sweater.

We went through a service entrance and took the back staircase, filthy with greasy handprints, up two flights. At the third-floor landing, Yellow held the door for me. "You'll have years to speculate about all of this." He avoided looking at me when he spoke. I smelled cleaning chemicals; the hallway outside the stairwell was dark. "Where are we?"

"Something I have to show you."

"Not again."

"Just go to the right. Second door."

I followed his directions, and he followed me. My jacket hung uneven from the gun's weight, and I tugged down on the opposite side. I passed the first door and approached the second, from which light fell through to the corridor's floor. Shadows moved and voices echoed. As I stepped into the doorway, I was blinded for a moment by the brightness. A ceiling fixture with three high-wattage bulbs and a cluster of floor lamps illuminated every corner. The room's windows were papered over, and rain lashed against them. Along the walls dozens of chairs were stacked one upon another; piles of table linens and round tabletops leaned against the dark windows. In the room's center sat a table, its round top covered by a white cloth. The cloth lay over a human figure, turning it into a landscape, a snow-covered mountain range, head and feet the highest peaks. At either end stood Seventy and Screwdriver.

I cleared my throat. So did they.

Seventy placed a hand on the tabletop. For a long moment, I thought he would pull back the cloth in some sort of magical reveal. Even though I'd already seen the Body, the idea disturbed me. I didn't want to see it again. I knew I needed to see it again. I wondered when I'd begun to think of it as "it."

Instead Seventy used the table for support. "How goes your investigation?"

I let out a breath that sounded like a tire deflating. "Well, I did meet a woman."

"You *saw* a woman."

"Yes. With you. Who is she?"

Seventy and Screwdriver looked at each other. Seventy's posture spoke of secrets, but Screwdriver released a shuddering breath that reminded me of Sober, and I caught a whiff of his grim determination. I wanted to ask questions I knew he wouldn't answer. Voices, nasal and angry, came from outside—parrots just beyond the papered windows, arguing about investment opportunities.

Seventy said, "When you've met her, you can say you met her."

"I get it. Who is she?"

"I'm not trying to be difficult. You'll understand when you meet her. There's a huge difference between seeing her and meeting her," Seventy said. "And a larger difference between meeting her and knowing her."

"All right, so I saw her. I'll meet her later." I tried one more time. "Who the fuck is she?"

Yellow, who was still standing behind me, placed a hand on my shoulder. "Be kind. Avoid your normal pedantic, condescending tone. She can't stand it."

I was disappointed that the drinks I'd had downstairs were wearing thin, and Yellow's comment pushed me toward surly. "You would know."

Screwdriver said sharply, "Watch your mouth."

Seventy raised a hand. "Enough. We're all on the same side here."

Any thoughts I'd had of revealing the gun to them disappeared. Either they knew I had it, in which case I'd be revealing something as obvious to them as my shoe size, or I'd be tipping my hand. Why I felt I had or needed a "hand," I didn't know. But I did, and I kept it hidden.

Seventy took hold of the cloth. With all the spontaneity of someone who had waited thirty-odd years to utter a line from a play, he said, "It's time for you to see the next great piece of our puzzle." Then he pulled off the cloth.

As I'd feared, I had to look at the Body, which had become a he again to me. He lay there, eyes half open, hands to his sides in a supplicant position, with an expression of almost willful acceptance of his fate. Practically shrugging at death. I'd witnessed supposed saints laid in tombs with less beatific expressions.

The Body's beard resembled the Drunk's, though more neatly trimmed. His clothes were rumpled and askew, revealing the parrot tattoo on his wrist. I looked quickly at Screwdriver's and Seventy's wrists to see if I could catch a sign of it there. They both somehow chose that moment to tug cuffs lower.

Yellow guided me forward so we all stood like the points on a compass. As we listened to the thunder, I glanced from Yellow, slightly hostile but also somewhat sympathetic, to Seventy, the elderly statesman of the group, to Screwdriver, who struck me as grim and threatening. I wanted to examine the Body's face to see if he shared my imperfect profile but couldn't make myself. "So."

"Dipshit," said Yellow as he took hold of the Body's head. "So you're looking at this." He turned it to the side. At the base of the neck was a bullet hole—large enough for two fingers— with blue-black bruising around it.

Seventy pointed at the wound, his finger shaking at the end of a tremoring arm. "He was shot. We were shot. You will be shot."

Yellow took hold of my shoulder. "You. You will be shot."

I dug my hands into my jacket pockets and wrapped my right one around the too-heavy gun. It was slick under my fingers. My stomach tightened with disgust as I realized that everyone here was a liar. "Why didn't you show me this earlier?"

Yellow straightened to our full height and said, "Because we didn't show you until now."

"It's something we all remembered." Seventy let go of the table. He vacillated between looking like the most frail and the most competent of us.

I said, "Shot in the back."

"No." Seventy, voice calm, hands shaking. "That's the exit wound. Entry is under the chin."

Screwdriver, apparently serenely capable of touching the Body as often as necessary, tilted the head so that I could see the hairs on his chin. What I noticed at first were the stray whisker clippings that rested on his collar, as if just trimmed. Screwdriver pointed to the hole lost in the beard. We all nodded.

I said, "Gun?"

"We don't know." Yellow shook his head. "Probably a .22."

I knew nothing about guns. I should read up, I thought. "Do you know about guns?"

"Enough. I read up. Researched. Picked up a few things."

"Picked up a few things about guns or picked up a few guns?"

He raised his eyes to me. "What?"

I'd said too much. "Nothing, I was just wondering. Never mind." He certainly didn't seem to know about the gun. In fact, he seemed rather confused. I kept my hands in my pockets, teetering between panic that I looked like I was hiding something and panic that I would end up lying dead on a dinner table in a third-floor storage room. Still leaning over the Body, I made myself look at his face. The nose had my bump. This was me. Would be me.

Screwdriver cleared his throat. From my perspective he was the three on a clock. Yellow was the nine, Seventy the twelve.

Eyes so wet they could lick me, Seventy studied me across the table. "Something's not right here."

I met his gaze. "What?"

"This isn't how I remember things. I'm getting confused."

Yellow nodded. "Me, too."

Screwdriver, also nodding, rubbed at his temples.

Yellow looked at me. "You should have known already that he was shot."

I rubbed the gun in my pocket. "How should I have known?" I'd never wanted to look at something as much as I wanted to look at that gun at that moment.

Seventy gripped the edge of the table for support. "This can't fall apart. Not now."

Screwdriver grabbed a chair from the nearest stack and set it on the floor. He helped Seventy sit. Seventy patted his arm with affection, as a father would a son. Was I really to get so old that I thought of myself as a child? I wondered. Then I remembered that the corpse on the table before me was a possible answer to my question.

Seventy took deep breaths and held his hands over his eyes. "I need a drink."

Both Screwdriver and Yellow looked from him to me with wide eyes. Yellow gestured to my jacket. "You're the only one with anything."

With great reluctance I let go of the gun. I feared they would see through my pocket, as if my hand had offered it protection. I pulled the flask, newly heavy with scotch, and handed it to Yellow. He unscrewed the cap and tilted the flask toward Seventy's nose like smelling salts, as if the odor alone would be enough. I knew it wouldn't be.

"Go on, give it to him," I said. It was the first time I'd told an Elder what to do, the first time one had ever listened. This felt different. The confusion and fear on their faces put me in control. I was no longer tethered, I reminded myself. They didn't know what I might do. Of course, neither did I.

Yellow wrapped Seventy's old fingers around the flask and held them there until they grasped on their own. When he let go, his hands shook a little. Seventy's eyes were closed, wet running onto his cheeks—not tears, something thicker. He put the flask to his heavy lips and tilted it back. Scotch poured into his mouth, and he choked, spit it out, coughed again. I watched him with absurd fascination. He tipped it gently this time, gulped it down, stopped, and then tipped again.

Yellow took hold of the old man's hand, pulled the flask away. "I think that's enough."

Seventy gave up the flask with effort, and Yellow passed it to me. I took a sip from it. He had emptied more than half. I promised myself to go back down and fill it. Perhaps steal a bottle.

Seventy looked up at me. "The good scotch."

"Of course." I wiped the flask mouth and recapped it.

"You will have to hurry down to refill that. The Brats are about to run low."

Yellow didn't like us chatting about alcohol. He shot me daggers as he patted Seventy on the back. "What's wrong? What happened?"

Seventy shuddered. "I've got some bad twinning going on. A lot of history that's severed." He looked from Yellow to Screwdriver and back. "Things aren't as they should be. I remember both of your perspectives, but this isn't how this played out. It's getting muddy here. As if we're all untethered."

"That's just what he said, 'untethered.'" Yellow pointing a finger at me. "When we were outside."

"Did I?" A silly denial. It was all I had.

Yellow frowned at me. "Don't pretend you don't remember." I wondered at what point I became so humorless.

Seventy ran a hand over his face. "Suffering with youth. That's all I've ever done."

"What can we do?" Fear was Yellow's driving force. I wondered if he had some stake closer to this than even I did.

"Nothing to do." Seventy listened to the rain on the window, eyes unfocused. I thought I heard wheels grinding deep inside his head. "We figure this out. The murder, the untethering."

The four of us each had our own death to prevent, but each of us was too myopic to consider anyone but himself. Each of us in that room was a ball of self-centered anxiety, a nervous animal waiting for the opportunity to claw. Yellow, twitching with panic, kept himself at a distance, his arms folded defensively. "But what caused it all?"

"Well I think that's obvious." Screwdriver locked my gaze and then turned away. I was somehow at fault, or would be, soon, but he wasn't blaming me. I suddenly felt I could trust Screwdriver. His anxiety was softened by a sadness. He approached this as so much business to deal with, and yet when he looked at me, it was with sympathy.

Yellow snapped at me, "What the fuck did you do?"

Seventy raised a hand. "Stop it. He doesn't know. All he knows is what has happened, not how it's different. It's Nose and Savior all over again. You do know about the nose?"

I kept my hand near my pocket. "Yes. I know about the nose."

"Good." Seventy nodded to himself. To Yellow he said, "Now, you should take him upstairs."

Yellow did such a comic double take that I nearly laughed. "What? I remember he doesn't see it until—"

Seventy stopped him with another raised hand. "Don't you see? Events are already out of our recall. Sticking to your memory doesn't help, and keeping another piece of information from him only increases the chance that he won't find it. We should have shown him the bullet hole downstairs. Something isn't working, and we need to force the issue."

Seventy's voice was small, but both Yellow and Screwdriver lowered their heads and took it in. Screwdriver looked slightly nauseated, and I wondered if it was because he was older, that, like Seventy, he was getting more confusion of memory, more twins running through his head. We were all so much the same person in our paranoia and fear—so many identical expressions passing over our faces, our hands dipped into pockets at the same angle—that for a moment it struck me as funny.

Finally Yellow put a hand on Seventy's shoulder. "You stay here and rest. Go downstairs when you feel better." He didn't need to tell anyone that he meant for Screwdriver to stay there with Seventy. To me, over his shoulder, "Come on. There's something else you need to know."

"And then?"

"And then you're on your own. Things have unraveled here. We have nothing else to show you." He marched out of the room.

Seventy gave me a smile. "You can do this. Don't worry."

I nodded and followed Yellow out the door.

Seventy called to me, "Keep an eye out for a gun."

I stopped and looked back at him. Was there something

in his face that said he knew? Yellow, from the hallway, said, "What if he's already found it?"

I watched Seventy watch me. "Have you?"

"No."

Neither Seventy nor Screwdriver blinked.

Yellow said, "What if he's lying?"

Seventy thought a moment, then scratched at his chin. "If he's lying, he'd better have a damn good reason."

Yellow returned to the doorway, stood shoulder to shoulder with me. "Do you? Have a reason?"

"If, and I'm not saying I did, but if I'd found a gun, wouldn't it be wise to keep it to myself to be certain of where it came from? Wouldn't it create more panic if word of it leaked out?"

Screwdriver smiled. "Actually, if I were you and I'd found a gun, I'd lie, because I wouldn't be sure whom I could trust. No knowing who shot the Body."

I stared at Screwdriver, waited for some wink or twitch telling me that he and I were somehow still tethered, but no sign came. My trust of him, founded on nothing, grew. Of all of us in the room, he and I thought the most alike. Yellow was the strange gap. Closer to me in age but inexplicable in his misunderstanding and lack of patience.

I was good at lying to myself. Always had been. "In any event, I haven't found a gun." It weighed down my jacket, probably about to rip through my pocket and thud to the floor.

Seventy waved us away. "Take him upstairs. Get it done."

Yellow swallowed his remaining argument and turned to the dark hall. "Come on." He waited for me at the stairwell, his face painted in shadow. I tried to keep my face blank of any expression as I passed. Before I could go through the door, he grabbed my arm and squeezed. "I don't know what you did, but if I find that you've ruined this. . . ."

"You'll what?"

His threat hung in the air between us. I saw the realization in his face: He'd just threatened me, the one who was supposed to die. I wondered if he could recall the suspicion of him that had just bloomed in my head.

"I just don't—" He let go of my arm. "I'm sorry. Look. It all gets very confusing. The paradoxes are coming constantly now. Little things set them off. It's very unsettling. I have memories of this working so smoothly, of everything going as we had planned it. But now. . . . Everything seems so fucked up."

I waited for him to say something else. His eyes appeared to lock onto something in the stairwell corner, but when I looked, there was nothing there. I said, "Are you done?"

He regarded me as if just remembering I was there. "Yes. Yes, I'm 'done.'" His anger was back. "You know, it really is unfortunate it's you who has to deal with this. It's too bad it's not someone older."

"Why's that?"

"Because from what I remember, at your age you don't have the capacity to imagine what this is like for anyone but yourself. You don't really grasp the full scope of what's happening. You're still too much of a selfish prick."

I glanced down at my shadow, my hands shaking. "What is it that I didn't understand in seeing the Body in there?"

Light fell on Yellow's face. He was pale, his lips quivering. His hands shook, too. Both our hands shook. "That's not just you in there. It's me. It's all of us. If the timeline follows the path we imagine it will, it's not just you who will die. I'll cease to be. So will they. The moment you fail, the moment you catch up with him, that might be it." He gestured back toward the room we'd left, toward the Body. "Everyone older than you is terrified."

My brain was slush. "How can it happen?" I asked. "How can you all even be here if. . . ?"

"None of us know."

He turned and took the stairs two steps at a time, his footsteps calling from farther and farther up. I watched my shadow on the stairwell floor. Cracks in the paint and mortar revealed the wire and the wooden studs behind the wall. I felt like that wall. My surface was shattered, and what was left behind barely held itself together. Yellow and the others saw my path leading to their destruction, but if I was right and I was no longer tethered to any of them, then it was only me who was going to die.

I followed Yellow up the steps.

By the time I found him on the fifth floor, I was exhausted and could think of nothing except sitting for a few minutes, but Yellow's impatience kept me moving. Halfway down the hall, Yellow stopped and put his hand on a doorknob—Room 503. "You'll want to see this," he said. "Hurry. I need to get downstairs."

He opened the door, and Yellow and I both squinted into the bright light that spilled out. The room was fully made up, as if the hotel were still functioning and not close to collapse. Three lights blazed—one on the ceiling, a table lamp near the bed, and a floor lamp. Above the neatly made bed was a painting of the ocean. Poorly done. The windows were curtained instead of papered over. The wallpaper, old and worn, had been mended in places with what looked like packing tape. It showed yellow flowers, peonies, layered one atop another, ceiling to floor. The room had a warm, sunlit glow.

On the dresser, next to an unused ashtray, sat a large plastic key ring. I walked to the side table and opened a drawer. A Bible and two pens rattled at the bottom. I touched the wallpaper, toyed with the taped patches. Up close the walls were the worse for wear, the paper faded and stained by please-don't-think-about-it. The bed's baseboard was banged up, and the nearby chair was dented along the edges. The room was shabby. It was also carefully staged, manicured as best as it could be, and smelled of ammonia and furniture wax. The rug was stained but vacuumed.

I tried to swallow. "Are there any other rooms like this?"

Yellow seemed afraid to cross the threshold. "No." He stood in the hallway, hands in pockets. He appeared older than I'd originally thought. And more tired. "Look in the closet," he said.

"What's in the closet?"

"Open it and find out."

"You're being childish."

Yellow shook his head. "I disagree. I think *you're* being childish."

The closet door was massive. I took hold of the cold crystal knob and turned it. The knob came off in my hand. As if it were a bloody knife, I dropped it. From inside the closet came a clattering as the knob on the other side fell to the floor.

"Are you kidding me?" Yellow joined me as I tried to fit the knob's shaft back into the hole. "This didn't happen when Seventy showed me."

"Don't come unhinged," I said. "It's only a knob."

"Only a knob?" He was sweating and rubbed at his temples. I pulled out my flask and offered it to him. He accepted it, started to take a drink, then stopped himself and handed the flask back to me. As I drank, he knelt down to work the doorknob into place. I drank half of what was left and repocketed it, exploring the rest of the room as he tinkered. The dresser drawers were empty. As I bent to look beneath the bed, the gun in my pocket swung and knocked against my side. I'd forgotten it was there. No I hadn't. How could I? All it did was let me know it was there. The whiskey warmed in my stomach.

At last Yellow stood. "There. Now. Open the door."

"You open it. You're right next to it."

His face flushed. "Just open the damn door." He stepped out of the way, back to the hall where he'd hidden in plain sight before, as if the threshold gave him protection from whatever was inside. He shrank by the moment, as if his hair were thinning and graying while I watched. He seemed consumed by his yellow sweater, almost comical, a man in a large, limp banana suit.

I turned the knob hard and pulled. Inside the closet was a television atop a small cart. Cables spilled from the back, some connecting to a videotape player, others connecting to a small silver camera on a tripod stand. It was a decades-old mini–tape recorder. Sometimes decrepitude doesn't inhibit function. The entire contraption leaned into the corner, lens aimed up over my head, open-irised. I knelt to take a closer look. The television was thirteen inches, flat-screened. Scratches on the floor showed how often the cart had been wheeled forward. I plugged the cord into a nearby outlet and turned on the set, which popped to blue-lit life, its speakers emitting a low hiss. When nothing else happened, I tapped the up and down channel buttons. Nothing. I stood to examine the back of the set. There was no antenna. I returned the set to its original input, which I assumed was the camera. A cable lay on the closet floor, and I connected it to the TV. A small red light appeared on the camera, and the blue TV screen turned to gray, INPUT 1 visible in the corner.

I pressed "play."

On the screen appeared the bed behind me. The perspective was from just inside the closet, as if it had been shot from exactly where the camera stood now. I sat down on the bedspread's black-and-red floral print and waited for something to appear on-screen. Just as I was beginning to fear that the video would prove to be a long study of the rose-printed bedspread, a figure crossed in front of the camera. It was me, older, growing a beard, still in the same suit. He was harrowed by exhaustion, more done in than the Body. He sat on the bed and faced the camera, and so I found myself staring into my own face. Looking at another me was like looking into a mirror that didn't cast a reflection in reverse, as it ought to. It occurred to me that I was more used to seeing myself like that than in an actual mirror, that the collection of me that filled the hotel was a series of broken mirrors moving among themselves, hoping to find the one that worked properly, that produced a vision of what was true. I rubbed elbows with my own vanity.

Video me pulled a brown paper bag toward him and rummaged through it, removed a bottle of whiskey. The bag dropped to the floor, and he kicked it under the bed. Corpse-still, bottle on his lap, he stared at me from inside the set.

I glanced down at my own foot. The edge of a brown paper bag was just visible by my heel. I reached beneath the bed and pulled the worn bag toward me. A half-full liter bottle of whiskey fell into my hand. *Gifts arrive in many shades of amber,* I thought. Beneath the whiskey was a small videotape, still in its wrapper. The right size for the video camera. I held it in my palm and looked back at the screen. Video's bottle, now open, perched on his knee. He jerked his head toward the door. I took his signal and looked at the door.

Yellow watched me from the hall. If he could see, or had seen, the video, he made no move to reveal it. His face was screwed up with curiosity. Despite the questions I could see rattling in his head, he said nothing.

Video was waiting for me. I marveled at dark circles beneath his eyes. He gestured, urgent, waved a hand in the direction of the door as if saying, *Go on, go ahead.*

I turned back to Yellow. "Did you watch this?"

"Are you crazy? This place reeks of paradoxes. I never saw it before, so I shouldn't have seen it now. Seventy didn't even remember seeing any of this shit."

"He didn't?"

"Did I fucking slur my words? No. You probably shouldn't have seen it either."

"We're not tethered. Don't worry about it."

"You still shouldn't be watching." He shifted away from

the door. The rug, which looked dry, made a squishing sound beneath his feet.

"Why bring me here?"

Yellow's hands fluttered. "Because Seventy said I should. I don't know why." His distress was somehow comforting.

On the screen Video raised his bottle to me, offered a silent toast. I opened mine in return and took a drink. I choked a little, and so did Video. I wondered if he might not be between me and the Drunk. His perspective was hard to place.

After Video drank, he reached into his pocket and pulled out the still-wrapped videotape, the one I held. He placed a finger to his lips and then pocketed it. I took another swig from the bottle and put the hard plastic cassette into my pocket. It clicked against the gun. At the door Yellow watched me.

I held the bottle out toward him. "Drink?"

He shook his head. "I can't believe you're watching that."

"Some good stuff on here." I hoped my bravado was thicker than it felt. "It's a bit racy."

"You would know."

I gulped whiskey through a smile. "Yes I would." I'd pissed him off.

On the closet television, Video toasted me once more. I was near the bottom of the bottle when he reached the halfway mark and recapped. He wrapped the bottle in the brown bag, took a pen from his pocket and wrote across the front of the bag, tightened the wrap, then shoved it under the bed, where I had found it moments earlier. I turned the bag over. I hadn't noticed the writing the first time; the script was so small and the pen so light against the brown paper.

It read, "*In case of emergency, break glass.*"

I finished the bottle, recapped it, and stuck it into my jacket's inner pocket. Between the loaded gun, the microvideotape, and the empty whiskey bottle, I was gathering a heavy little collection.

To no one, myself, everyone, I said, "Okay, enough of this. Let's get out of here."

"You're drunk." Yellow stood off from the doorway, hidden in the dark.

I stood and did my best not to fall. "Not fully." The whiskey had been effective. I *was* drunk.

He said, "You're chewing the inside of your cheek." It was a technique I'd learned to sober myself.

I couldn't see Yellow's face in the shadows. The room tilted around me a little. "I need a bathroom."

He pointed behind me. The bathroom door was ajar, and the white tile looked cool and inviting. I hesitated. At the door Yellow continued to hover. I suddenly feared that he'd known more than he let on, and I wanted to get away from him. I'd been too cavalier in watching the tape. Video had known that Yellow was in my doorway, but I still didn't like it. It was possible that Video and I were tethered, that he was on the right side of the Body and still connected to me. I both hoped and feared that was the case.

I said, "Listen, you can go."

"No, that's fine. I can wait."

"You want to hear me puke? Is that it? Relive old times?" He didn't move. "Is there something else?"

"What do you mean?"

"Another room? Some other thing I don't know about? You said this was it."

"Yeah, this was it."

"Then fuck off."

His face twitched. I couldn't recall ever talking to an Elder like this. In the past I'd felt anger toward Elders, given myself the pleasure of horrible fantasies about my older selves, then felt some embarrassment later when I approached those ages and saw certain glimmers in Youngsters' eyes. But this was different. A simple expletive and I felt so much better. Untethered or not, I wouldn't feel guilty about that.

Yellow stepped away from the door and called back to me, "You're on your own now. Good luck, you drunk piece of shit."

Self-loathing ran in both directions, I realized. I could hate both who I had been and who I would become. It was efficient.

When he was gone, I moved quickly to the closet to eject the tape from the machine, then crushed it between my heel and the bathroom floor. The spool unwound, spiraled across the white tiles. There might have been more on the tape, but I relied on Video's knowing that I prematurely smashed it. I gathered the plastic shards and flushed them down the toilet. Before I could put the second tape into the camera, I heard a squish of footsteps in the hallway. I stowed the tape and returned to the bathroom, made a grand show of it—ran the water, splashed my face, soaked my hair and slicked it back, gargled loudly, spit louder, turned off the water, and flushed the toilet a second time—before I left the bathroom.

The woman from the ballroom was standing in the doorway. "Always have to slip out, don't you?" She gave me a conspirator's smile. Her face made me forget the worried frenzy of the evening, among other things.

I tried to give my own conspiratorial smile in return but felt a lecherous grin lock onto my face. It wouldn't let go. "I think I'm starting to hate crowds." Just then the floor shook with thunder, and I imagined that I could feel the music from the ballroom bumping its way up through the superstructure.

She crossed the room. Her bright eyes were lined with dark makeup that made them stand out even more than I'm sure they normally would. Her dress was a complicated silk arrangement—red waves emerged and disappeared. A split seam ran up one thigh, and it flashed at me once, twice, I prayed for a third as she crossed to the foot of the bed and sat down. She turned and looked over her shoulder. The parrots tattooed there spoke to me.

I wiped my hands on the towel I held. I didn't remember picking it up, but nothing comes from nothing, so there you go. I sat beside her. There wasn't much room, but she didn't move away.

"I was just washing my face. It gets pretty hot in that ballroom," I told her.

She nodded, quiet, as if trying to recall something. Her eyes roamed the ceiling. I got the feeling that she knew all my answers even though I hadn't heard her questions. We both faced the open closet, the blank television screen. I wished I had shut that door, even though she acted as if she'd seen it all before.

"What were you watching?" Her voice was silk scraping silk.

"Nothing, really." The unused tape in my pocket pressed

heavily against my hip. It gave an embarrassing throb. "Just using the washroom."

"Washroom." She laughed. So many of her questions sounded like answers, and they all seemed to amuse her. Her voice dropped to an even silkier volume, so that I almost had to read her lips. "You were watching something about me, weren't you?"

I couldn't believe I'd destroyed the tape before watching to the end. Was it too late to retrieve the pieces from the plumbing and somehow reconstruct it?

She laughed as I blushed. I kept my mouth shut and let her lean in a bit closer, let her press a bare shoulder into mine. Her breath was sweet—from rum, I thought—and her hair smelled of flowers. I looked at the peonies on the wallpaper, faded and yellow, and tried to remember what peonies smelled like. She smiled at me. Her hand touched my knee, ran upward to my thigh. The gun, only an inch from her hand, seemed to pulse. She studied the lines of my jaw and neck, leaned in and touched my lips with hers. Our breaths mixed.

Her hands ran up my sides and drew me against her. She withdrew before I knew the kiss was over, and I watched her eyes harden as she leaned away. She examined my face. For just a moment, she ran her fingers over my cheek, up toward my temple and forehead, tender, as if caring for something only she saw. Her long nails sketched lightning trails on my skin that continued to vibrate even after her hand left my face. She pulled back my sleeve, and her fingers danced over the pale skin on my wrist. She smiled at it sadly, stood, and straightened her skirt. Red rose up her neck.

"That will make you follow me," she said.

"Excuse me?"

"It's important that you meet me and that you follow me." She sounded like she was reciting a mantra.

"Why would your kissing me make me follow?" I sounded more accusing than I meant to. I saw a veil fall between us in her eyes.

"Because you've never been with anyone like me. That's what you'll say."

"Don't be ridiculous." My denial did nothing to dispel the truth of her comment. "Who invited you anyway?"

"No one yet." Her lips continued to move after these words. She was still speaking, in a whisper I couldn't understand. She stopped and tilted her head. For a moment she looked like one of the parrots tattooed on her shoulder, black eye watching me. Then her gaze fell on my lapel. "Your clock. Wrong time." The color drained from her face, and I could practically hear her bird heart fluttering to escape her chest.

I stood and held out my hand. "Are you all right?"

She didn't answer, just turned and walked from the room. The echo of her voice—"Wrong time, wrong time"—followed her out the door.

I trailed her down the hall, watching her avoid rips in the carpet and squeaky floorboards as if she'd walked these halls for years.

She approached the elevator, and I was about to sputter that she shouldn't waste her time when she pulled open the grate and climbed in. She didn't slam the door in my face, though this may be due to the door's catching on a frayed edge of carpet. I smiled at her, kicked the door free of the carpet, and yanked it shut behind me. We both faced forward, toward the gate, and she cleared her throat.

"Can you press the button, please?"

I pressed the button, stammered an apology, and the elevator, which was apparently working again, began its creaky descent. The buttons in front of me wavered in and out of focus, and I wondered what might be wrong with them— something with the electricity, perhaps. Then I remembered the bottle of whiskey I'd just finished. The meatballs from earlier had cushioned its fall, but now it was settling into me and finding its way to my head.

The elevator clicked past four and three easily enough. Halfway between the second and first floors, it gave a whine and a shudder. The floor pitched forward as if we'd caught on something, and she fell into my back. We both hit the gate, me first, hard, and my hand slipped through a gap and slapped the slowly moving shaft wall. It was smooth and gray, and little cobwebs hung across its surface, clung to my hand and sleeve, dragged along behind my fingers. She pressed into my back. We hung against the gate like two bats, and the elevator shook again and stopped. The woman had righted herself and apologized for falling into me.

"I think we've got greater worries," I said.

We were stuck between floors. Light poured in through the one-foot gap at our feet and threw our ankles' shadows against the rear wall. Above a thick slab of concrete was the darkness of the second floor. Music and voices leaked upward from the first.

The woman squatted down into her heels, peered through the gap, and called for help. There was no answer.

She looked at me. "How are we going to get out of here?"

I burped a semisolid, wet, and sour burp, swallowed what I could, and coughed on the rest. When I could breathe again, I said, "How should I know?"

"You must have some recollection of our getting stuck in here."

"What the hell are you talking about?"

She stared at me as if realizing for the first moment that she was alone in an elevator with a man-shaped bag of feces. "Isn't that a roomful of younger yous we're listening to right now?"

"Oh, that." I waved a hand, and much of my torso followed it. Finishing that bottle had been a big mistake. "No. Things haven't been going according to memory tonight. Not for me. But even if I do remember this in a year, I'll have to let it happen."

"Why?"

"Rule number three."

She smiled. She hadn't smiled since the moment in the room when she thought I was someone older. "You and your rules."

"You know my rules?" I didn't tell people my rules. I didn't tell people much of anything about me, assuming I even spoke to them at all.

"I know of them."

"Ah." This was a rather vague response, but as the car was swirling around me, it was all I could manage.

"So what do we do?"

I'd been in odd situations with women before, but this situation reverberated in a way that made me uncomfortable. I sat on the floor. The elevator hung at a nauseous angle.

The woman stared down at me, one hand against a wall. "I asked you, what do we do?"

I shut my eyes. The elevator stopped spinning briefly. I thought we might get away with staying there for a while, that she might understand that I needed to be still, to hide from everyone else. I don't know why I had this fantasy—delusion, really—that she cared about my needs at all. She burst that impression by muttering, "I don't want to die in this elevator."

I opened my eyes. "What does that mean?"

"What?"

"Die in this elevator? Who are you, by the way? I can't keep thinking of you as just 'the Woman.'"

"The Woman?"

I waved a hand in the air to dispel her anger. She shook her head and looked up toward the ceiling, as if remembering something unpleasant. Her voice, sad and resigned, came from far away. "I'm Lily."

"Lily. Nice to meet you." I held out a hand, and she turned toward me just as I stole a glance at her breasts. Her green eyes pinned me against the wall. "How did you get here, Lily?"

She stopped to consider her own words. "I received an invitation."

"Impossible. There are no invitations."

"Not from you."

I waited for her to continue. She didn't. She understood me in a way that made me afraid. She knew I was weak and scared. She didn't like it but accepted it nonetheless. I wondered when I would find her and how I would convince her to follow me to the party. Would she be familiar with me as an old man? Did I really have to wait that long, if I made it that long?

I fumbled with the elevator's control panel beside the door but couldn't even get it open. I gave up and squatted, thought about where I might get sick inconspicuously.

Lily parroted herself. "How are we going to get out of here?"

"Seriously, can't we just rest a bit?"

"Get the fuck up and help me get this gate open."

I stood and brushed myself off. Head swirling, I put one hand against the wall and tugged at the gate with the other. I noticed a clean spot on the tile floor where a powerful cleaning solution had stripped not only the dirt but the polish. Somehow I knew that it had been a bloodstain, cleaned with effort by an Elder. Screwdriver, most likely. He wore an air of shitwork. I sensed Lily's eyes following mine to the floor, and I looked away. Would she panic if she knew that one of me would die in the car earlier that night?

I rattled the gate. It made a lot of noise but drew no attention. Conversation from the first floor didn't stop, and the disco music seemed to grow louder. I rattled the gate again, and Lily put a hand on my shoulder.

"Let's get the gate open."

She used the spike of her heel to hook the lower latch and wrench it free of the catch. I held the bottom of the gate clear, and she worked at the upper latch, jumping to reach it. She leapt again and again, with a determination I might have never had in my entire life. In a way I didn't care if I got out of the elevator. In just one heel, she fell into me several times. I ended up keeping a hand on her waist to steady her.

"I almost got it that time," she said, face flushed and damp with sweat. She glanced down at my hand. I pulled it away.

She struck the latch again. It held as if welded shut. Unless someone came to open it for us, we were truly stuck. Lily knelt back down, put her head into the opening, and shouted. She screamed. She pleaded. The music grew louder.

"What are they all doing down there? How much time can someone spend with himself?"

She looked at me as if I should have the answer. After a moment I realized that maybe I should. "It's a party. I like music. Loud music, apparently."

"Has there ever been trouble like this with the elevator before?"

Before I could answer, there were voices above us. "Hold on. We'll have you out in a second." Someone forced open the second-floor door. I looked up past the legs and tried to see the face. The voices that carried down to us included some so high-pitched they must be prepubescent. They made my skin crawl. When would I be so stupid that I would bring children into this?

The alcohol rushed over me in waves. "Get something under that latch and pop it out." The elevator seemed to shrink around me, and I wondered if it was conceivable that I had intentionally poisoned myself with the whiskey. I stumbled and fell against the wall.

Lily grabbed my arm. "You're not well."

"No. I'm fine." I watched the youthful shadows over her shoulder. "Listen. Do me a favor. Don't talk to them. All right?"

"Why, what's wrong?"

"They shouldn't be here. I haven't figured out how they

all got here. Some are too young. I don't know what they're capable of."

Her hard eyes softened a bit. "Right. Okay. Now, let's try to get out of here."

Who was she? She was handling this better than I was.

That was when the whiskey had its way with me. As the elevator car turned sideways and darkened in a frenzy of childish hands.

I WOKE UP being hauled by a dozen struggling pairs of little hands, head hanging, legs swinging, heels catching on steps. Above me, upside down, was Lily, knees flashing as she climbed stairs, a pair of teenagers holding her elbows. I felt a pang of jealousy. I let my eyes close again, catching a last brief glimpse of Lily's legs in the parade of me.

Before I passed out for the second time, I heard her say, "If you look up my skirt again, I'll break your nose."

Images of broken noses swam in the darkness before me. It was a reassuring vision, and when I woke for the second time, I found myself struggling to scratch my nose. Something kept my arm pinned. I groaned and opened my eyes.

I lay on my side with my hands tied behind my back. Whatever I'd been tied with was cutting into my wrists. Lily was pressed against me, back-to-back, and our fingers touched. Some kind of wires bound her wrists. I stopped struggling and silently prayed that the dark room would cease its steady rotation.

A flash of lightning came through the peeled paper on the window. We were in a hotel room stripped bare to the lath and floorboards. Bits of wood and broken tile covered the floor. Around us a dozen youthful figures of me formed a wide arc. Some seemed as young as seven or eight, crowded together for security or fear. The hushed rattle of conversation among them made me think of birds.

I cleared my throat. "You've all broken a number of the convention rules, you know." I sounded froggier than I would have liked, but the message still struck home. The Prepubes looked at one another with the concern children show at an adult's displeasure. "Someone untie me now so we can get back downstairs."

A teenager's voice, deep and cracking, called from near the door, "We're supposed to keep you here. It won't be long."

Lightning flashed again, and in the brief light I saw the fear in their eyes. They knew that what they were doing was wrong. That was the appeal, what made them do it. I wondered who it was who took their childhoods away from them by inviting them here.

"Who's the oldest here?"

The group parted, and a single teen stood by himself. He was awkward, thin, hands buried deep in his jean pockets as if he was unsure what to do with them. I didn't remember seeing him at the party before, and I understood why. Pale light from the street caught the glimmer of braces on his teeth, an otherworldly silver smile. It was me when I was eighteen. The year I'd begun my work on the raft.

I asked him, "What are we doing here?" My eyes wanted to shut again. In moments of panic, my body's reaction is to shut down, to find a safety in lack of energy. Lethargy must be a genetic defense. The cells that don't move don't get hurt.

The Inventor ran a hand across the unruly hair that crowned his head. "Just wait a few minutes, okay? He'll be here soon."

"Someone's got you on the wrong track. You shouldn't even be here."

He looked to the floor. "I belong here more than anyone. I came up with it."

His voice was deeper than mine. I wondered about hormones and their effect on the body. Overcompensating for youth with excess maturity.

I said, "Listen. There's no need for me to be tied up. And this nice lady doesn't belong here."

He said, "I talk to you while you try to escape, and then we fight, and I knock you down hard and kill you."

Some of the children were crying.

"What?"

He hesitated. His voice shook when he answered. "You heard me. If you don't do exactly as I say, I'll kill you." Children fluttered nearby. I scanned their faces and saw mixtures of fear, worry, excitement. Nowhere did I see recognition. They thought of me as someone other than themselves. I imagined they saw the same lack of recognition in my eyes.

"What makes you think you kill me?"

"I've seen it a dozen times." His hand waved over the group. "Some of them run. A lot of them stay. They've all seen what I've seen. Only one here hasn't."

He indicated the smallest of the crowd, a six-year-old. He stood nearest the windows, as scared of the dark as he was of me and the others around him. I wondered if he had any concept of what was happening. I wanted to grab him and take him back to the books and puzzles that I knew littered the floor of his room.

I suddenly remembered being six, playing in my second-floor bedroom in the hundred-year-old house. Outside the window a large spruce grew. Walls painted sky blue, a midnight blue bedspread with stitchwork scars. Me on the floor, on hands and knees, surrounded by toy cars. All of them have a story, in my mind, as they drive under my hand to places I haven't bothered to give names. I remember lifting the mattress and placing the cars, one at a time, under it. I did this again and again, car after car, until they were all gone, all clustered together under the mattress, not having gone anywhere other than in my imagination. Pretending to have a place to go made it so much easier to get there.

I imagined now that instead of playing with cars this six-year-old remembers the raft, the nausea that the trip induces, the flash of darkness. Arriving somewhere wet and dark, getting out and running through trees in Central Park, or in deserted alleys downtown, crying while Elders shepherd him through this ruined city. Not old Elders. These elders are only a few years further along than he is, but that's enough. And I see them take him to a man of eighteen years, the Inventor, for whom this new memory would be wrapping over the old one. I wondered at the older children's inability to console, to empathize. Before them stood a fearful child, and they did nothing for him, nothing for themselves. Their own version of rule number four. I thought of me breaking my nose.

Fingers played along the wires that bound my wrists. Lily.

"Harsh," I said to the Inventor. "Scaring a little boy like that."

"You won't distract me." He didn't even look at the child. "I remember being him and screaming. I'll get over it."

I clearly wasn't tethered to this one either. I'd never been that child. "You won't help his suffering because you suffered? Do you realize that it's you who's *making* him suffer?"

Lily had the twist of metal undone. I tried to wriggle my wrists without being too obvious. The storm was reaching its peak; it had to be near midnight. Every time the lightning burst through the window, I was certain that one of the dozen children would see her working on the wire and call out.

The Inventor said, "You're arguing about the color of the chips during a losing poker game. It's happening as it happened, as it is supposed to happen."

"That's bullshit." Some of the children looked to one another, the glimmer of fear mixed with amazement at the bad word I'd thrown at their leader. "You know I'm right. All of you. You know you didn't come here as kids. You know you were brought here by someone who had no right."

"But that person is you," the Inventor said, arms wide to include the whole group. "It's always been you. You know that."

"Not me. I never went back."

"Didn't you?"

"No."

"I think you did. I know you did. We all do. You went back so that we could do this. So we could stop you."

"What the hell are you talking about?" The fog inside my head refused to lift.

The Inventor reached into his back pocket and pulled out a gun. I immediately recognized it and moaned.

Lily gasped. "Jesus."

The Inventor stood in a wide gap the others created. He towered over everyone else, his face gone black in the sudden darkness. I pulled hard at my wrists and tried not to wince.

The Inventor said, "I want to know what happened to your nose."

Lily stopped working on my wrists. "What?"

"He was in a panic. He ran into a bathroom to check his nose in a mirror. Something important happened, and we want to know what. Hurry, she's almost done with your binds."

At that, Lily started working again.

"Listen to me," the Inventor went on. "Unless you tell me what is going on, I'm going to have to hit you with this and kill you. I don't want that."

"If you kill me, then you know you'll be killing yourself."

He said nothing. Lily finished with the wire, and my hands fell away from each other. The group of children had already begun to back away. They'd always known the precise moment of my escape and had done nothing to prevent it. They were even more slavish to rule number four than I had been.

I said, "Give me that gun." As I said it, something knocked against my hip. It was the gun I carried. So the gun he held wasn't the one I'd found. These children had no idea what they were doing. *Amateurs,* I thought.

"It won't really be killing myself. There has to be some way around it." I could hear his internal logic buttressing his words. He'd been through this puzzle. As many times as there were kids in the room, he'd witnessed my "death." Twelve years? I'd only just this night been shown the Body, and they'd worked for a lifetime to understand the intricacies of their actions. I worried that this one might be right: What if killing me didn't really matter?

"How can you be so sure you're not killing yourself?"

"Because of the Elders."

"I'm an Elder."

"Only subjectively. I'm talking objectively. Those who are really old. Older than you."

"What about them?"

"If killing you really did kill me, then they couldn't be here."

I nodded slowly. "That would make sense if it weren't possible to become untethered."

He shook his head. "That still doesn't make sense. I've thought about it since he heard you say it." He gestured toward the smallest boy, who now cowered in the corner. "Go ahead and give your explanation. I've got a response. Hurry up. I'm going to have to kill you in a moment."

This one was painful to talk to. I was too tired and drunk to think clearly. I needed to get away from him and catch my breath. "Untethered means that your actions here could predicate a new reality for you. One that puts you on a different track from the Elders."

"You're making that up. I'm not sure if you're just drunk or crazy."

Lily walked around me, her heels grinding bits of rubble.

"This has gone on long enough. He won't shoot. How could he?"

The Inventor said, to himself, to me, "This is it." His eyes on mine, he raised his gun. The group of children began to scream and run. Everyone but Lily, me, and my six-year-old self knew what was coming and wanted to get away from it.

I lunged past Lily and reached for his gun but missed. The whiskey still bounced around in my head, and I wasn't sure I was moving in a straight line. He pulled the gun away and spun in place. As the weapon came around to complete the circle, he raised it and smashed me in the temple. Stars burst in my vision, and I staggered into a wall.

The Inventor muttered, "That won't really kill you."

Screams burbled darkly around me for several moments, minutes, perhaps a lifetime. Voices, all my own, washed over me without meaning. I only knew the blood in my mouth and the grit of the floor in my cheek, the feeling of limbs oddly buoyant. I slept and dreamed of black rocks underwater. A voice whispered soundlessly, then again. I opened my eyes.

Lily knelt beside me, her hands on my head. Something hot and sticky ran down my temple. "Hold still, you're bleeding." She rummaged through my pockets, removed the videotape, and dropped it. She started toward the other pocket, where my gun was, and I grabbed her hand.

"What are you looking for?"

"Something to stop the bleeding."

"Here." I pulled my empty pocket inside out and ripped it from its seams. So much for the Suit, I thought. She finished tearing the pouch of fabric free and pressed it against my head.

The room around us was empty. Everyone else, every child and Youngster, had gone. Even the storm had moved on, although in the distance thunder echoed up the canyons of the city. I lay on the floor for several minutes, maybe a quarter hour, Lily pressing the thin fabric to my head, her free hand stroking my temple. I closed my eyes and listened to the storm recede. In the past I had done this, closed my eyes and listened to the storm fall away as the party downstairs wound down, imagined the century earlier when I'd arrived. In my mind's eye, I could see others of me, around tables speckled with nearly finished drinks, heads tilted left and right, ears searching for that last reverberant peal of thunder, the end of the spattered rain.

I reached for Lily's hand. "Where'd everyone go?"

She nodded, as if answering an unasked question. "They started screaming. The little ones especially. Older kids grabbed younger ones, and they tore out of here. The last one to leave was the one who hit you." She looked back at the doorway as if seeing him there now. She was not affected by multiple versions of me, only by my actions. She made my head spin. It was like I was a balloon, floating, and everyone else held my strings.

I said, "Who the fuck are you?"

Her eyes stayed on the door, searched for things I couldn't imagine. "I told you. I'm Lily."

I shook my head, and the room shook along with it. "That explains nothing."

Her hand held my cheek. "It'll have to do."

I tried to sit up. The room made one lazy turn, then settled down. My head had left a rather large hole in the plaster where I'd ricocheted off the wall.

"Why won't you tell me? It's me, for Christ's sake. You act like I don't know it's someone older than me who invited you."

"He made me promise."

"Break the promise. I promise, he'll forgive you. I already do."

"It's not that easy."

"Why?"

"He trusted me. He made me promise. And I've already hurt him enough."

Even through the dark, I could see a flicker in her eyes. She was protecting something she thought worth the effort. The fact that it was me made me ashamed. I hadn't even been willing to protect myself, as the screaming six-year-old would attest.

She helped me to my feet. While I was out, the hall lights had come fully on, and her face looked sculpted and clean, out of place in the decrepit room. I had no idea where in the hotel we were. We headed toward the rear stairway, which was silent. I headed upstairs. Lily followed, pulling at my coat.

"I think we should go back to the ballroom," she whispered. I didn't respond, kept climbing. After another floor she said, "None of them would help the little one." She said this with a secretive hush to her voice, as if she were afraid to let herself hear it. Unbidden, up popped an image of my face at six, eyes full of tears, nickname hovering above like an ad on the side of a bus: Little One. What was it that compelled me to reduce them to labels? I wondered, and then just as quickly I wondered why I thought of them as "them" when they were in fact "me," again and again and always.

There was a noise below, and for a moment I thought the

Inventor might have returned. Instead a rat bounded up the steps and, with no fear, scurried between us through the open door. We watched its bald tail disappear. That rat had a better idea of where it was going than I did. I wished for a plan, but all I could think of was Seventy.

I said, "I saw you with an Elder. Red tie, black cane." She didn't answer. "I want you to go tell him to meet me in the room where we met our friend. Say it just like that."

She gripped the railing. "What if the children find me?"

"They'll be terrified, hiding and afraid to see you. If they're anything like I was." As I said it, I realized I wasn't sure it was true. "Just tell him. Please."

She nodded and held out her hand. I took it, and she gave me a gentle squeeze. "Good luck."

THE BODY'S ROOM was locked. I wanted to break in the door, but we were only two floors removed from the party—an unexplained crash would bring me running.

If the Elders all assumed I had this under control, their confidence was misplaced. They relied on logic that I knew would eventually fail. For them the fact that they were even here mitigated the threat of the death. But I understood that the adjustment of a single element had more drastic changes. My nose had broken and not broken, and I'd both casually recognized this and drawn attention to it. The latter adjustment had brought about the hunt for answers that the Inventor was now involved in, the stampede of children, the modification of my—our—childhoods. Elements could change, be twisted, and have impacts beyond my imagining. This meant that the death could still happen. I was confident it would. And Seventy's confidence, his assurance, even his presence mystified me.

I found a doorway down the hall from the Body's room and crouched in the shadows. Two floors up, electricity blazed, but this floor wallowed in darkness. I watched the door and counted minutes, listened to water trickle in the walls. Lily would have reached Seventy by now and would have made herself clear. He was old. He walked with a cane. He'd navigate slowly up the steps. I waited ten minutes. I would wait ten more, I thought, then leave. Five minutes into the second ten, the stairwell door opened, revealing the silhouettes of Seventy and Screwdriver. I, for reasons I chose to ignore, reached into my pocket and held the gun.

Screwdriver reached the Body's door first. He keyed the lock and opened it, turned on the light and held the door open for Seventy. I stepped out of the dark and approached them. Screwdriver saw me first and gave a simple nod. I nodded back. He was a few years older than me, but I saw in his face a grim determination I knew I'd always lacked. I wondered if it was being forged now.

Seventy was not as warm to me. "What the fuck have you been doing?"

"Trying to find out why I die. How was dinner?"

Screwdriver laughed. Seventy shot him a glare but then started to laugh himself. "You know the meatballs are all dried out." His smile fell, and he looked older than seventy. Perhaps he should have been labeled Eighty? I'd stick with Seventy until I knew for sure.

"Everything has gone to shit down there," he said. "The Youngsters are out of control. They're actually threatening people. They've laid off now, but for a while it looked like us against them. And they keep multiplying. There were never this many here before."

"And they're young." Screwdriver crossed his arms, and I noticed dirt smeared across his shirtsleeves. I wondered where he'd been. "There were never kids here."

"They know that something is up," I said. "They want in."

Seventy shook his head. "Christ, no. Don't tell them anything. And what the fuck happened to your head?"

"I was hit."

Screwdriver grunted. Seventy worried the knob of his cane. "Who hit you?" he asked, trying to keep his voice calm.

"The Inventor."

Seventy nodded. "We were a bit arrogant back then. He must have figured out that you were up to something."

"Not him. I think he's answering to someone else."

"Who?"

"The Nose, maybe. Look. I know you brought in Lily. She shouldn't have been here in the first place, but now that things are falling apart, we need to get her out of here."

Seventy stared at the floor. "I didn't bring her."

I didn't expect an answer, but I asked anyway. "Who did?"

I looked from Seventy to Screwdriver. Screwdriver pointed down at the Body. I'd forgotten he was there. I drew back the sheet. He had nothing to add. I was beginning to feel anger at him for getting killed. Anger at me. "All right, so what?" I said. "One of you must remember where it was she came from."

Seventy wiped at his face with an open palm. "That's just the thing. We don't. Now that we're not tethered, that girl could be from anywhere. She refuses to even say." He shrugged. "I tried to convince her to leave." Was I really going to be so passive at his age?

I re-covered the Body, the sheet tented over his face. What had he been thinking, bringing that woman here? If in fact it had been him. I didn't believe I could fully trust either of these two. At least they hadn't brought the one I really didn't trust. "Where's Yellow?"

Seventy chuckled. "He was busy. We're trying to keep some semblance of normalcy down there. In fact, you should come down. The movies are about to start."

"Christ, no."

"It's tradition," Seventy said pointedly. "You come make an appearance, and then you get back to work."

I reached into my pockets. One hand slid through the hole where the pocket had been ripped out; the other fell against the gun. I remembered that the pocket lining was stuck to my forehead and yanked the fabric from my temple. The pocket, black and sticky, smelled of sweat and blood. I noticed the filth on my hands. Dirt filled the nails and creases. It made them look old.

I said, "I've got Youngsters threatening me. Right now half of them probably think they killed me. How come I have to figure out all this shit by myself? How about some of you guys pull some of the weight?"

Seventy circled the perimeter of the room and stopped near the door, eyes vacant, mind probably replaying events. I felt sorry for speaking and didn't want to hear a reply. I knew whatever he had to say would fall at my feet like a dead thing, stinking.

Finally he said, "I've waited, year after year, to figure out how it happened. Worked to put together pieces. But the death kept creeping up. And fingers have begun to point at you. I used to think you were the killer. I don't think so anymore, though, because you're not as done in as some of the others. If you were blacking out, or out of control, maybe, but you're not. So unless it's premeditated, it's not you." He smacked his cane against the floor. "We don't know who the killer is. That's the main reason we keep coming back here. You know. This thing stopped being fun almost from the first year. From this point on, it's nothing but work. We've all been trying to piece things together to figure out what happened. So if we can't provide you with answers, it's because we worked hard to keep from upsetting the balance of things." He pointed the cane at me, and I didn't care for how sharp it looked at the end. "We maintained the balance, until you. Balance is something you didn't care for, and at this stage the apples are bouncing from the applecart too quick to count. Well done. Now, if you don't think you can stop bitching about having to save our life"—and he gestured from Screwdriver to the Body to himself, his finger swirling to include the floors beneath us—"then maybe you could just focus on saving your own."

Seventy turned and left. Screwdriver watched me for a moment. He opened his mouth as if to speak, then thought better of it. He held up the door key and smiled. He placed it in the keyhole and walked away. The key, the room, the Body were mine now, my responsibility.

I felt awkward staying there with him. I walked to the hall, shut the door, and locked it.

From the stairway I heard echoed laughter. The movies had begun.

ON MY WAY to the ballroom, following the sounds of films I knew too well to want to see again, I passed the men's room. I ducked in to wash my face, clean my head wound, try to find something in the mirror that reminded me of me. What I found was a flooded floor, blood on a sink, and signs of epic failure on the part of myselves to remember to flush. I stood before a sink with a perpetually running faucet and splashed water over my face and hair for the second time that night. I watched a face I ought to have recognized emerge in the mirror.

The movies started after midnight. Time-travel pictures, both small-budget films and blockbusters, all of them laughable for one reason or another. I watched them in the crowded ballroom, which would quiet down when they started, projected on the wall, the cracks of the plaster adding depth to films that otherwise lacked any. The time travel depicted was spectacular or dangerous. Nothing like time travel actually was in my experience, as banal as moving from one room to the next, watching ice melt, as banal as becoming hungry again, catching a cold, noticing a recession of hairline, a growth of nails, hair, paunch. Time travel was a simple slide sideways instead of forward. It was, I'd discovered when the raft had first hummed to life, no different, in any notable way, from doing nothing. We forget, I think, that we are born to travel through time, to trip into the next moment over the bump of the present, to keep looking over our shoulder to find that bump, understand it, and in doing so trip over the next. And on. And on.

No matter how often I saw some of the films—and no doubt the alcohol helped lubricate the humor—the serious foibles of the travelers, the difficulties they endured in their adventures, never ceased to be absurd. Depictions of traveling through time as if it could be an experience in itself. As if a brain designed to perceive only slow forward progression could magically decipher backward travel, as if color and swirling images, glimpses of moments happened or about to happen danced in a kaleidoscope. As if there were anything but darkness and the roar of blood in your ears, as if there were anything different from the normal panic of living. And so I laughed year after year at the movie heroes, their dangers and discoveries. Threats always came from outside, and in monstrous form. Obstacles appeared as questions of timing, not choice. Logical inconsistencies abounded. How could they not? I laughed most at these, as I do now at my own. Only now do I realize that logical inconsistencies are what allow for us to travel in time in the first place, keep us tripping forward or—like me—sometimes backward or sideways. I was blind to my own illogic and still am, though now by choice. Sometimes to discover a solution is to forget the problem.

Now I entered the ballroom and found an unfamiliar scene.

The room was divided into two groups. The Elders sat as near to the projected image as they could, the bottom of the film on the wall fuzzy with their hair as they reached across one another for popcorn. Behind them circled the Youngsters, rattling like disturbed sparrows. Their number had grown, and behind me came the slap of sneakers on hardwood as more arrived. From the ages of six to perhaps twenty-six, there must have been a hundred. More. Multiples of every age stood in clumps, fought one another over cookies and candy, crunched popcorn underfoot, nudged one another as older Youngsters squealed past. Only the really small ones, the six- and seven-year-olds, seemed worried or frightened. I tried to see if I could spot the youngest one, the one who'd witnessed my "death" in such a shattering way, but couldn't locate him in their crowds. More children ran past me and found themselves. The noise was unnerving.

"Don't just stand there," said a voice beside me. Yellow placed a hand on my shoulder. "They've been looking for you ever since they heard you weren't really dead. Get with the others. At the center." His face was dirty and his sweater torn. His mouth was bleeding.

"What happened to you?"

"I got jumped. They wanted information." He nodded toward the children. "It's not safe to be by yourself any longer. Get with the group." His hand at my back was insistent.

He escorted me toward the Elders, the floor sticky with

spilled drinks. All conversation stopped. Only the whiny dialogue and electronic sound effects of the movie droned on.

I felt conspicuous, a giant target. I regretted visiting the men's room. I looked less thrown about, less wounded. The Youngsters might excuse themselves for their actions, convince themselves that the damage they inflicted was less than real, that they could get away with more of the same. Or worse. I held on to the gun in my pocket as I walked. I really needed a drink. My flask was gone, fallen down some rabbit hole, but ahead I saw several bottles passed between older hands.

Elders parted to allow me into the heart of their circle. Then aging faces closed in around me and the questions began.

A sixty-year-old in a dark blue blazer shook his finger at me, spit hanging from his lips. "What have you done?"

"You've been drinking again?" I asked. I observed. I hoped.

Angry recriminations from all sides, often slurred. Again and again the same question: "What have you done?"

"Nothing that should have come to this." I closed my eyes briefly to escape their rheumy glares. Beyond the thin wall of gray or graying heads bubbled the growing mass of children, silent, curious, trying to listen in to our conversation. "A Youngster did this."

Seventy held up a hand. "As I said before, now is not a time for blame. No one is to blame."

"Bullshit," said Blazer. "We know who's to blame. This young shit fucked it up. All he had to do—"

"All he had to do is something we haven't managed in years of trying." Seventy's attempt to smile like a grandfather failed. "You know what we know. And we know nothing. He at least has been trying to find out what happened."

Blazer and the others waved Seventy's assurances away. "What has he found, then?"

The Elders waited for me to explain. On the wall above our heads, a large spaceship was shaking itself apart as it tried to return to its own time, the crew hanging on to computer consoles as they pretended to quake with the vessel's motion. An extra in the back of the shot conspicuously moved in the wrong direction, giving a strong impression of bad choreography.

I took a deep breath. "There was the furnished room."

Blazer laughed. "We know about the room. We showed it to you."

Yellow said, "Yes, but he watched the tape."

Blazer fell silent, his face stone.

I realized I didn't want to reveal what I had seen on the tape, or the second tape's existence. "Yes, it was of me. Older. Not much. I was drinking."

A voice from the back called out, "Where's the Drunk?"

A murmur ran through the Elders. Elbows and shoulders knocked against one another as they spun to locate the Drunk. Their anger grew by the moment, a storm that builds energy from itself. They no longer snarled only at me but also at each other, a stomped foot leading to a thrown punch, a shove answering a glare. An Elder fell to the ground in front of me. I stooped and helped the old man to his feet. It was Seventy. He looked up at me, a sad smile on his face.

"We all just want to live," he said. "I wish we deserved it."

"He's not here." Blazer yelled, and others soon joined in. "He's not here." Some took this as a cue to go hunting. Groups of Youngsters, somehow better organized, splintered off to follow, even though I doubted they knew who the Elders were looking for. I hoped a confrontation wouldn't take place somewhere in the hotel's dark hallways.

Seventy, trying to regain long-lost control, raised a hand. "It doesn't matter where the Drunk is now. The Body is already a body. What matters is what he, or someone else, has left behind." This brought silence. In this group no one was as old as Seventy. I wondered what this meant. If he was the end of my years, if there was only him and no further, what had he learned? Sad, I thought, that just when I finally became comfortable with life, as he appeared to be, that would be the end. To me he said, "What have you found?"

All eyes were on me. I had to tell them something of the truth. I relied on the massive paradoxes we were all awash in to keep my next lie from being too obvious. If any of them here had more information than I expected, it wouldn't take long to find out. "The Youngsters have a gun."

The group became absolutely still. Eyes left me, searched one another, the same aghast expression reflected back and back and back, each sure that one of the others was responsible.

An elder with nearly white hair licked his lips. "It's the gun that shot the Body?"

"I assume."

"And you're sure it was a gun?"

"It looked a lot like one just before they hit me with it."

"Good God, they're armed?"

Children filled half the ballroom now, and I could see clogged hallways beyond the two sets of double doors, children jumping to see what fun was being had in our besieged group.

I lowered my voice. "They are still bound by their expected memories. Unlike you, who know that this is a paradox, they remember only these current events. Remember that. They are not afraid to hurt or kill. They tried to kill me."

Blazer leaned in. "Why can't we recall what you're experiencing? Why are we all untethered?"

They huddled like a flock of terrified sheep. Being untethered from me they had dealt with. Being untethered from one another made them afraid.

"The Body was our link," I said.

Blazer growled, "We need an observer. Someone to watch the Suit." This as if I weren't there. "Someone we can rely on, someone who we know is on our side." I knew he meant "our side of the death." At least I think he meant that.

Seventy said, "We don't want to get in his way. He's more motivated than any of us. After all, he'll be the one to feel the bullet. One of us would slow him up and confuse him."

Voices shouted Seventy down.

Blazer pointed at Yellow. "He should go, too. Everywhere that one goes."

Yellow was scared. "I don't think—"

More shouts of agreement. They converged on Yellow and Seventy. Again I was an afterthought. A hand grabbed my elbow, and I was dragged from the center of the group. Screwdriver. He led me to the door beside the bar. On the wall above us, the captain of the time-travel vessel congratulated himself for a job well done.

Screwdriver opened the door. Lily stood on the other side. "Hurry, before they realize you're gone." His face was white. He was worried he'd made a mistake.

"Why?" I asked.

"They'd kill you to save themselves." He was staring at Lily, as if he wanted to grab her and hide her away for himself. "And besides, she convinced me."

I walked through the door. Lily smiled at me, then at Screwdriver, who shut the door behind us.

"Why did he help me?" I asked her.

"I pointed out to him that if they were really all on the same side as you, then they would have your scar."

"What scar?"

She touched my temple. "This thing. It's going to be permanent. And I haven't seen any of them with it."

I worried about what that might mean.

"Let's go," I said. I didn't know where we would hide but knew we must. The Elders were getting as feverish as the Youngsters. Panic leaked in like fluid through the hotel's cracks. Lily and I moved along the dark hallway toward the kitchen's service entrance. Large looping graffiti clung to the dingy walls, piecemeal caricatures, murals, indecipherable turf markers. I had ignored the paint for years. Blindness can be chosen. Not until I ran along the hall with Lily did a word catch my eye. *Scar.* The word was part of a longer message splashed on the wall in red. It had been painted with a brush instead of a spray can, which gave it an anachronistic urgency the canned messages lacked.

I stopped and read the whole message: *A scar is something you can trust.*

Lily retraced uneven steps toward me. She looked back the way we'd come, worry evident on her face. I took her cue and moved on.

Farther down the hallway, I spotted another sentence: *Can't move ahead without the Body.*

It was as if the dead man upstairs had called to me, reached out through wires and walls to grip my shoulder and whisper into my ear.

I said, "We have to go upstairs."

"What?"

"We can hide upstairs. I know a room. I have the key." I reached into my pocket and felt past the gun to the key that Screwdriver had given me. As I did so, I realized that the videotape was missing. "We need to find the room where the Youngsters held us. I dropped something there."

Her face was pale and clear in the dark hall. "Upstairs. One more trip upstairs. I don't want to, but let's go."

I said, "What are you talking about?"

She didn't answer. She looked at me with eyes too bright for such a dark hall, and I forgot my questions, questions about why she trusted me and why she accepted so many of me running through the halls of a dead hotel, what it was that made her stand next to me and take my hand and say, "Okay, yes, let's go upstairs."

We turned and ran together, the messages lingering in my head. I thought of scars and a body that were part of my timeline now, perhaps always had been, if only I'd paid attention before. Might I have seen them when I was twenty, thirty, thirty-five? Could I have seen them and glanced away, convinced myself that the struggle of an Elder was not my struggle and the suffering of Youngsters beneath contempt? As I ran, I recognized my own sinister nature for the first time, my blindness and my anger, my self-hate, and it scared me.

I ran with Lily's hand in mine. Her eyes flashed in the dark, reflected some light I couldn't see.

I caught the spare shape of more letters in the dark, more slashes and splashes of the red brush. Words a foot tall covered the walls of the stairway, overlapping so that I caught only fragments. I tried to decipher even a single word but couldn't make sense of anything except individual letters.

Lily suddenly sagged against me, heavier than her weight. Her eyes scanned the walls, her face tortured by what she saw. My curiosity about what the words said was overwhelmed by my desire to flee. I held her against me. "What's wrong?"

She whispered, "These messages. They remind me of something." Her hand was cold and her grip weak.

"What?"

She shook her head. "I don't know yet."

I lugged her up the stairs, trying to cover her eyes with my hand, but she pulled it away. We reached the second floor, and she gripped the door's edge tight, sobbing. She hung from the doorframe, slowly gaining strength as she read, and when at last she turned to me and said she was ready to go, I saw that a door inside her had closed.

I asked, "What did it say?" I knew she couldn't answer. I may have asked just to make sure she wouldn't.

She shook her head, tears at the corners of her eyes. She took my hand, and even though she'd been dizzy and sick only minutes before, her grip was strong now, reminding me of our situation. She turned and led the way down the hall to the Body, led me to a room she'd never seen.

Outside the door I searched my jacket for the key, slipped deep into the lining through another hole. I was decaying like the building around us—a little bit at a time, but to an inevitable ruin.

I opened the door, and she stepped in. The Body rested as he should, on the table under the weak bulb, the sheet tucked around him. I shut and locked the door. Lily slowly drew the sheet from the dead man. She wasn't shocked, not in the slightest, only took his hand and held it, squeezing so tightly that her hand turned white. Her fingers played over the tattoo on his wrist.

"He's so cold," she said.

"He's been there for hours."

She nodded. "He has your scar."

Without looking I knew she was right, but I walked to his side and saw the scar, a faded smudge of whiter skin, a crescent above his temple. I looked down at his face, my face, truly mine, at damage I only now realized hurt, and couldn't look away.

The window paper had been torn off, and the sky outside was turning light. It was the color of mud. I wondered if Lily had ever seen the sky blue, as I had, as I could at any moment if only I boarded the raft.

"I'm sorry you've been dragged into this," I said. "It's something I should have figured out on my own."

"You can't do this alone. That's why it's happening this way." She put the Body's hand back under the sheet and came to stand near me in the pale light. Before I could react, she had placed her head against my shoulder and leaned her body against mine. It fit as if it had always been there, as if my bones had grown around her figure. Her hands met behind me and reached for the muscles of my back. I returned her embrace and held her tight against me. My urgency scared me. I tugged at her dress, yanked it above her waist, and she pulled at it with me, then worked at the buckle of my belt, tore at the front of my pants to release me so that I could enter her. When I had, we stood against the wall, arms knotted around each other, my knees bent and hers stretched to tiptoe. We stood still a moment, and I searched her eyes for the light I'd seen there before; I felt for it with the part of me inside her and couldn't find it there either, and I told myself that I imagined it, that it hadn't really been there at all, even though I knew it had been. The proof was that she looked away from me to lose herself in the moment, pressed herself against me without seeing me. We breathed ragged and tasted each other's tongue. It didn't take long. I withdrew from her, smelling her skin on mine, and we both fixed our clothes. We looked from the Body to the pale window and at each other. She raised a hand to me and began to speak, but there was a voice at the door. It was me, probably no more than ten years old.

"Hurry up," he said. "I don't like this floor."

"Don't worry about it." The second voice was older. "There's no one here anyway." There was a crash of old boards breaking. "See, this stuff is just junk."

"I still don't like it." The doorknob jiggled. "Hey, this one's locked."

I took Lily's hand. We backed toward the window, her palm as wet in my hand as mine was in hers. Between us and the rattling doorknob lay the Body, an artifact, his silence balancing out the panic I felt at the hunting party on the other side of the door. Another voice had joined the first two, a deeper one—a teenager, who immediately took action.

"Wait here," he said. "Let's see if we can't bust it down."

I whispered to Lily, "Did you see any fire axes or tools in the halls? Was there anything they might use?" She looked at me, her eyes blank and fearful. She might not even have understood the question. I glanced around the room. Behind us was the partly covered window, its thick butcher paper held on with brittle masking tape. I tried the window latch. Years of rust bit into my fingers. I searched the room in growing desperation, and near the foot of the table I spotted a long screwdriver. A gift from Screwdriver. I held it before me like a dagger, pointed at the door.

"What are you going to do?" Lily's eyes locked on the screwdriver.

I couldn't attack children, not even if I was in danger. Besides, if I were really going to use a weapon against them, I had the pistol in my pocket. Instead I turned back toward the window, worked the tip of the screwdriver beneath the latch, and started to pry at it, levering it back and forth. The old metal began to give almost immediately, but it was twisted in upon itself enough to keep the window locked shut. "Chances are they won't get in here anyway."

At that the door shuddered beneath a heavy blow. I hoped Lily wouldn't sense my fear as I scanned the window for another way out. Dust and old paint flecks floated in the low shaft of light spilling through the gap of the window cover. A second blow shook the door, a crack appearing from top to bottom. Quiet counting leaked from the other side, a hushed *one and two,* and with *three* the third crashing blow came.

Hoping the paper was thick enough to keep the glass from raining down on us, I stabbed the screwdriver through the middle of the pane like a needle into a blister. The window shattered with a jingling crash, and the voices in the hallway stopped. I stepped back and brought my foot up to kick out the remaining glass, and the paper and the tape fell, a soft chiming off the side of the building.

Another crash against the door, and another. They'd heard the glass, and it had motivated them. I grabbed Lily's hand.

"Ready?" I asked, even though it was more command than question. She had no choice, nor did I. I leaned out the window and hauled myself onto the rusted fire escape. When I was fully outside, Lily followed. It creaked under our weight. Past the abandoned buildings to the east, the sun leaked through a strip between clouds. I looked up and then down. Beneath us the fire escape had rusted away and come off the building. Too far to drop; we had to go up.

We climbed.

Up close, the walls of the hotel were worse than I'd imagined. Acid rain and the slow, gentle impact of debris left the stones porous, like coral or a sponge. I pulled Lily closer to the rusted rail of the escape ladder. Beneath us the window bubbled with faces, all mine, of various ages, and their shouts climbed after us. Most of them were too scared to venture onto the fire escape. The two who did, in their early teens, all legs and awkward elbows, made the entire structure creak and settle. A bolt somewhere burst with a loud snap, and the ladder shifted beneath me. Lily, climbing ahead of me, looked down. "Oh, God," she said.

The teens on the ladder beneath us were armed. Each carried the pistol, my pistol, the one the Inventor had used to hit me, and they all aimed theirs up. A hand from the window—older, I thought—grabbed the nearest and shook him. Both teens stood back and gazed up at us. The scaffold moaned and began to shift again, and I knew we had only moments of climbing before it freed itself from the building.

"One more floor," I called up to Lily. She didn't respond. Hazarding another look below, I saw teens crowding the third-floor platform, fearful of climbing but unaware that they were in danger of collapsing it under their growing weight. The eldest held the others back, as if afraid he might be responsible for their loss. I realized that in fact he was, as was I. I took my own pistol from my pocket and lowered it, aimed at the street far below them, far away from any of them, and fired a single shot. It had the desired effect. The children—for they were just children—fell over one another to get to the window. I wondered for a second after the Body—what might they think. I knew they'd treat him with respect, but only out of fear. He would seem ancient to them and his connection to them tangential at best. I thought of their crowded rooms, their confused plans, the collisions of memories conflicting with new events. Each of them was alone. Each of them fought to be heard in a chorus. I pictured them clogging the doorway, filling the hall, and looking at one another, panic on their faces, worry in their hearts about what a dead body meant to them. How could they return home to a normal life after this? Untethered from one another because they'd been brought here, no longer even tethered to their own days and lives, no longer able to deal with the realities of their childhood after seeing what they'd seen here. They would go back to being children, planted in their normal routines, but they would know of this place and this time, know of the Body, of me, of Lily, and it would taint them and their days. Each of them would think it right to return here again and again, to continue to change events, to muddy their life and memories. A cold realization closed around my heart. I was no different.

The scaffold jolted, and another bolt broke. A red dust speckled down on us. Lily coughed. She looked at me, her eyes dark. "It's letting go."

"Get to a window," I said.

She climbed the steps to the next platform, and I followed. The scaffold groaned. Outside a window black with old newsprint, mildewed to unreadable, we held hands, and I removed the screwdriver from my pocket. For a moment I hesitated. In the window's imperfect reflection, I couldn't see how bad I felt. I saw only a man and woman, dressed for a party, holding hands. In the reflection my suit still inspired awe. What if we didn't need to face any of the troubles I foresaw? The Body might be avoided if I simply hid, ran away, and never returned, ever, to the hotel. My youth might be wasted poring over every room of the hotel looking for me, but that could last only so long. An army of me would eventually limp home in retreat. Lily and I could go anywhere; we had limitless options.

I thought all this in the time I studied a blessed reflection of myself and Lily, and then the scaffold began to separate from the building and I brought the screwdriver into the glass, pierced it with a nearly perfect wound.

"Kick it in." Lily cried.

I raised a foot and attacked the window. The scaffold's complaints sounded human. The ancient metal beneath us sagged, abandoned its rigid shape. It twisted like rope. We gripped the railings to stay upright as the floor curved like a lolling tongue. Finally the glass gave, and I threw Lily into the opening just as the scaffold let go. I fell forward to grab the window edge. Glass bit into my arm, and a bar of metal caught me across the back as it fell to the ground below. I screamed, or tried, and held on, Lily gripping my arm. Beneath me the shriek rising from the collapsing scaffold ended, and we were washed in silence. Both of us labored at hard, uneven breaths.

"Help me up," I said.

We pulled me into the room.

THIS ROOM WAS just as the others—lousy with dust and plaster grit. Lily and I lay for a minute on broken glass. Too tired to move, I watched the rise and fall of her chest. As her breath slowed, so did mine, and we climbed to our feet, picked glass from our skin and clothes.

"They'll know where we are," she said.

We left the room, headed away from the stairwell toward the end of the hotel. A noise behind us made me turn, certain it was Youngsters already bursting from the stairs. There was nothing there, some dust settling from the ceiling, the building exhaling.

Lily led me through the halls. It occurred to me that I should ask what she knew of the hotel, what it was that made her run so assuredly. Just then I saw another batch of graffiti: *Dumb waiters tell no tales* →→. The arrows pointed around a corner to what looked like a dead end, a cluster of three doors.

"Hurry," Lily said.

I glanced behind us again. We'd made a number of turns, and I couldn't remember how to get back. "What are we doing here?"

A noise skidded up the hallway after us. It was a little boy's voice, calling that he'd heard something. At that moment, as an adult, I understood the boy's panic. I reached for Lily.

"They're coming," I said.

She tugged at the rusted latch of the small half door mounted on the wall beside us—a dumbwaiter. "Give me your screwdriver."

I handed it to her, and she worked at the latch until at last it snapped open. The dumbwaiter car was not there, but the ropes that held it were. She wrapped my hand around them. "Climb down to three."

"How will I know what floor I'm on?"

She hesitated. "You're right. Go to the bottom. We'll start from the ground floor."

I took the rope in numb fingers and towed myself through the small doorway. It was like crawling into a vertical coffin, and I worried that if the rope snapped, I would twist in the cramped shaft and tie myself into a knot of flesh and bone. I held the ropes tight and tried to lower myself down. When I'd gone a few feet, Lily climbed in after me and drew the door closed, dipping us into darkness.

The shaft was cold and wet. Mildew clouded the air, fighting with the dark for dominance, and I found myself more than willing to slide down great lengths of the rope in near free fall. Water dripped on my face. Lily descended as quickly as I did, catching my head and hands with her heels. At last I landed hard on something solid and hollow.

There was no door in the shaft there. I whispered up to Lily, "I think we're on the dumbwaiter."

"Break it."

I began to stomp on the dumbwaiter and prayed that the sound would not call out to the Youngsters. The old wood splintered with a wet crack, and I fell into the small car. I kicked at the door and then kicked the pieces of the dumbwaiter out onto the dark kitchen floor. I followed them out, snagging myself on the splintered edges of the car, and Lily emerged after me. Dirt and grime streaked up her legs and arms. I knew I was in a similar condition.

"We're going to have to get to that room." I heard exhaustion in my voice. My speech slurred even though the alcohol had burned off hours earlier, and my mouth was dry, my tongue clicking against my teeth and lips.

The kitchen had been scrubbed clean whenever the hotel had been vacated. There was no grease, no smoke stains on the ceiling. All the cupboards were closed tight. Other than a thin layer of dust, it was immaculate. I opened a cupboard and found nothing, not even a roach.

Lily tried the faucet. It produced a rivet-gun staccato, but no water came from it. I wouldn't have drunk the water regardless. "I need something to drink," she said.

"Let's see if we can get to the bar."

"That's not what I meant."

I lied. "I know. But there's water there, and ice." Possibly, I thought. I'd spent much of my first year preparing for this event, traveling back and forth with trays of food, coolers of ice, cases of alcohol and bottled water. I'd estimated how much I would eat and drink, and then I'd doubled that amount and spent weeks bringing it all to this morning, the morning of the party. I'd done everything myself; not a single Elder had ever appeared to help—but why would one? I already knew that the Inventor had prepared for the party alone, set up the bar, the food tables, napkins, utensils laid out just so. Everyone else showed up later and ate and drank it all, then pissed and shit it away. By this time, this late in the evening, I doubted there was any water left, let alone ice. But she didn't appear to know that.

We made our way down a hall to the kitchen's ballroom entrance—double-hinged doors with round windows. The dark ballroom was lit only by a movie playing on the wall. In the light from the projection, I could see two dozen audience members slouching in chairs. The room behind them, where the Youngsters had held their war dance, was empty. Was I really so ignorant as a youth that I wouldn't leave even one lookout? Apparently.

I leaned against the door, and it moaned open. Lily held back a moment, and I took her hand and gave it a reassuring tug. We stepped into the ballroom. I approached the scattered spectators, who sat in little clusters of two or three. Decades of me, tired and sleeping. I recalled having watched every film projected until the sun rose, but now on the wall played a film I'd never seen. The swinging movie image showed a stairwell full of rubble, the shadow of the cameraman as he staggered toward a window and nearly fell out to the city street below. The image captured me, and I had begun to focus on it when a voice called from behind me.

"You'll want to get out of here."

I turned to face Seventy. He held the projector's remote and paused the film. No one else stirred.

I indicated the others. "Won't they mind?"

He shook his head. "They're asleep. Nothing on their minds to keep them awake. Unlike me. What's happened?"

I told him of the invasion of the Body's room and our flight.

He rubbed at his chin. "I didn't realize they were that dangerous. They told us not to leave here or they'd kill us. We don't believe them, but we're old and tired enough to listen." He shrugged at those sleeping around us. "It's late for us to be up."

"You're up." It sounded like an accusation.

"I had to speak with you." His mouth wrinkled into a smile. "Lucky me. What are you doing back here?"

"There's a tape."

Lily's heels scraped against the floor behind me. "What is so important about this damned tape?"

Seventy straightened himself against his cane. He glowed in her presence. I'm sure she noticed it, too. I regarded him with a mix of pity and understanding. He must realize how he looked, but he was fearless in his admiration of her. I respected that.

"I don't know what is on the tape," I said. "But it will be important enough for me to leave behind so that I'd find it."

Lily nodded as if she understood. I marveled again at her calm in the face of my chronology.

Seventy walked back to his chair but didn't sit down. "You should try to find that tape as soon as possible. But we need a diversion. I have an idea." He drew the remote from his pocket and turned off the projector. The room fell into almost complete darkness. Only one of the chandeliers was partially lit, and as I watched, one bulb burst, bouncing orange sparks that faded to red, then black. Phosphene trails slid across in my vision as I heard someone approach.

Seventy said, "You need to do us a favor."

Screwdriver joined us, eyes on Lily. "What is it?"

"The Youngsters are hunting him and more dangerous than we thought. Can you provide a distraction?"

"I can." Screwdriver looked at me with a neutral gaze. "Give me your jacket."

I hesitated. Lily already knew about the gun, but neither Seventy nor Screwdriver had seen it. I reached into my pocket and clamped a hand around it.

Seventy's eyes narrowed. "What's wrong?"

"Nothing." I withdrew my hand and the gun with it. Screwdriver's eyes flared. He struck at my shoulder, and I lowered the gun and took a step back.

"What the hell is he doing with that?" Several of the sleeping figures stirred.

Seventy looked down at the gun as if it were covered in blood. I waited for a withering comment. Instead Seventy said, "No. He's right to carry it. Obviously if the Youngsters are armed, he should be, too. You must have gotten this from one of them?" His eyes locked onto mine. I felt no need to answer but did anyway, with the lie he'd given me.

"Yes. One of them dropped it." Behind me I heard Lily's silence and wondered why she helped me carry the lie.

Screwdriver looked tired. "I still don't trust him."

Despite my lies I was offended. "At what point does my fuse get so short?"

Seventy said, "It was a slow burn." He laughed and gave

Screwdriver a reassuring nod. To me he said, "We don't have time for this. Give him your jacket."

I removed my jacket and stood holding the gun and the extra timepiece I'd found near the penthouse. As Seventy and Screwdriver watched me repocket these items, I tried to see if they shared a scar where I'd been struck. Seventy's old skin was impossible to read. Screwdriver was poorly lit, but I thought I could see a hint of a faded line.

With my jacket on, even with different pants and the close-cropped hair, Screwdriver had effectively become me. We looked at each other a moment, his eyes bouncing from me to Lily and back. His hands ran through the pockets, searching for things that weren't there, things I couldn't be sure he remembered, as we were no longer tethered. "What floor do you need to get to?"

"Four," I answered.

"I'll try to keep them on five and six, then."

I nodded, and he turned without another word. Seventy watched him leave. "Don't lose that." He pointed at the extra timepiece in my hand.

"I won't."

He sat down on his chair. "Go find that tape."

Beyond the ballroom doors, the stairs sounded with Screwdriver's footsteps. I crossed the room to the bar and reached over for a bottle.

"You won't need that," Seventy called. "You don't have time for a drink."

I ignored him. When I turned around, the glow of the projector had returned. Frozen on the wall was a decrepit stairway, white paint peeling, metal handrail rusted. A shadow like that of a woman's arm hung on the wall. Beneath the rectangle of the image, caught in its reflection, was the group of men I would become, maybe. Sleeping through the commotion, the panicked chase upstairs, the frantic search for answers about their own dead Body. In the light of the projector, hair of differing lengths and shades of gray—grayer here, whiter there—fluttered in competing drafts. Was I really that indifferent to my own suffering? I wondered. I thought of the boy and how I had failed to comfort him in any meaningful way.

I gripped the bottle of whiskey tight at its neck and marched past the sleeping men. "Where are Yellow and the Drunk?"

Seventy held the remote ready. "Off somewhere tending to their wounds, I'm sure." He was waiting for me to leave before running the video. Still a private man, I thought of myself, even when only being entertained.

"What wounds does Yellow have?"

Seventy smiled. "Only those you haven't healed yet."

Still angry, I took Lily's hand, and we left the room. As the door shut, I heard the old man resume his movies.

WHEN WE REACHED the fourth floor, I had little recollection of where we had been held hostage. Lily was likewise unsure. Last time we'd come to this floor, I'd been unconscious and she'd been terrified and bound. I closed my eyes and conjured a dizzy picture of that room, the boys circled around us. In my memory there were streetlights outside the window.

"It has to be on the side of the building facing the street," I said. We turned right, stepping lightly around rubble and ceiling plaster. This floor was in worse repair than others. Water damage from leaking pipes had caused a great collapse. Musky odors hung in the air, and mold grew along the walls. I walked with one hand outstretched, afraid of what I couldn't see, despite the predawn sunlight trickling through several doorways. Room after room revealed disheveled furnishings and ripped window covers.

"They've been here," Lily said.

"Who?"

"The children. They've been looking for us. Torn every room apart to find us."

She was right. I marveled at my own pursuit. These Youngsters were more determined than I remembered ever having been. The fanaticism of one, one old enough to feel the danger of being untethered, of having removed his connection to the rest, was enough to drive them all.

We passed room after room, glanced in at floors covered with glass and plaster, paper and wood. Nothing remained to remind one of a hotel other than numbers on the doors. Above us thundered footsteps, raised voices shouting. Screwdriver was one floor up, and the chase was on.

"We have to hurry," I told Lily. "If they catch him, it will take them just a few seconds to realize they have the wrong man." We moved to the next room. It was there, among pieces of glass, that Lily found the tape. Her hand shook as she handed it to me.

I watched her try to hide her eyes. "What is it?"

"Nothing. Let's go." She left the room, and I followed.

Back through the wet halls we rushed. We'd almost reached the main stairs when voices called from behind us. Youngsters had spotted us. They squealed, as if it were a game, squealed and screamed and grinned like hungry dogs.

I grabbed Lily's hand, and we ran.

Tripping down the stairs, we reached the third floor and rushed along a hallway. They'd expect me to try to get to the ground floor, I thought, not hide on the third. We ran past the Body's room, which now stood open, the sheet on the floor, the Body abandoned and uncared for on the table. At the smaller staircase at the end of the hallway, I heard noises below us, calls of children, high on panic and power. Where was Screwdriver? I thought. Why hadn't he been able to keep them away longer?

We headed upstairs, thinking to double back to the main stairway, but at the landing outside the fourth floor I heard voices, and we continued up. The light grew as we climbed. Lily leaned to look up. "If we reach the top, it ends there."

Before I could ask what she meant, I heard footsteps below us. I leaned over the railing and peered down through the squared spiral of stairs. My shadow fell large before me, down the floors. In the center of it, looking back up at me, I saw myself. It was the Nose.

To Lily I whispered, "Get up and climb." We made our way up the stairs, stumbling on glass and plaster, our footfalls mixing with those of the Nose behind us. He didn't call out. He didn't say anything. He worked to gain on us, his breathing fast and hard, and I heard the call of the gun he carried as it hit the handrail. My exhausted, hungover body burned with the effort. Lily and I tripped each other in our rush. My hand on her arm, I tried to balance her. Finally we reached the top, the penthouse landing. To our right yawned the mouth of the elevator, to our left the door of the apartment that I'd only ever been in once, twelve hours earlier. In the dark it had seemed deserted, but now I saw the unmistakable signs that someone had been living here. The floors were worn but clean, the drop cloths over the furniture a temporary protection. New drywall sheets lay on the floor, and a bucket of dried plaster with trowel sat near the door. Repairs were under way.

In the kitchen the service exit was painted shut. I quickly

searched the rooms, looked out the windows. Outside, the fire escape still clung to the upper floors of the hotel. I ran back to the apartment's entrance and found Lily looking down the stairs.

"He's stopped," she said. "I think he's waiting for more of them."

I tugged at Lily to follow. "Come on. We'll go back down the fire escape."

"It collapsed."

"Not all of it. We can get down a floor or two."

She looked from me to the stairs and back. "If he's stopped, maybe he's not that dangerous. Maybe we can talk to him."

"He's got a gun."

"So do you."

I tapped my leg with the revolver. "That's different. I need it."

"For what?"

"To keep him away from us."

She reached out to brush my cheek. "You know, the only one who's fired a gun around here is you. They haven't—"

"Listen to me. They're dangerous. They don't know what's at stake."

"They saw the body."

She was right. They had seen the Body. Their quest for answers had been transformed, the moment they found the Body, into something else. I tried to imagine what I would be thinking if as a child I'd been shown the cadaver I would become.

"Whether they've seen it or not is beside the point," I said. "Things have spiraled out of control. We've got to get out of here."

Footfalls echoed in the stairway. I grabbed her hand and pulled her through the main room. Dawn chose that moment to arrive, and direct sunlight coming through the wide windows blinded us. I moved on instinct, swinging the window into the room. I was leaning out to survey the fire escape when a loud snapping sound erupted from the kitchen. It could only be the painted door breaking open. My eyes still blurry from the bright sunlight, I saw my arm rise on its own, the gun suddenly weightless in my hand. I aimed at the dark gap of the kitchen doorway. For a terrible moment, nothing happened. When at last a figure stepped into view, I thumbed back the hammer. My eyes cleared enough to see the same gun in the other man's hand.

"I'll kill her," he said.

I squeezed the trigger.

The gun sounded a double shot, though my hand jerked only once. I watched him collapse, watched him fold over at the waist like an empty suit. His head hit the floor hard, and he moaned as his body crashed down around him like a collection of parts. I wasn't breathing. I realized that I was looking at the black suit I now wore, that the jacket I'd given to Screwdriver was on the floor, wrapped around the man I'd shot. I stepped toward him, more frightened than I'd ever been in my life, and grabbed a shoulder. I was sure it would be Screwdriver, but when I turned him over, the face was wrong—more haggard. A gash oozed blood at his temple at the same place the Inventor had struck me. Blood dripped from the whiskers of his chin, the bullet wound in his neck lost beneath the unruly beard, blood flowing down his front, dyeing his shirt. I gulped for air. I clutched at his collar and shook him, tried to make the empty, blank eyes focus on me, but they didn't move. I felt his chest, and my bloodied hand came away without a heartbeat. It was the Drunk. In his hand was the pistol I also held, smoke twisting from the barrels of both. He had faced me, had aimed at me, yet his bullet had missed.

I turned to look at Lily and found her lying on the floor, a red-black puddle growing beneath her.

I think I screamed. I must have. I want to have done so.

I crawled to her, spreading blood across the floor in streaks. Her eyes were wet with tears.

"Take me home. I want to go home." Her voice was thin and airless. I reached around her, found the exit wound at her back. I tried to hold it closed with my palm, my tears dripping onto her red dress. Behind me came footsteps. I turned around as Seventy and Yellow stepped into the suite from the hallway. Behind them was Screwdriver, my jacket in hand, face flushed and sweaty, masked in anguish. He knelt beside me. Lily looked up at me and sighed.

"Take me home," she repeated.

Screwdriver started to lift her from me, and Yellow had to pull my hands away. He helped me to my feet but would not let me follow. Screwdriver paused as Lily said something to him. He nodded and turned around. I heard a tapping and realized that my hands were shaking, the gun knocking out a message against the floor. I tried to let go of it, but my fingers refused.

"She wants her things."

Seventy waved him away. "We'll bring it. You take her home."

Screwdriver handed me the jacket, as if in payment for Lily, collected her against his chest, and left. Before me were the bloodied floorboards where she had lain.

Yellow turned his attention to the Drunk. "He's dead."

Seventy gave a withering look. "We knew he would be. Take him upstairs. We'll send him to yesterday in my raft."

Yellow nodded, hauled the Drunk into a sitting position, and then rolled the Drunk's body over his shoulder. With great effort he rose into a crouch, bearing the body to the stairs, the Drunk's feet dragging behind him. Seventy and I were alone in the penthouse living room, blood smeared across the floor. We listened as the sounds of Yellow's struggle moved up. The roof door opened, and I was surprised that an alarm sounded, so like the one I'd heard when the elevator descended. It stopped after a moment. At my feet was the Drunk's gun and in my hand my own. I knelt and picked up his, identical to mine but coated in dirt and missing one more bullet. I looked at my own gun and realized that the bullet in line to fire next would be the bullet to kill Lily. I was cold and shaking.

Seventy, his lined face tired, said, "Okay. Now that that's over with, let's get out of here."

Seventy and I walked through the hotel halls. I lost track of where we were, and Seventy never said. I carried both revolvers, one in each hand, both warm as if ready for more shooting, as if there were anyone else here as dangerous as I was. We passed plaster holes and bared latticework, door after door, all identical. Somehow the Youngsters' search had not come this way.

At last Seventy stopped in front of a door and handed me a key. "Open that up, will you?"

I shifted both guns to one hand and opened the door. It was the finished room, where I had watched the video on the miniature TV, where Lily had first kissed me. I tried to hand him the key, but he refused it.

"Keep it," he said. He looked tired enough to fall. "Empty your pockets." He sat on the bed, in the exact spot where I had earlier.

"Why?" I fought the urge to vomit on the floor and instead squeezed my eyes closed. Lily's image lurked behind my eyelids, crumpled, bleeding.

"Empty your goddamned pockets. She's dying."

I put the guns on the bed first, followed by the twin timepieces, six months different, then used tissues and spare buttons. The tape was last, and the only thing he took.

"Keep the guns," he said.

"I can't."

"You better."

I said, "I won't. I can't. Not after what—"

Seventy raised his silver-knobbed cane and pointed it at me, like a wand, as if his will might fly from it and turn me into a frog or a table lamp. "You take those guns with you when you leave here or I'll beat you so you can't chew snot."

I took the guns from the bed and stuck one into my remaining jacket pocket, the other into my waistband at my back. I didn't want to bear their weight.

Seventy stepped into the closet, out of my view. I stood next to the bed looking at the items I'd carried with me. Change from different eras. Buttons that had come with the suit. I'd traveled years beyond my lifetime, beyond the lifetimes of anyone I'd known as a child. I'd gone back to watch seeds planted and then moved forward to see centuries-old wood taken from the same spot. I'd met children who had no idea I'd later walk over their graves and the graves of their children's children; I'd met them and watched them play games they thought would never end. And all I carried around were the buttons that came with the jacket I'd ruined. Nausea boiled inside me.

Seventy pulled the camera out of the closet and off the tripod and held it out to me. "Here, this is hers. She asked for it. Take it to her."

"I don't know where she is."

"The building across the alley, just next door. She lives there."

I took the camera and held it at my side. "Why did she come here? Who invited her?"

Seventy stood beside the bed. "We did. I did. You. You will. She came because that's what happened."

Suddenly I was seeing the room through a dark circle at arm's length, a hole the size of a plate. My breathing was too loud in my ears, and the walls moved around me. I needed to leave. I reached out with my free hand and felt for the door. Before I left, Seventy said, "You should hurry. She doesn't have long."

"What do I do now?"

"How about you stop her from coming here? How about you keep her the fuck away from this hotel?"

I left him in the room, standing next to the bed, heavy on his cane, with my buttons and ancient coins lying around him like treasure. Perhaps he'd remember where they came from. At that moment I had no idea.

EARLY-MORNING SUNLIGHT poured between the buildings in large shafts. People were out, in groups of twos and threes, moving among mounds of garbage and debris that had piled up during the night's storm. Some were beginning to clear rubble from the street and collect it in large barrels. Behind me rumbled a flatbed truck. I was surprised to see a vehicle running.

The entrance to the neighboring building was open, without even a door. I scanned for signs of where Screwdriver might have taken Lily and found a set of stairs and an out-of-service elevator. Climbing the stairs, I was overcome by the repetition of it. Not the fact that every floor was just like the previous and the next but the feeling that I knew the building and this stairway. I looked on through the small circle of my vision, certain that when I finally reached the top, I'd find Lily and then pass out. Consciousness was only borrowed for the climb. I watched steps go by beneath me, the dirty white linoleum spotted with black circles of still-wet blood. The struggle to focus was exhausting. I stumbled and caught myself on the sill of an open window. Below me scrambled tiny figures on rain-washed streets. I remembered to climb. A shadow moved in the square of light ahead of me—a man burdened with something heavy. A woman's arm, hanging over his own, swung to the rhythm of his walk. It was Screwdriver, and he turned to look down the stairway at me.

"Help me, would you?"

As fast as I could, which felt not fast at all, I climbed the last six stairs to the landing at the top floor. I helped him carry Lily's inert body into a large apartment. Screwdriver led us down a hallway and into a bedroom where a bare mattress on a pallet lay at the center. We placed her on the bed, and I sat on the floor.

Lily's voice was a secret. "Bring me that needle."

The tunnel I watched the world through swung around the room. Nothing connected to anything; I caught only glimpses of early daylight bursting through windows, crumpled bedsheets, water-damaged walls, a collection of old liquor bottles. At last something moved past me, through my line of sight, and my eyes followed. Screwdriver rummaged through a pile atop a paper-covered table, returning with a small, shining statue, like a squid with its tentacles spiraled around its body. As he walked back to Lily, I could see that the object was twisting as he carried it, opening at the base, the arms opening to reveal a long silver needle.

My voice, thick in my throat: "What are you doing?"

Screwdriver didn't answer. He knelt over Lily, hands

shaking as he gave her the device. Lily took the object, raised it to her head. I couldn't see what she did with the needle— Screwdriver blocked her from my view—but she moaned as a whirring sound came from the device. Her feet traced slow arcs across the bed. I felt sick. At last the sound stopped and her body relaxed. She held up the device and said something to Screwdriver as he took it from her.

His voice quivered. "I'm so sorry." He looked over his shoulder at me, eyes red and tearful. Their whispers crawled along the edges of the room and under the sparse furniture, just out of reach. As I strained to hear, my vision blossomed, and I took a deep, shuddering breath. The room came into focus.

Screwdriver, crying, leaned down to kiss Lily on the forehead. Then he stood and walked to me, the small, shining device bright silver in his outstretched hand. "She wants you to have this."

I looked at it, unsure I even wanted to touch it. "What is it?"

"Take it. She'll explain it to you." His voice crackled.

I took it, started at the chill it held. "Can you help me find a doctor?"

He shook his head. He was barely holding himself together. "I'm leaving now. She wants you to take care of her."

I shook my head, just as he had. Identical. "Stay. Please."

His breaths came short and fast. "I can't stay. I can't see her die again."

Again.

Behind him Lily talked to herself in bubbling whispers.

"Why me? What can I do?" I was desperate for his help.

"She trusts you."

"She barely knows me." I knew that this was wrong the

moment I said it. The words pinched in my chest and made me twitch.

Screwdriver almost reached for the device in my hand. He didn't want to leave it. That made me want to keep it more. He said, "You can do this. Know that."

Lily muttered from her bed, hands stretched toward the ceiling as if to catch something. I knelt beside her. She lowered her hands and held her side, blood leaking between her fingers and soaking into her mattress.

I looked over my shoulder at Screwdriver. He was in shock, no different from me, eyes narrowed and face pale. He shook his head and turned away. "Fix this." He sounded as if saying those words severed a part of him. He didn't look back as he left. Watching him leave made me feel as if I were leaving, as if I were abandoning Lily. I thought I could hear him gasping for breath on his way out. Her hand reached over and found mine, fingers sticky with blood. The room smelled of copper. She looked up at me and said something. I leaned in, straining past roaring blood in my ears to hear her voice.

"Not him," she said. "You."

"Why me? I mean, why not him, too? We both can help you."

She spoke again, her voice so weak it was only air, and I had to force myself to hear her, will myself to understand. I heard her more through the skin than through my ears, her breath brushing the hairs on my cheek—soft, wordless promises of trust and love that were unearned. Her eyes were on me but looked through me, too wide, too seeing, her lips slightly parted. I leaned in and kissed her eyes and then her mouth, a deep kiss for me, only me, because she was gone. Lily had died the moment her breath brushed my cheek, I knew it. I sat with her and listened to the sounds of voices through open windows—parrots or people, I couldn't say—close but indecipherable, no longer hidden under the labor of her breath.

Guilt weighed me down. I waited for my shaking to stop. When it did, I found myself holding something in each hand: in one, the small silver device, the squid, whose oblong glass head was now full of pale pink liquid; in the other, the video camera. The power light on. I felt the gentle hum of it, and realized that Seventy had turned it on and set it to record before handing it over. I looked into the lens for a moment, realized that it would be recording me then, catch me looking into it, and I turned it away. As I did, I felt a tug at my cheek, the cheek that had felt Lily's dying breath, and I felt for an instant that the camera had taken something from me. I dropped the camera onto the table and reached up to touch my cheek. It was cold. I climbed into Lily's low bed, lay beside her, and fell asleep.

I woke at midday to the sound of laughter. The sun stood overhead, and the apartment was hot and filled with indirect light. I went to a window to find it already open. Below, in the alley between her building and the hotel, a crowd had formed around the fire-escape scaffold ruin. Groups of men worked on the twisted metal in concert, brandishing small handsaws, laughter rising at jokes I couldn't hear. They seasoned themselves with bits of rust. In minutes they had the steps and ladders in parts and the parts loaded into wagons and old shopping carts. Most of the men pulled their wagons themselves; one had a large dog attached to a harness, its tongue hanging low despite the shade. In the short time they'd worked, the scaffold had been deconstructed, nothing left behind but bits too thin and brittle to be of value, and a paprika-colored dusting on the ground.

I watched the street a moment, surprised that I had caught these scrap collectors. A handful of pedestrians passed through the alley. They wore suits or coveralls, carried bags and umbrellas. They looked suspiciously like commuters, and if the city weren't a ruin, I might have thought this the end of the workday stream.

Among them hobbled a man on a cane. His white hair caught my eye, still at a distance, crossing toward this building. I nearly turned away before realizing it must be Seventy, that he could only be coming for me. I tried to leave the room, but Lily's body lying before me became a barrier I could not cross. I choked on guilt. Such a short time before I had lain next to her, and now I could barely look at her. I sat on the floor and waited for Seventy. I waited a long time.

When his face appeared at the door, he said, "Can I speak to you outside?"

"I'd rather not leave her."

"It will be just a moment."

I edged around the perimeter of the room and followed the old man to the stairs. The room had filled with light, and as a result the hallway seemed darker than tar. From somewhere downstairs a radio shouted out old songs, Top 40 hits from an era long gone quiet, but too fast, voices pitching up too high.

"Where's Screwdriver?"

Seventy laughed. "Is that what you called him?"

We refused to look at each other. The dark of the hallway obliged us.

"Lily's not dead in the past."

I said, "Don't you think I've already fucked things up enough?" I had meant just Lily, but the way Seventy was nodding I realized it could mean so much more.

"Oh, yes. You have. You fucked everything up very nicely. But now you know your goal has changed. Lily didn't deserve this. Fuck what happens to you. You're dead already. But Lily—"

"How?"

"All you have to do is keep her from going to the hotel. One of us invites her. Stop that invitation. How hard can that be?"

I watched the floor between us. The songs on the radio fuzzed out and were replaced by voices speaking Chinese.

"Shit," I said.

He nodded. "You've got no fucking choice." He gripped his cane like a club, as he had before.

"You gonna threaten me again?"

"Don't have to. There's a whole group of Elders who are ready to kick the shit out of you if you try to chicken out."

I put on the jacket. "Why can't one of you do it?"

"We don't need to go back," he said simply. "We already know you do."

I laughed and returned to the room where Lily lay, surveying it for anything I might have dropped. On the table was the strange silver device, the only thing she'd given me. I took that. I lifted the video camera, popped out the tape and pocketed it.

From the door Seventy held out a hand. "I'll take the tape."

"Why?"

"Because it's mine."

I pulled the tape out, thought that I could snap open the cassette and rip the tape before he could stop me. I handed it to him, certain it was the wrong thing to do. At her sink I ran a glass under the weak stream of dirty water, filled it, and drank, then refilled and drank again. I'd need to get food but didn't want to look through her cupboards.

The hallway was empty, Seventy already gone. I didn't see him or any Elders on my way to the raft. Truth was I didn't look for them. Instead I focused on my own hunger and the weight of the guns and the odd metallic squid in my pocket. How far back I needed to go was a guess. I thought six months would be sufficient. As if to confirm this, my hand dipped into my pocket and hit the extra timepiece I carried. Of course six months was enough. It already had been. I worried the watch I'd found meant I was doomed to another failure.

I'd have to find someplace long-term to set the raft. I'd figure that out when I got there.

I PARKED THE raft atop the hotel. I'd never done that before, not even when I scouted it.

The fall day was clear and cool, and it was just after dawn when I arrived. Exhaustion from nearly twenty-four hours without sleep made me careless, and I nearly fell from the raft. My back hurt, and I stumbled as I walked. I was very hungry and felt slightly drunk but couldn't remember the last drink I'd had.

An alarm blared when I opened the rooftop door, but the buzz seemed to come from a distance, as did my footsteps and the rattle of the handrail. They were like sounds traveling through water. I descended, counting the steps without meaning to, trying to ignore the sense that something was wrong. The feeling grew slowly, and empty corners pulled at my attention. I kept expecting to see figures lurking or unexplainable shadows.

The fifth floor was where the graffiti had begun last night, six months from now. The red-painted messages on the walls were gone, or rather hadn't been painted yet. I stood for a moment, stared at the cracked wall, and almost dropped off to sleep standing. I didn't want it to be as simple as it had to be: If I never put the messages up on the wall, they would never appear. I leaned against the railing and watched a spider climb a thread between me and the wall. Sunlight rainbowed along the silk. Without warning, the spider stopped and toppled from the strand, a fresh line tied to the first. It nearly reached the floor before slowing, then climbed again.

I sat on a step and emptied my pockets. I had the guns, the device, and a key. It was for 503, the furnished room. I would go there, I thought, rest, and then I'd find food on the streets, and then I'd find Lily.

The key fit. I expected the key to fit, but nothing else. I knew instinctively that the room it opened to wouldn't be anything except the peeled wallpaper and bared lattice behind the plaster, knew in that moment that I would be the one to refurbish it the way I'd found it last night. I wondered how long it would take to find the furnishings and to make the room presentable. It would be, I knew, an undertaking.

I was wrong. The room was finished and as clean as I'd found it the first time, six months in the future. My shock was nothing compared to my exhaustion. I stepped in and fell onto the bed. Sleep came quickly, but even in my dreams I was tired and hunting.

I woke slowly, not knowing the room for a blissful moment, then sinking into recognition. I'd fallen asleep so fast that I was still dressed, on top of the bedcovers, the door still open.

I went to the bathroom, washed my face, drank water to fill my stomach, and returned to bed, afraid to close my eyes. The light outside was low. Dusk or dawn, I couldn't tell. I checked my watch and found I'd slept for twenty hours, through to the next morning. My stomach hurt, and I pushed the curtains away from the window. Below me morning walkers were already out, dressed for jobs the city didn't look like it could support: ties and jackets, tweed skirts, black leather shoes.

I went down to the street and crossed the alley to the neighboring building. It was, as it would be when Lily was shot, open. I wound my way up the stairs to her door. I knocked before I knew what I would say. I was hungry to the point of illness, my stomach turned upon itself with sharp spasms. I held myself up against the doorjamb and knocked again. After a minute, footsteps clicked toward the door. A man's voice came through.

"I've got a fucking gun. Get the fuck out." The voice was thick with sleep. I'd seen nothing in Lily's apartment to make me think she lived with anyone. In fact it had been almost bare, unlived in, as if she'd just appeared there one day.

I put my hand against the door, as if to feel it for warmth. I said, "I'm looking for Lily. I think she lives here."

A pause and then locks grinding, four, from top to bottom. The door swung away from my hand. Before me stood a man, thin, hinting at transparent, long past sixty years, bones propping the flesh of his stubbly face, hand wrapped around a pistol not unlike my own. His short white hair was swept all to one side from sleep. Beyond him stood garbage, piled waist-deep in most places, even higher in some. Old newspapers stacked to the ceiling. Radio parts lining shelves along the room's perimeter. Boxes of old lamp parts—coiled cords, finials, shade holders, bulb sockets like empty eyes. A sheet lay on the floor, a pillow nearby, his head's imprint deep at its center.

Stupid with hunger and exhaustion, I said, "I'm looking for Lily."

"I know," he said. "You said that. She's not here. Never has been."

"You live here alone?"

He looked back at the room, as if to check for other occupants, as if unsure himself. "Why don't you come inside," he said as he wandered into the room, distracted by something I couldn't see or hear. I closed the door behind me. He went to his sheet and sat cross-legged on it, rubbed a hand over his hair, perhaps to get blood flowing, to reawaken from what must feel like a strange dream, me arriving at his door and demanding to see a woman he didn't know. I looked for a place to sit but found none. I opted to lean against a stack of crates, but when I did so, the entire stack shifted and I almost fell.

The man smiled. "Be careful, alright? I keep an ordered house." He laughed at his own joke and searched the floor around him until he found a bottle with amber liquid in it. He pulled a stopper free and took long gulps from the nearly empty bottle. He looked at me, not so much daring me to ask for a share as needing me to, as if he'd share with me anything he had, but he'd be damned if he'd offer. I joined him in his drink by taking my flask from my pocket and removing its stopper. He smiled and raised his bottle to me. My nearly empty flask didn't stop me from matching his draw from the bottle, and when we lowered our drinks, he shuddered and blew out a whistle.

"Shit, that's awful."

"Why drink it, then?"

"Nothing else to do with it." He laughed again. "So who's this Lily you're after?"

I moved a mayonnaise jar filled with thumbtacks away from the edge of his table. Six months from now, it would be on Lily's counter. She might not be here yet, but she would be.

I said, "She's just a woman I met once. She lived here, or I thought she did."

"Lied to you?"

"No. Just the truth is a little. . . ." My hand waved in a circle, as if it explained anything.

He let me not finish my sentence. He looked at the two, maybe three gulps left in his bottle, and I could see his inner debate about finishing it now or saving it. I held up my flask to him. "Try this. It's twelve-year-old scotch."

He hesitated to take it. "You sure?"

"Consider it a housewarming present."

He smiled and unstoppered the flask. He sniffed at the mouth before tasting it, eyes closed and smiling as he drank. He tilted his entire head back, and I felt a pang at his taking so much. When he had finished it, he pulled the flask away slowly, then lowered his head. "Yes, that's old all right." He smiled at me. "I do know a girl, but she's not your Lily. Least I don't think so. But she can help you."

I looked around at the collection of scrap metal and paper, glass jars filled with pins and paper clips. Finding food was all that mattered. "I'm not interested in hiring a—"

His face fell. "She isn't a prostitute. Won't sleep with you, not even if you had money. No." His fingers fanned as if preparing for a magic trick. "She helps you remember those things that you forgot made you happy. She remembers things for you."

Desperate to vanquish his loneliness, he sought to keep me by offering help, but his needs were outweighed by mine. I was used to waiting for history to catch up to me, to staking out events. I'd spent days waiting for battles, weeks waiting for births. To fully appreciate assassinations, one needed months. I needed to be here when Lily arrived, and it would be easier to keep watch on the apartment if invited in. I was too tired and grieved to feel callous for using him. The only thing I craved more than forgetting the image of Lily crumpled on the floor was sleep, but to encourage allegiance I would go to meet this woman. I asked him his name.

"I'm Phil," he said.

"All right, Phil," I said. "Where is she?"

We walked through Times Square and down the center of Broadway. To either side of us, the sidewalks were filled with crowds, not moving anywhere, only looking at one another with uninterested eyes. These were vendors without customers. Thousands of bracelets, key chains, plated watches, necklaces, and earrings sparkled in hundreds of open briefcases, trinkets identical from one to the next. Salesmen watched one another wander by, shadows with clearinghouse savings. A few cars passed through, ancient, rusted, and nearly as done in as their drivers. They drove through intersections with flashing yellow lights, passed the ruins of theaters sporting worn posters and marquees dripping letters.

Phil walked ahead of me, talking constantly, his words

cutting the current of people to either side. Despite the sun the air was cool and people around us were wrapped in light jackets and lengths of fabric. I realized that some wore curtains, or pieces of curtains, from the theaters. On one corner Phil stopped to see the end of a street performance—four gray-haired old men break-dancing on cardboard flats. They spun in place, slowly, like the hands of a dying clock, until one moaned and came to a stop. The others went to his side but refused to touch him. His arm was cast at an unnatural angle. Onlookers from the crowd tried to help, but the dancers themselves disappeared into the crowd, as if fearing reprisal.

Phil motioned to me to continue south. "They've never been able to come up with a better ending," he said.

"That's part of the routine?"

He shrugged. "It's all I ever see of them. It's for the tourists, mainly. They give the 'hurt' one some money, and he goes home to the others."

I looked around us and wondered how to tell the tourists from the locals. Above us advertisements flashed. We turned east on Forty-second Street. More traffic came through here, bicycles and hansom cabs. We retreated to the sidewalk and headed toward a cluster of trees. Construction equipment roared around us. A team of orange-vested workers jackhammered a hole into the concrete in the middle of the street. A large man with a potted tree jumped from the back of an idling flatbed. With a blade in one hand, he cut open the plastic pot and pulled the sapling free, its potting soil white with roots grown tight to the pot's shape. He dropped the tree into the fresh hole, and the others began to shovel dirt around it. Another worker pulled a hose from the nearest fire hydrant, already leaking water into the gutter. He threw the hose onto the newly planted tree's base even before the others had finished covering the roots, and then they all moved on quickly, only one of them remaining behind to finish the job, smoothing, tamping with his shovel, dropping to his knees to spread earth back into the hole, placing as carefully as he could the remains of the concrete over the open dirt, making for a rough display of the small ginkgo. When he finished, I finally noticed the other trees they had planted. The street was cluttered with roughly circular holes, each sprouting a small, nearly dead ginkgo. They stood in uneven rows along Bryant Park and beyond. I was reminded of cemeteries that grew from battlefields, the parks that grew from cemeteries, and I sank into the urge to check my hands for dried blood. They were clean, somehow, but shaking. The small green leaves brushed at our shoulders as we threaded our way, with the rest of the pedestrians, into the overgrown rectangle of Bryant Park.

Ginkgoes and sweet gum filled the park's lawn. Saplings, some five feet taller than those just planted, covered the lawn leading to the back of the large gray expanse of the public library. Green folding chairs, many of them broken, sat in clusters; conversation filtered through the trees, laughter.

Phil nodded and smiled, either to himself or to the voices in the shadows, as he walked toward an information booth at the corner of the library building. "We've got to check in with Emma first. She knows where most of the girls are."

Emma's girth filled the small booth entirely. I wondered how she forced her way inside each day, or if she ever left. Two black chopsticks held a wispy coil of gray-blond hair in place above a still-pretty face. We stood close enough to know that her thickly layered perfume didn't hide her natural odor.

Emma looked up and smiled. "Phil, how are you?" I realized at once that she was a person with whom one shared secrets, without coercion.

"Emma, I need to find Eden."

Emma's eyebrows rose.

"Not for me." He presented me with a grand wave of his arm. "For him."

Emma tried to be nonchalant in her appraisal of me. I became conscious of the pistol's weight in my pocket and paled at the thought of what I'd so recently done with it.

She said, "I'm afraid Eden is no longer around."

Phil nodded, not really understanding for a moment, and when he did, his head kept bobbing. "What? She left?"

Emma pulled a bag of licorice from beneath the counter, leaned back to make room for it between herself and the old wood, and placed it on her lap. "Left or otherwise. Not sure."

"Oh, that's too bad. What are her regulars doing?"

Emma laughed. "Trying to remember on their own."

Phil's eyes bounced between her face and the bag of licorice. She relented and offered the bag to him. He took a handful, probably as many as he thought he could get away with, then turned to me, offering from his small stash. I needed food, but not the way Emma looked at me. I waved it away.

I said, "Thanks anyhow, but I'm going to head back."

Emma leaned forward. Apparently my refusing her candies improved me in her estimation. "You look horrible, sweetie. You need someplace to stay?"

"No, I'm up at the hotel."

Both Emma and Phil stopped chewing, black licorice bits stuck in their teeth. Phil swallowed and nearly choked. "The Boltzmann? Next to my building? That hotel?"

I said that was the one.

Emma put her licorice away, placed her elbows on the uneven counter in her booth, and leaned heavily onto it. The boards groaned. "Honey, that hotel is haunted."

Phil nodded again. "Weird stuff in there. Someone walking around. Voices. Lights at night. But no one goes in. No one comes out."

"I think I'll be okay."

Behind us the crew filled a hole with a suffering cherry tree. A young woman wandered past and stopped, knelt beneath the new tree, and watched the crew begin work on another spot some ten feet away. She curled onto her side in the fluttering shade and closed her eyes. I tried not to notice how she held her hands across her stomach as Lily had when shot.

Phil said to Emma, "What about my girl? I can't recall if she's working tonight."

Emma removed a pad of paper from a nail on the wall, scanned the scribbles. "She's off." Somehow it sounded forced. As if what she said was both truth and lie. "Want me to get her a message?"

"Yes. Send her home with a fifth. Put it on my tab."

"You know, it's getting hard to lift your tab."

Phil reached through the window to touch Emma's hand. "It's not the size of the tab, darlin', it's what you do with it."

They both chuckled. Emma's laugh made her face prettier. "Pervert," she said. "I know what you want. Want me to rip your tab right off."

Phil winced. "You do know how to make a man feel like he owes money. I'm good for it—you know I always pay my debts."

"It's the only reason I talk to you." Her bright and happy eyes scanned his face, then rolled, still happy, in my direction. Phil's teasing must have reminded her how she trusted him and his judgment. "You look like you could use a meal. Go to the information booth inside Grand Central and tell them I sent you. They'll hook you up. You'll have to work for it, but you'll be fed."

An instinct rose in me, the desire to turn and run, to protect myself somehow from anyone's help, to own and bury myself in guilt, but on its heels came the need to lose myself in some mindless task. I thanked her for the offer.

Phil thanked Emma, too, and we walked east toward the public library. He said, "I've got an appointment to set up, so you go get your food and I'll see you later. Do yourself a favor. Don't stay in that hotel. It's a bad place. You can stay in my building till you find one of your own."

"There's room in your place?" I imagined myself sleeping between piles of newspapers and old doorknobs.

He shrugged. "In one of the other floors, yeah."

It took me a moment to realize he meant that the entire building was his. "You live in that building alone?"

"Not alone. Me and my daughter. It was a good choice. Off the beaten path." He shook my hand. "I'll see you later. Just let yourself in. Knock before you come to my rooms." He turned at the corner of Fifth and headed uptown. He'd disappeared behind wandering pedestrians before he'd gone a block.

I stood at the corner and watched people swarm north and

south. Behind me lurked the library, its gray stones covered in a mossy green growth, the steps rotten with books and people, a swarming mass. Wagons teetering with books descended makeshift wooden ramps toward the street. I headed toward Grand Central Station and found myself in a procession of book-laden wagons. Through the station's nearest entrance, I walked past storefronts without glass in the windows, baked goods and clothing on display. Behind me a clatter. A wagon had overturned, its load of books spilling down the ramp. The red-faced wagoneer swore and scurried to gather the books. Those behind him hurried him on with laughter. I turned and walked off.

The hallways of the terminal were dark, bulbs flickering, burned, or missing. It was less crowded than the streets outside. I followed signs toward the main concourse with its looming ceilings and marble arches. Across the main floor stood pallets of wood, each stacked with books. When the books reached six feet, another pallet was laid on the pile and the stacking began again. Hundreds, perhaps thousands of books were piled in this way. Stepladders on caster wheels rolled between the columns, workers carried armloads of books to the upper tiers, others held the ladders steady as books were placed or pulled. At their tops, three tiers high, just out of reach of a person stretched toward toppling off the ladder, another pallet, and then scaffolding that reached to within an arm's length of the ceiling. Atop the scaffolds lay men and women with buckets of paint. They lay on their backs, brushes above them, paint dripping down on them. The green ceiling, covered with depictions of the zodiac constellations, was being obliterated, hidden beneath new black paint. Farther along the room, where the black paint was older and already done drying, the teams of painters made marks nearly invisible from the floor. I watched, the light from the massive steel-and-glass walls at either end barely enough for me to make out their work.

The famous clock atop the information booth had broken at some point; all its faces showed different times. I stood beneath the nearest clock face, my own slack and stupid, until a woman approached me. She was old, bent to a question mark, gray hair pulled back, face youthful. She said, "Honey, are you okay?"

I'm not sure what I said, and I tried to smile despite my confusion. The woman smiled in return and held my elbow, steered me to the shuttered ticket windows. My head swam with hunger and the smells of gasoline, ozone, and horse manure. "Emma sent me."

The woman smiled. "Oh, did she? Well, you must be a good worker, then. Follow me." She led me across the wide room toward the open doors to the track platforms. The smells grew stronger, and I caught the sounds of horses neighing and clicking their shoes on concrete. The platforms hissed with engines hidden in lightless tunnels. She asked me to wait a moment and disappeared into the darkness. When she returned, still smiling, we headed back through the main concourse and up the stairs at one end, metronome footsteps leading me. Above us massive windows filtered yellow light.

"Get something to eat and then come back downstairs. Tell them I sent you. I'm Emily."

I thanked Emily and walked into Cipriani Dolci, a restaurant overlooking the main room.

The restaurant was half full. Low, whispered conversations rolled from the dark tables. Exhaustion and hunger weighed on me like chains. I saw everything through a tunnel, a cloudy circle at the end swung spotlightlike over white plates, partially eaten meals, and dining customers.

Someone took my arm and guided me to a table. I braced myself against the chair back, looked up at an unsmiling face topped with red hair. "Who sent you?" He had an Irish brogue.

"Emily."

"All right. What'll you have?"

I didn't know what to say. I had no menu. I had no money, if they even used money these days. The floor tilted beneath me.

He said, "How about a ham sandwich?"

I must have agreed, for several minutes later one materialized before me, a pickle and a glass of water as well. I ate without tasting, finished the water and three glasses that followed. My eyes focused on the wine bottles lining the back wall. My flask was with Phil, possibly for good. I was tempted to ask for a drink, then dismissed the idea. The waiter returned to clear my table and asked, "Feel better?"

I did and told him so. He waved me away when I said I didn't know how to pay. "Emily knows."

I stood, thanked him, and headed for the steps, exhausted but no longer near collapse. I had to find Emily. The light from windows cast halos over the patrons I passed. I saw now that their faces were speckled with dirt and paint. Some were gaunt enough to mistake for shadows. Several glanced up at me, nodded in camaraderie I didn't share.

I found my way back down to the concourse. Emily strolled across the marble floor to me, leisurely with age.

"Now that you're fed, feel like working?"

I was glad for something to keep me moving. Anything other than thinking about what had happened to Lily, what lay ahead for me and her, if I found her in time. I saw no way out of my debt.

I nodded, and she led me to a group of three men. All three turned toward her, respectful. She spoke quietly to one, and he gestured for me to follow. Emily waved good-bye, and I trailed after the man in silence. Outside, the day had grown hot. Crowds of people, many with cameras and video equipment, jostled one another down the street. We dove into the current, my guide showing no patience as he used an elbow to create a gap between pedestrians. Each step was a battle. We fought our way to the middle of Forty-second Street, where the crowds thinned for wagons and the occasional car or bus.

My guide shouted over his shoulder, "Fucking tourists," as a bus nearly crushed us. At his outburst bus passengers swung toward us to take his picture. He raised a fist, and up shot his middle finger. When they'd rolled away, he called, "Come on," and broke into a trot. He rounded onto Fifth and walked a block. At an uninteresting glass-fronted building, he hammered on a window. The door swung open, and a blue-uniformed man leaned out. He smiled at my guide. "Hey, Jonah."

My guide, Jonah, said, "Got another mule."

The thought of doing nothing more than physical labor was enticing. I didn't want to think or feel.

The guard nodded, one hand on a hip-holstered pistol, and pulled the door closed again. He returned with a child's red wagon loaded with books. Jonah turned to me. "Go on. Take it."

I grasped the handle and thanked the guard. He said, "When you come back, just knock, but knock hard." His tired eyes tried to smile at me.

I turned to follow Jonah back to Grand Central. Tourists swarmed, filling the opposite sidewalk and a good portion of Fifth Avenue, camera-flashing and street-map-fluttering. They spoke languages I'd never heard, some I could have sworn were dead or at least close to dying, their skin covering the spectrum from blue-black to albino white. Their eyes squinted up at the decayed buildings, the tattered ads, the failing scaffolds. Above them windows yawned, taunted with curtains blowing in unfelt breezes, figures of somewhat human aspect drifting behind. Double-decker buses stopped in the middle of the street, hissed hydraulic fluid at the intersection, and more people spilled out. They took pictures of themselves riding the library lions. Laughter erupted from children as they chased one another and put their hands on the lions' chins, as if one might actually roar and snap.

Jonah walked without looking back. I tried to keep up but kept losing books and had to retreat to gather them. A short woman with a street map clutched tight in her fist took pity and chased after me with two I'd missed. I thanked her, but she spoke no English, only smiled and nodded. Nearly back at the station, I spotted my guide bobbing forward a block ahead. He stopped to wait for me at the station entrance, where he held the door open. "That's what you have to deal with. That shit."

I thought of the woman who'd helped me. "It's not so bad."

"Tell me that in half an hour." He laughed mirthlessly and followed my wagon down the ramp.

Emily saw me right away and waved me over. She looked at the wagon of books and said, "Didn't lose any, did you?" I told her I hadn't. "Good. Now, bring them over here." She walked toward one of the four massive piles of books. "Look for spaces that need to be filled in," she said. She pulled a book from my wagon and slid it into place, already searching for another spot. The next book she grabbed was squat and thick. She had to move a few books, filling smaller spaces to open one wide enough. "It's okay to move books. The most important thing is that you not leave a gap unfilled for too long."

I noticed men and women among the stacks with long lists written by hand on pads of yellow paper. Pencils tucked behind ears, shopping bags hung from wrists, they wandered, eyes rolling over the great piles until they spotted a volume, pulled it free, and placed it in one of many shopping bags too heavy with books, then crossed the item from their list and moved on. When they could carry no more, they hauled them to the terminals' dark doorways, where train engine hisses rose and fell, seasoned with the neighing of horses.

I watched the people take books away. "What is this?"

Emily picked another two books from the wagon. "We're the book exchange."

I stared at her, not understanding.

She said, "We get search requests and send the books on to those who need them. We used to run it from the main library, but it was simpler to do it from here. Could you hurry up and place some books? We don't want this stack to topple."

I looked up at the scaffolds, the painters working on top. "What are they doing?"

She followed my gaze. "Painting the new zodiac. Much more accurate."

I didn't ask how the zodiac had changed. The scaffold above me swayed, and I grabbed two books and found spaces to sandwich them in. When my wagon was nearly empty, I said to Emily, "If we place the books randomly, how are they ever found again?"

She smiled. "The books just seem to know to go where they'll be found."

Despite having eaten, I couldn't focus enough to understand the system, and in light of what I had done and what lay ahead, I found the confusion of the room, the tasks, the ease with which everyone accepted me, refreshing. If I'd stopped to think about the strangeness of this, I might have fallen into old habits, old needs to piece together the puzzle. I decided that here was a puzzle that simply didn't matter to me. Here was something I didn't understand, a mystery I would leave behind me unsolved. There were bigger problems to worry me.

When my wagon was finished, Emily brushed her hands on her skirt. "Okay, now you know what's going on. Go back to the library and get another wagon. We'll be doing this until the sun gets low. You'll have to move quickly."

As I pulled the wagon back toward the entrance, I walked by the clock again. Some of the hands had moved, but as I watched, I could see that some moved too fast.

"What's wrong with this clock?" I called to Emily.

She shrugged. "It's been like that for years. Someone altered it, and no one turned it back. It's kind of helpful, actually." She smiled at what must have been a joke shared by the workers. "It always seems to know what time you need it to be."

A school of tourists, mouths gaping, surrounded the information booth and snapped pictures of themselves standing in front of it smiling. I wondered what time the clock would show in the pictures, or if it would show any time at all.

I worked until it was too dark to see the stacks clearly, and the painters climbed down from their scaffolds. A new collection of workers arrived, swinging brooms and mops among the steady stream of vacant-looking tourists. Emily waved me over to the exit.

"You did a good job today, thank you." She held a brown bag out to me. "Here's some supper. If you're up for it, we could use you tomorrow."

I said I would be back. I didn't know why. The work had calmed me a bit, and other than watching Phil's building for signs of Lily, I didn't know what to do with myself. I'd been exhausted when I'd arrived, and now I realized I'd also been lonely. The people bringing the wagonloads of books, all as tired and focused on working for their meals as I was, provided a different sort of companionship than I'd had in a long time.

I HEADED WEST. The sun glowered in the low spaces between the buildings. I walked past the new trees of Bryant Park. Thin, sickly branches waved in the breeze dusting Forty-second Street with ash. Voices chattered through the trees and followed me west. I waited for fluttering green and gray wings of parrots fleeing my intrusion, their words close enough that I could make out single words and phrases. I kept turning to look behind me but saw none. "Only hurts a moment," one said. "Great, great weather," came the reply. I was tired enough to sleep, but I felt a need to talk, or at least to listen. Phil seemed the type willing to go on at length just for the sound of his own voice.

Music echoed down the stairs of his building. A radio played a quiet song, a woman singing words I couldn't make out. I remembered the images of the video I'd seen and then accidentally filmed on the stairway, the shadows of Screw-driver, me, carrying Lily's body up the steps. For a moment I was overcome with guilt and grief in equal measure. They washed up my legs like a rising tide, and I swayed in their current. I felt no better knowing that in this time she was alive.

The climb was finishing me off. A small slice of light leaked below Phil's door, and I wondered if he had drunk himself to sleep. I held the rail and steadied myself. When I could breathe again, I walked to the door and knocked gently.

Immediately the singing stopped. The music continued. I had interrupted not a radio but a woman performing, and I regretted being there. I almost turned to go when the woman called out, "Who is it?"

Not knowing what else to say, I answered, "I'm a friend of Phil's. I can come back."

Footsteps and the clank of falling junk. She approached the door, turned the locks. "No, it's okay," she called through. "He mentioned that someone might stop by."

The bolts pulled back, the door opened. Lily stood in the doorway. Candles, too many to count, lit her from behind.

"I'm Sara. Phil's daughter." She reached her hand out to me, and I took it. She let go of mine again even as I willed her not to. "He mentioned he'd made a friend today. I thought he'd made you up. He sometimes does that."

"I do not, you lying girl," Phil's voice, thick with alcohol, burbled. His arm waved from beyond a junk- and candle-laden table. Lily, now Sara, walked back into the room, the door open to me, her bare feet making no sound on the hardwood floor. Suddenly terrified, I entered. The heat of the candles wrapped around my head, and their perfume watered my eyes. I struggled to see Sara as she moved through the room's dark corners. I lost her in the shadows and waited for her to reemerge. The sound of her grew faint, and I heard whispered voices again just outside the window.

Phil lifted himself to a sitting position and held a jelly jar half full of amber liquid up to me. "My friends are never imaginary. Only my enemies." He took a sip and then began to laugh until he had to lie back down. He disappeared behind the table. Sara melted into yellow candlelight, her face lit from beneath, and smiled.

"He's been enjoying a bottle of whiskey."

I nodded. "He enjoyed some I had with me earlier today."

She laughed. "I should have known he met someone. He was in such a good mood." She gestured for me to find a place to sit. My brown paper bag crinkled, the sides dark with grease. I offered her some of my dinner, not knowing what it was but certain I wanted to share it with her. She refused. I opened the bag and found three pieces of baked chicken and a triangle of cornbread. I apologized for my hunger and started to eat. Phil, lying on his back, began to talk. What he said sounded like the middle of a sentence begun hours earlier, a river of thoughts someone else had released, and I was left to find my way into the conversation without help. After a minute I realized he was musing about the uses of the many objects of his apartment once he was done cataloging them.

"I just need to make sure not to lose track of anything," he said. "Once I get through the minutiae, the small stuff, I'll be ready to open it up to the public. This is the stuff they need. Emma's always saying that, she's always saying how she doesn't have this or that. Well, I've got it. I've got it all, but it needs to be listed and organized, and then it'll be ready to go back to work."

Sara nodded and leaned forward to stroke his hair. "That's right," she whispered. He closed his eyes. His drink, sitting on his chest, moved up and down with his breath.

Candlelight glowed through Sara's long white cotton shirt, revealed the shape of her body. I let my eyes linger, perhaps too long—she caught me looking. I tried to appear interested in chicken bones as I tossed them into the bag.

Phil, his eyes closed, said, "Have you seen my things?"

Sara smiled, a patient I-have-to-answer-this-so-often smile, and I smiled back. She said, "Yes, you know I have."

"Not you, girl." His eyes struggled open and rolled awkwardly to find me. "You. Have you seen my things?"

I looked around me. "Yes," I said. "They're very nice?" My compliment twisted out of my mouth as a question. I looked at Sara to see if I was on the right path. She winked at me through the low light.

Phil became upset, thrashed on the floor like a dying fish until he had turned onto his side, craned his neck to see me. "No, no. This is just crap. The sorting area. I mean my real things. The good ones. Have you seen them?" His eyes watered. Hard sounds clicked in his chest as he spoke. To Sara, his voice impossibly deep and filled with gravel, "Take him and show him. Would you, sweetheart?"

Sara uncoiled and rose from the floor. "Of course." She searched for shoes under the table. I gathered the remnants of my meal and crushed the bag into a ball. Unsure where to put it, I carried it with me, followed Sara to the door. She stopped and called over her shoulder, "We'll be back in a few minutes." Phil mumbled and waved, ushering us out.

Sara carried a small lantern. I followed, my mind racing. Seeing her was harder than I'd imagined it would be. This was Lily, but not yet, calling herself another name and caretaking her alcoholic father. This was the same set of stairs I'd watched Screwdriver carry her up.

At the third floor, she stopped at a door and turned to me. I could hear a smile through the dark when she said, "Get ready for his great collection of things." Her laugh was slightly cruel. She opened the door, and we stepped inside.

The third-floor apartment was more densely cluttered than the one Phil lived in. The items were bigger, more organized, closer to clean. A line of refrigerators blocked the windows. A rebuilt car engine sat atop cinder blocks two feet from the door. The walls were dotted with nails and hooks on which hung assorted devices. Battery-powered screwdrivers, electric toothbrushes, music players, each in a sealed plastic bag and pierced onto the hook or nail. Each item was labeled or tagged, numbers and letters separated by dashes written in a looping hand, a catalog system that perhaps only Phil understood. Maybe not even him. Bookshelves stood in the room at seemingly random locations, each stacked with some particular item. Cans of beans, unopened battery packs, stacks of pristine telephone directories. The bookcases stood mute in the dark room; the lantern cast their shadows one way and then the other. I felt as if we'd snuck into a cemetery and looked over the names of dead we didn't know, as if the things on these shelves were mysteries from a time unknown to anyone.

Sara set the lantern on the floor. "Welcome to Phil's room of things." She approached the shelves of beans and took one down, searched through her pockets for a can opener, and pried the top free. "Impressed yet?" She went to the kitchenette in the corner, found a spoon in the sink, and began to eat the beans from the can. "Come on in. He'll quiz you about this stuff, so you'd better look around."

I was entering a sacred space; Phil's devotion made it special. Sara leaned against a kitchen counter and watched me as she ate. I surveyed clean blenders, shiny toasters, cords tucked in tight coils, boxes of forks, spoons, knives, no two alike but each polished to a shine even in the dark. Some of the nails in the nearest wall held photographs in frames, old pictures—a child laughing in a park, a woman on a boat, a man over a computer keyboard, a strange hat on his head and a curious smile on his face. From others dangled ballpoint pens still in bubble packs, children's action figures, three pristine white bathroom tiles. At the center of the wall, a dark spot caught my eye. I leaned in. I was only inches from the item when I realized what it was. Inside the plastic bag, sealed tight against moisture and age and time, untouched for who knew how long, was the gun—the one I now had in my jacket pocket— as well as six bullets.

My hand sank into my pocket and wrapped around the same grip and trigger at which I looked. I held my breath a moment, felt my guilt and my hatred of the thing roll inside me, and then I pulled myself back. I turned away from the wall, guilty needles in my head, and found Sara gone. Across the room from me was a hallway, another unspace, dark and rattling with sounds of someone moving. I followed the sounds, left the lantern behind me, and felt myself sink into the darkness. The air was thick and still, the windows closed. I breathed through my mouth to avoid smells of mildew, mold, rot. In between me and the streetlit windows, I saw Sara's figure float across the room. I heard the squeak of bed springs.

Her voice cut into the darkness. "So what do you think of his things?"

"I don't know. Some are better than others."

"That's true. I don't care for the weapons."

I agreed.

Several long moments scurried between us, me in the doorway of the black room and her sitting on an unseen bed, springs mousing out minor protests—nothing compared to what I imagined they might do, could do, I was certain, if I joined her. I held out a hand and steadied myself with the doorframe.

She said, "You know I'm not his daughter, right?"

"No, I didn't." At first I found this a relief. Then I realized all the complications it implied in her relationship with Phil. "What—"

"I work for him."

I didn't think I wanted to hear this. I wanted her to stop talking, to let me retreat to my fantasy of the eccentric collector's daughter. Now I could only think of what he paid her for.

"Listen, I should really—"

"I'm not a prostitute."

I held the doorframe and sought some way to decipher her words. She let me float free for a minute, maybe two, before she continued. "I'm an actress. I help people reenact relationships or moments from their past. I've been Phil's daughter for five years, but he gives me enough freedom to work other clients into my schedule. I'm available for you if you want. I could see in your face that you have something you've replayed in your head over and over. I can help with that. Help you get past it."

The bed springs woke again as she stood. Her head and shoulders rose into view before the empty pane of the window, and I started at how close she was.

"Let me know if you want to talk more," she said. "I do both role replacement, like with Phil, or direct reenactment."

"What's the difference?"

"Role replacement is me playing the part without a context. We just go about our time as if I'm your missing person. Reenactment is a specific moment, which we play out as it happened. That costs more."

I nodded as if any of this made sense. Her voice sounded so close; I wished it would go away. Her breath touched my neck. Her hands found my arm, and she gently forced me loose from the doorframe, to open the space for her to exit. Our bodies had been intimately close for only a moment. I took in a breath of her and said, "You aren't really named Sara."

"No," she said. She was more visible in the lamplight now, and her smile made me remember how sweet she tasted when I kissed her. "Sara was Phil's daughter. She died twenty years ago. I'm just holding her place."

I waited for her to tell me her name, to release the sound of Lily to me, and I was also somehow hoping this wasn't the woman I'd met in the hotel. Yet it was—there was the same intellect, the same understanding, sad and tired, of how things worked. She knew the world too well, and she was past worrying about it. At last, just as she started to turn from me, I realized I had to ask her myself. "What is your name?"

She didn't stop her turn or look back to me, only kept moving down the hall to the lighted room and its layers of things no one missed. "Jessica," she said. "But don't call me that. No one calls me that. Not for a long time." Somehow I could hear the truth in what she said, same as I heard the truth in everything she'd said, even the things that hadn't been true.

I called down the hall. "Sara?"

A long pause. It was her game that we were playing, but she was somehow uncomfortable with it. Finally, a yes in answer.

I said, "If I were to invite you to go somewhere with me, a trip, out of the city, would you go?"

"Of course not."

A series of unspoken reasons floated past. She didn't know me, she couldn't leave Phil, and a thousand unknowns.

There was a clatter as she threw the empty can into the sink. "Don't take anything, he'll know," Jessica's voice called from the stairway. "If you want to hire me just look for me here." Her steps clicked down the stairs, and I was left alone with an old man's obsessions and the realization that my own wants and desires had not only been awakened but stolen by someone who didn't exist. Lily had been but imagination, no different than Sara was for Phil. I'd known nothing of her, nothing of her past or why she'd suddenly appeared. Yet even knowing that someone I didn't have any chance of saving had been lost, and that the person I'd watch die in six months was someone I wouldn't even know—even that didn't make me want to leave. If anything, I wanted Lily, a shadow of an idea, more than ever.

My shoes scraped out a rhythm on the steps as I descended to the ground floor and found my way across the alley to the hotel. It was haunted, Phil had said, and I knew why. It was filled with ghosts I'd put there, ones who had no business being anywhere. The basement door to the hotel was open, the lights of the first few floors already burning. I walked to the finished room and opened it with my key. The bed groaned as I lay on it and sank into sleep.

DAYS UNROLLED, GREW shorter, and I passed them working at the library, hauling wagonloads of books to Grand Central, propping up scaffolds that wobbled as librarians drew volumes from the piles, carrying them to the dark train platforms to be pulled upstate to other librarians. I tried counting time in tasks instead of hours or days, all my tasks the small parts of one larger: getting Sara away from the city. The smaller would lead to the larger, as minutes build hours. I had time. I always had.

It took the painters nearly three weeks to traverse the length of the main waiting room. The platforms and scaffolds drifted slowly across the floor as the shifting piles of books were adjusted slightly, consciously or not. Books pulled free and replaced, the pile a little further along. Assistants delivered food or fresh paint, stalked the floor on stilts to reach the pulleys and ladders that rattled at the scaffolds' sides.

Some days the painters couldn't reach an unedited spot and sat cross-legged under their illustrated sky. They smoked or slept, their snores echoing from the ceiling, their dreams probably filled with fumes from the painted stars overhead. Below them the piles of books melted away, like giant cubes of ice, pieces dripped away and disappeared. The piles grew smaller. One of the scaffolds nearly collapsed, and I and several wagon pullers had to reinforce it.

When the last star was finally painted, the aqua-green ceiling gone, the old zodiac replaced, the scaffolds were dismantled, and with them the last of the original book piles. Instead we built up two new piles at the eastern end of the terminal. Almost immediately the painters and the assistants began to reassemble the scaffolds on our new piles of books. That very evening the painters commenced the labor of painting the stars again, this time with midnight blue paint rather than black. The stars they used this time were not small points but rather large, childish crosses like asterisks. I had been coming for three weeks and stopped and watched the ceiling begin to change again, to be rewritten once more over the new artistic design. I had not heard discussion among the artists or seen any rendered plans exchanged—to my eye it was eerie and spontaneous. I stood, ate a sandwich the bartender had provided, and watched the work. Parrots had gotten into the building and circled along the perimeter, asking about bus routes and weather patterns. Emily found me staring at the sky.

I asked, "Why have they started over?"

She laughed. "You don't look up much, do you?"

I wondered what she meant but didn't say anything.

"No sky they paint up there is true. Not even the first one they painted over. The sky has changed again. The zodiac was useless. They had no choice but to start again." She stood a few minutes and watched the work with me. After a time she drifted away.

I watched the painters, chewing in silence. At the center of the room, the four-faced clock glowed solemnly. From where I stood, I could see two of the faces, and as I occasionally checked them to see their time slowly unwind, I recognized why they felt so familiar. From my pocket I fished out my timepiece. The hands from the two clockfaces matched four of the hands on my timepiece. The clock had been altered to perform like my watch. I sensed Seventy's work in this. Some kind of message.

Perhaps this is why I was only curious and not confused by the artists' repainting of the ceiling: I was like them. I crossed myself out and started over again and again. My party was proof, the deaths I'd caused in self-driven conspiracy were proof, and so, too, was the dizzying reality that at some point I came back—how soon would I, how far back had I—and adjusted the clock so that it counted moments for no one but me and the woman I would kill. I stared at the clock until I could breathe again.

I shook my head as I wondered how many ways I could fuck myself over.

IN THE EVENINGS I visited Phil, and sometimes Sara. I rarely spoke to Sara alone, but when I did, the conversations were quiet and unimportant. I felt nervous around her. She never brought the sale of her services up again, but I saw them in practice every day. I didn't know how expansive their act was until the night I found a note taped to the hotel door. The note, written in Sara's clean hand, read, *"Dinner party at 8. Please come."* I heard Phil's voice dictate the last line: *"Please bring drink."*

I had never reclaimed my flask from Phil, but I returned to the raft atop the hotel to find the bottle of whiskey I'd taken weeks before from the bar while the Elders slept under the film projector's light. In my room I showered, dressed, and left the hotel through the main exit.

Phil's apartment was packed, two dozen people filling the space available, toes touching, glasses and jars sloshing drinks on pant legs and dresses. Laughter poured out the door into the hallway. Emma lounged in a chair near the door and reached out to touch my elbow. I thanked her for finding me my job with Emily, and she shrugged. "You look like a man who always has options." She pointed to the tables near the windows. "They have food and drink over there. Too far for me, but you go."

I said I'd bring her back something and struggled past people who smiled or glowered depending on how heavily I stepped on their feet. Two librarians from the station smiled and waved. The food was picked over. I placed my bottle of whiskey on the table, unopened, found a small glass jar I hoped was clean, and filled it with water. When I turned, I found myself face-to-face with Phil. He looked at my drink, then at me. "Gin? You brought gin?"

"Water." I held the glass up between us. We regarded each other through the distortion. "I brought the whiskey."

"Ah, yes. Okay." He wasn't drunk yet. I wondered how he managed to function so well without food. I had never seen him eat, only drink. "I can't stand gin. Have you seen Sara?"

"Not yet."

"She was looking for you." His eyes fought to focus on trays laden with moldy cheese and stale crackers. His chagrin was obvious. "I think . . . ah, you know—"

I didn't, and didn't ask for an explanation, since I knew I wouldn't get a clear one. Phil exposed truths the way clouds exposed the sun—accidental, brief, and sudden. He dipped his nose into a few bottles, made a gasp of discovery, and filled his glass to the top with a thin red liquid. He smiled at me over the stuff, took a drink, grimaced, and smiled again, deeper.

"Sara needs someone to watch over."

"What do you mean?"

"I mean she's a caretaker. She needs a project. That's why she stays with me. I can't pay her much." He stopped; embarrassment flushed his cheeks. I pretended not to have heard or understood, didn't react to his revelation that she was a hire, not an heir. He sipped his drink and started again. "She knows I need her, so she stays. But she needs more than just me."

Someone bumped him from behind, and his red drink splashed out of the cup. He spun to shout a long string of obscenities, then either forgot we'd been talking or decided he'd said enough and staggered away through the tangled guests.

I left the food table with my plate for Emma. More people had arrived, and walking a straight line through the room was impossible. I drifted to a stop against Phil's table, staring into a sea of baby-food jars full of washers and screwdriver tips. Unable to move, I reached forward and passed the plate to a woman on the other side of the table and asked her to hand it to Emma. It disappeared, and from beyond the wall of people came her shout of appreciation.

The woman across the table, older than Phil and weathered in a way that said she spent days under the sun, smiled at me and said, "That was very kind of you."

I shrugged. "I promised her I would."

"A man who keeps his promises."

"Some of them."

She laughed and then looked past me. "I hate to ask. But could you get me some water?"

So it began, the conveyer belt of refreshments passed around the room. The cheeses were followed by crackers. Fruit salad, grilled asparagus, chocolate in large bricks that needed to be chiseled into edible splinters, a bowl of tuna salad with walnuts mixed in. I began to see food I was sure hadn't been at the table when I'd arrived. A roast turkey on a carving board was raised over people's heads and passed like a sacrifice from hand to hand. A gravy boat followed. Half a layer cake. Pewter jugs sloshing with punch; old milk bottles filled with juices from grapes, apples, oranges; carafes of wine, red and white. Food passed over me, along either side. Where had it come from? The stores I'd seen were mostly vacant. Empty plates began to drift back. Shouts of thanks rose from the corners of the room. I handed platters bare save for grease and bones to the two other library workers. They solemnly took the refuse and piled it onto the table. When all the serving was done, the din of the crowd hushed to the sounds of smacking lips and occasional moans of gastric pleasure. A belch came from someone behind me. All around the room, strangers shared dishes and even meals. A petite young woman who somehow had ended up holding her heavy plate with both hands laughed as three men around her took turns feeding her with their spoons. Strawberry mousse dripped from her chin.

I watched and sipped my water. When a juice bottle came by, I poured what was left into my glass and handed the empty container to the nearest worker. He struggled to find a spot for it. We laughed when he placed it under the table.

"Where did this stuff come from?" he asked. "I don't remember handing half this stuff out." I wasn't alone in confusion and felt a flush of belonging.

The woman with the sunburned face was eating an apple. "See what you started?" she said. "Just because you kept your promise."

Phil, fully drunk now, emerged from the crowd and swept his jars off the table so he could climb on top. The shattering glass called the room to order and settled at our feet as everyone turned to face the commotion. Eating stopped and conversations ended midword. He opened his mouth to speak, but nothing came out. Pointing a finger at the crowd, he spun around to take it all in and tried to speak again, his voice breaking. "You're all here, right?" Everyone agreed, some laughed. I watched him sway and felt embarrassment for him. "Right," he said. "So. There's work to do. All this stuff needs to be taken care of. I've spoken briefly to each of you, about what you need to handle, but now's the time to do it."

Murmurs snaked through the crowd. Emma caught my eye, raised her eyebrows, and shook her head. I was reaching up to take hold of Phil's hand when someone stopped me. It was Sara. She held my elbow, her green eyes searching mine as I waited for an explanation that didn't arrive.

Phil continued his monologue. "There comes a time when a man realizes that he wasn't always here, and won't always be here. There comes a time for gathering and a time for letting go. I've reached both points at once. It happens that way sometimes. Not for everyone. I wouldn't expect anyone to understand, but that's where I am." People looked at their plates and whispered to one another. A current of embarrassment washed over the crowd.

From the back came a drunk call: "What the fuck are you talking about, Phil?"

Phil's flushed face swung to the heckler. His angry smile threatened to crack his face, and tears ran from his eyes.

He said, "I'm dying, you fucks."

Even the dinnerware fell mute. The flap of wings from the dark street sounded through the windows. Footsteps clattered in the doorway. In ones and twos, guests slipped out. As space opened between people, they were free to turn away from Phil and roll their eyes. I stayed beside the table, looking up at him. Sara still held my arm.

Phil said, "It's been happening for some time, but I can feel it coming now. It's time for me to get these things back into the world, and that's where all of you come in. I've asked each of you to take care of something, to make sure it's ready when it's needed."

Phil was carved stone, gave no sign he saw the exodus, no sign he knew that the room was half as full. Cool air spilled through the windows. Candles extinguished themselves, drowned in their own wax. The people who remained muttered jokes behind hands, mocked him. As the three workmen passed behind me, headed toward the door, I heard one say, "Just like every other Phil party."

The gathering frayed away to nothing. Someone slept on a chair in the corner. Emma stayed beside the door, her face wet, hands twisting on her lap.

"You'll know when the items are needed," Phil said. "Each of them was needed before and will be again. It's the way of the world, it's—" He stopped and shuddered, wrapped his arms around himself. He looked down at me and Sara and whispered, "Help an old man down, would you?" Sara let go of my arm and reached up to take both of his. He half fell into her and lowered himself to a nearby chair. Sara stroked his hair, and I turned away, embarrassed.

Emma, watching me, called out, "Phil, if I'm to get those books to my booth, I'll need his help." She pointed at me and waved me over to her side. "You know I can't manage. We'll go get them and I'll be off, if that's okay with you?"

Phil smiled at Emma. "Of course. Good night, Emma."

I followed Emma into the hall. She said, "I'm supposed to take the phone books. As many as you can carry, I guess."

When we entered the apartment on the second floor, I found it untouched. Apparently none of the guests had come to take the heirlooms they'd been assigned. I hadn't expected them to, but it somehow shocked me nonetheless. I moved through the darkness, found the phone books stacked near the windows, and piled four in each arm, the most I found manageable.

Emma waited in the lobby, leaning against the doorjamb, breathing in what little air was moving through the streets. The heat of the day had gone with the sun, but what was left behind was humid and smelled of rot. "That can't be all."

"No. There are more. I can bring them in the morning."

"Fine." Her eyes said she didn't need them, nor would she ever.

She walked onto the dark street without fear but with great effort. At the corner by my hotel, she crossed the street. I smiled; even those who knew I lived there still believed it haunted. I looked up at the building and saw the usual flickering lights on several floors. The electricity came and went at random. I had learned not to trust the system from one day to the next. That night the hotel's uppermost floors burned bright, even the penthouse. I couldn't recall ever before seeing any lights higher than the fifth working.

We turned the corner onto Forty-second. I didn't know what I would say if it turned out Emma lived in her information booth itself. I was thankful when she stopped at a corner shop at Sixth Avenue and turned a key in the lock. The sounds of trains rattled beneath us, and singing came from the park across the street. We entered what had once been a coffee shop, before the coffee shops had been abandoned. The corner nearest the door was filled with copies of Emma's brochures, lists of spots of interest around the city and maps for newcomers. Emma insisted that tourists were the blood of the city and that as the premiere information booth she herself was the heart. I thought she was more of a spectacle, as much a site of interest as any of the abandoned buildings she told travelers how to get to.

Emma opened the door wide. "Just put them on a pile."

She turned on the lights, and the fluorescents above clicked twice and began to buzz at us. Empty glass pastry displays winked to life. On the far side of the counter was a twin bed and covered with rumpled blankets. Her eyes narrowed as I placed the phone books on her corner table. "Wouldn't you know it," she said. "They're all from different cities."

"I haven't seen a working phone since I got here." I realized after I said it that I had no idea if phones ever worked here, if they ever had during Emma's lifetime. For a moment I worried about what questions she might ask me now, but she just laughed.

"That's beside the point, as far as Phil's concerned." Her chuckle ended with a gasp and a sudden release of tears. "I'm sorry," she said. I stood behind her, watched her shoulders shake as she worked herself under control again.

"I'm sure Phil will be fine. He's still—"

She turned to me, laughing and crying, eyes merry. "I forgot, that was your first death announcement."

"First?"

"Yes. He's announced his death every few months for years. The first time I met him, he told me he was dying and we spent hours discussing it. That was seven years ago."

I felt relief at that, but Emma just continued to cry. "Why the tears?"

She took a great, quavering breath, released it in a puff, and wiped the wet from her face. "Because, other than the first time he told me, this is the first time I've believed him."

"Why?"

She nudged the books, on which my hand still rested. "He's never given his stuff away before."

We both looked at the phone books, dry paper turning to dust as we watched. Numbers for phones and people long gone from Philadelphia, Chicago, Dallas, and Seattle. Photos on the bindings of buildings we couldn't know still existed.

Emma pushed hair from her face. "You should go. And keep an eye on him. I don't think anyone else believed him. Except maybe Sara. Oh, God. What will she do?"

I didn't know what she would do, but I knew that Phil thought it would be me who would take care of her. I'd realized that of all the things he'd bestowed on various people, she was what he'd seen fit to give me.

I left Emma's place and walked back to the hotel. For a moment, standing at the entrance to the lobby, I debated returning to Phil's, but I could see that his building was dark. Instead I entered the hotel. Sitting in the lobby's cleanest chair, in the same black dress she'd been wearing earlier, was Sara. She looked at me over the top of a yellowed newspaper whose front page was covered in dramatic photos of what appeared to be a protest or a celebration.

A weight I hadn't been aware of fell away. "What are you doing here?"

She folded the paper, which nearly snapped in half. "Phil's not well."

"So he said. Emma said he does this occasionally."

Sara rolled her eyes. "She's right. He does this a few times a year. But tonight was different."

Around a corner from the empty concierge desk was the side entrance she'd come through the first time I'd seen her. I marveled that I'd never noticed her at the party in my youth. Even in just a simple black dress, she glowed like a bonfire among dry leaves.

She was shaking her head. "No one took anything he asked them to. It's made him sick. If you could come by tomorrow to look in on him. . . ?"

I said I would and wished her a good night. As I turned to walk away, she stood and said, "I've never seen your room."

I felt a sudden dread. I'd managed to convince myself that this woman, Sara, wouldn't have to become the Lily who would die in my arms if I could just keep a certain distance from her, never let her be anything but Sara, Phil's daughter. As if it wouldn't be me—some other version of me—to release the flood of bad choices that would bring her and the Body and the Drunk and maybe me, too, to the party where some or all of us would die. As if I could stand by, an observer in her time, and live . . . what? A normal life?

I was terrified by the idea of taking her upstairs with me. I was desperate for her to go upstairs with me. "What about the ghosts?" I asked.

She smiled. "We see fewer weird things now that you're here. At least I do. Phil still thinks he sees shadows in the penthouse." Her eyes darkened for a moment as she mentioned Phil. Under all the layers of lies, of self-protection and self-interest, there was genuine concern, a simple love that was rightly unconscious and unquestioned. I recognized, finally, that she needed to be away from Phil for the night, and that was why she'd come here. To be free from a man making himself sick with his collection of dead things.

I said, "I'm on the fifth floor."

She followed me, quiet to the point of reverence. The rustle of the newspaper was louder than either of us. We found the entire fifth floor ablaze with light. The hall was hot and cleaner than I'd ever seen it before. The walls looked scrubbed, and the rug was cleared of the splinters and pebbles I felt beneath my feet every morning. At my door I pulled the key from my pocket.

She said, "I hope it's darker inside." She was obviously trying to kill me with her flirting.

I opened the door for her. I thought of my promise to Phil and my promise to Seventy. I didn't owe Seventy anything. But to let Phil down would hurt.

Sara sat on the bed, and, without thinking, I shut the door. The ambient hallway light collapsed and vanished and we were left with the sliver of light from the bathroom.

"I have one of those," Sara said. In the low light, her eyes glinted, two bright points. "It's Phil's, but he gave it to me."

Not sure what she was talking about, I followed her gaze to the dresser. There sat the metallic device, the needle wrapped in squid arms, its head filled with the milky fluid. The one she would use the day she died in what had been Phil's apartment. I realized then what I should have sooner: Phil was actually going die.

I held up the device. "I've never discovered what it's for."

She averted her eyes. She knew but wouldn't say what it was. As I stared at her, she took the device and rolled it over in her palm, found a catch I hadn't seen—still couldn't, even though she'd pressed it in front of me—and the many twisted arms unwound, pulled away to reveal the long needle. She fingered another invisible button, and a small drop of opaque moisture formed at the tip. She carried it up to my neck and touched a spot just behind my ear.

"You insert it here. Do you want to try?"

"No. No, I don't know what it is." I was sick at the memory of what was in it.

Her fingers slid across my neck. "That's part of the fun. A rush of pain followed by recollections you shouldn't have." She gave a small pinch, as if to demonstrate the process.

"I'd rather not."

She shrugged. She looked down at the device in her hand, probably wondering how it could be so similar to the one Phil had given her. I felt the explanation rise in my throat, almost spoke it, and admonished myself. My only task was to not arrive at the party in several months, just go somewhere else and never invite her, and both she and I would be on different paths from the one I'd seen bleed out before me in the penthouse.

One problem lurked. I didn't want to go. Sara stood near to me, her breath fast as she touched the back of my neck; my own came faster. I sought out her hand to take the device. If memories floated in the liquid, they belonged to Lily, and she wasn't Lily. At least not yet.

She refused to let go of the syringe. "Let me have them." Her whisper soft as skin on skin. "Please. Let me remember something else tonight."

I tried to pull the device away from her. Her hand locked over it, and her fingers stopped moving in my hair. "Please."

This was it, I was sure. These memories would be what would drag her under. She'd remember her own death, she'd remember all the versions of me. No wonder she'd been so calm at the party—it was all flashback to her. Keeping her away from the device kept her away from the party.

"I have to keep them," I said. My heart clenched around a hollow in my chest.

"Why hold on to memories you don't even want?"

When I still wouldn't let go, she finally released the device. The liquid sloshed inside the vial. I should smash it, I thought. Right now, under my heel, let the dying memories soak into the ugly carpeting and dry to dust. But I couldn't. It was all I had of Lily. I held the cool glass bulb between shaking fingers and knew that as much as I wanted them gone, there was nothing I would do to get rid of them.

Sara sat back on the bed and turned away from me. She was crying. "That's the only thing I've ever been good at."

I waited for her to look at me, to continue. She did neither. "What is?"

She looked at me at last, but with eyes that said I should

already know the answer. "Being a lie collector." She played with the hem of her dress. "Phil was the first job I ever had in the city," she said. "He was my first and one of my only clients, because he didn't want the job to end. As far as he was concerned, it wasn't really a job." She didn't wipe her tears from her face. She didn't stop speaking either.

She'd come to the city to get away from something, but she wouldn't say what. She'd needed money, but the only jobs people offered she'd been unwilling to do. She'd become a squatter, hid in vacant rooms and searched through refuse bins behind restaurants for brown lettuce and hard bread. Occasionally she'd make a little money cleaning strangers' homes, spend it quickly on a large meal or a room with a bath. She passed her nights half awake, listening for people who would hurt her if they found her.

She grew so hungry that she begged from vendors. They sometimes took pity. Often they did not. One afternoon she entered a fruit-and-vegetable market and gathered a few things, hoped that maybe the clerk would turn away for a moment and she could run. The clerk only paid more attention to her, and when at last she knew there was no sneaking out, she surprised him and herself by carrying the items to the counter and demanding that he have the heart to help a starving woman.

"I need to eat something," she'd said. "I can't go another day without a meal. Please." When she'd said this, a small ring of other customers formed around her to watch. She pretended they weren't there, stared at the clerk, who looked away, afraid to meet her gaze.

"If I start feeding you, I'll have the whole city demanding

free food." He lacked sincerity. He knew she would disappear, not tell anyone. Still he refused.

A woman's voice came from behind Sara. "I'll pay for it."

Sara turned to face a white-haired woman, thick glasses squaring her gray-green eyes. Without another word, the woman placed a bill on the counter. She refused the clerk's change, gesturing to Sara. The clerk didn't make eye contact and didn't offer to bag the groceries. Sara gathered the bananas and apples in her hands and scurried to the door. She was too ashamed to look back at the woman, too stripped bare of who she'd been. She could only think about what she'd become, the very thing her family had told her she would.

She got a few blocks down Broadway before she was bumped and her purchases flew from her arms. Someone stepped on one of the bananas, crushed it into the sidewalk, and an apple shot from sight into the street. She yelled a curse at no one, everyone, knelt on the sidewalk and tried to gather the fruit. By the time she'd recaptured what was left, the white-haired woman had caught up to her.

She picked up the last apple but didn't offer it to Sara. "You're clearly starving, and the best you could do was fruit?"

Sara thought about dropping the fruit and running. She normally avoided conversations with people she didn't know, but she owed the woman for the meal. "I go after what's available."

The woman stood back, eyes roaming up and down Sara in silent evaluation. "I can probably get you a job. I can get you an audition at least."

"Audition?"

"It's an acting job. I'm Mana, by the way."

Mana took Sara to a diner and told her about the job over hamburgers. Sara ate hers in giant bites. She didn't taste most of the meat, limp lettuce, or hard white tomatoes. She relished it nonetheless. Mana told her the job was a short, improvised one-act performance, usually taking less than an hour a day. There were no announced shows. She would always be on call.

"You'll get a call and you go in immediately. No calling in sick. No excuses. You do your part, then you go home. It might be at any time during the day. I've worked as early as eight in the morning, as late as midnight."

Sara mopped a french fry around her plate. "There's nothing kinky about it?"

Mana smiled. "No. No one will touch you. It's me, a young man, and you. And the employer, the man who's paying us."

"What's his name?"

Mana stirred her soda with a straw as if weighing whether to release the name or not. "Phil."

Mana gave Sara a phone number and a twenty-dollar bill. "If you disappear, that's your choice, but there is money and security in this. As long as you do the work." Sara promised her she would call. At first she hadn't meant to, to do only as Mana suggested, to take the money and make it stretch a few days. Instead she found herself a decent meal and then a pay phone. The man who answered was clearly drunk, but she said, "I've heard there's a role for a young woman."

The man at the other end, the one who hadn't answered to the name Phil, coughed. "How old are you?"

"Twenty," she lied. "But I look younger. I look eighteen." She would be eighteen in six months. "I can also look older, if you need."

The man laughed. "Do you have the address?"

She wrote it down. He told her to arrive early in the morning. "Later than noon and you won't find me here."

She said she understood and hung up. Fearing she might be late, she headed to the trains and made her way uptown. In Grand Central she found a corner of the main concourse and tried to sleep, failed, listened instead to announcements about closed stations, canceled trains. She arrived at Phil's address well before noon the next day and knocked at the door. She was in one of the sections of the city that were beginning to empty out. Real estate available but not for sale. Squatters, or no one, claiming entire blocks, buildings staring down like empty skulls.

She knocked at the decrepit door again, then tried the handle. It was open. She stepped into an anonymous lobby, devoid of any furniture. She waited. After a few minutes, the tall figure of Phil emerged. He was hungover, his gray hair and beard pillow-tangled. He wore black pants and a T-shirt, no shoes, no socks. He smelled days removed from a bath. Phil raised a hand to Sara, tried and failed to smile, and said, "Good morning. Follow me."

The stairs were clean. She followed him in silence from landing to landing, each time thinking the next one must be it, only to find him turning to climb to another flight. At last, at the top of ten stories, he led her into a great room empty except for a long table and four straight-backed chairs. They were well used, paint-nicked and beaten. The chair at the table's head had been abused more than the others, gouges running the length of both arms. It was in this chair that Phil sat.

White paint covered everything in the room. Not just walls and doors and table. Countertops in the kitchen, windowsills, baseboards, sink, faucet, cupboards. Only the floor provided contrast, sanded bare and unpolished. The room had been scrubbed with bleach. It would never again retain the warmth of being lived in, be someone's home.

"Please, sit." He indicated the chair to his right. As she pulled it out, he held up a hand. "I'm sorry, before you do, please turn for me."

As she gave a slow pirouette before him, Sara reminded herself that Mana had said this was an audition. Phil was some kind of casting director, not a john. She had been looked at by men before, she knew what it felt like to be judged attractive. She knew that most people could find almost anything attractive; she might not fit their descriptions of perfect beauty but would most likely meet some carnal need, some appetite. This was different. From Phil she felt the need for something very specific, that he was checking for correspondence with a predetermined size and shape, like seeking a key for a lock. What that shape might be she couldn't guess, but she assured herself she already fit it in Mana's eyes. Most important, she was not afraid of Phil. She could feel that his hunger to do harm had been burned from him and what was left behind was worn through with rubbing against the world.

Phil nodded.

Sara sat and looked at him, became uncomfortable, and looked away. They sat in silence a minute, Phil watching Sara, Sara watching birds outside the window. Parrots, their green flashing in the gap of glass between the white walls. Phil smiled. He explained that the birds were generations removed from parrots set loose when a cargo crate broke open at JFK. The parrots had taken to the air and forged a new home— immigrants, like everyone else in the city—the originators of a new breed of city bird, competing with pigeons and sparrows. They wintered in hidden spaces, forgotten attics and cemetery mausoleums, survived despite their nature, which must have been telling them to head to warmer climates. Their progenitors had escaped and fled in fear, lived despite their terror and uncertainty. Now the parrots, long since expanded beyond Brooklyn into Queens and Manhattan, flew over the city with impunity, as at home as anything might be in New York, more at home than Sara or anyone like her. Phil believed that the parrots, as parrots will, had picked up words here and there as they roosted over the city. Phil said he liked to think the parrots remembered the things people had forced themselves to forget.

The windows of Phil's apartment looked out over the river to New Jersey. Sara marveled at the light spilling over the river, onto the other bank and beyond, as Phil stood and walked to the refrigerator, from which he pulled a Styrofoam container. He chose utensils from a drawer, placed the container before her, and then reclaimed his seat.

"Please eat," he said. "I'm sorry it's cold. Drink when you like."

Sara opened the container. Inside was sliced turkey breast, gray mashed potatoes with gravy, limp broccoli spears, and jellied cranberry sauce, all congealed into a cold, solid mass. But Sara was not used to eating full meals, or even many partial ones. She couldn't be sure, but she might have moaned in anticipation of the first bite; Phil let out a small laugh. By her third mouthful, she forgot that Phil was watching her. She ate the turkey almost entirely before dipping into the potatoes, pulling large scoops free of the mass, and swallowed without chewing. When the container was half empty, she began to slow. She finally remembered her host and looked up at him over her plate, smiling around the fork.

When he spoke, she realized that he was no longer seeing a girl he didn't know. He said, "What did you do in school today?"

She almost corrected him, reminded him that she was there for an audition. She opened her mouth to say this when she realized that this was the audition, that it had begun the moment he placed the food before her.

She told him the first of the many lies she would come to learn he longed to hear. "Fine," she said. "Nothing much going on." She searched for some memories of what school had been like, what her parents, if they had cared, might have wanted to hear if she'd gone to school regularly. "A couple of friends skipped out early." His eyes flashed with surprise—she'd thought Phil wanted to be the kind of parent who was confided in, but maybe he also wanted a well-behaved daughter. "They wanted me to go, but I couldn't. I had a test last period."

Phil smiled. "Good girl. How do you think you did?"

Sara pouted her lips, speared an unfortunate broccoli stem over and again. "Don't know for sure."

"You know." His tone was patient, practiced concern.

"It's hard. All those dates. I mean, come on, when am I ever going to need to know when some old man in France lived?"

"You never know what you might need. That's why you need it all."

She stabbed at the broccoli until she felt bad for it. "Well, if I didn't do so great, I can always ask for extra credit."

Phil shook his head and laughed. "You can't extra-credit yourself through life, Sara."

Up to that moment, he hadn't called her by name, any name. Nor had he asked what her name was at all. At that moment he baptized her Sara. She hadn't realized until that moment that she needed so badly to know that someone cared enough to name her. She smiled at him and said, "I know." She didn't say the word, but to think of him as "Father" wasn't unimaginable.

She finished the meal, every cold piece, as they talked of the minutiae of her pretend life. He asked about teachers she hadn't heard of, boys she'd never dated. She conjured details as she tapped her fork on the foam container. If she closed her eyes, she could picture the walls of the high school she'd never attended, filling in the stories with faces she collected from wandering the city streets. She discovered that "Sara" had good grades that could be better. She had friends who couldn't be closer. She had won and lost her heart countless times and knew that more ascents and declines lay ahead. By the time she'd finished the meal, she was sure of one thing: She wanted to stay with Phil, to be the girl he quizzed and coddled.

She put down the fork at the last bite and smiled at Phil. "It was delicious."

Phil tried to hide an answering smile. His demeanor had shifted, warmed. His eyes sought something to land on and kept fluttering back to her. Then, abruptly, he blinked a few times and the warmth vanished. Old barriers rose up again.

He stood and left the room without a sound, then returned with a cell phone, set it on the table beside her hand. She was afraid to look at it, let alone touch it. He pulled a roll of money from his pocket and peeled off two bills illustrated with the faces of men she didn't recognize, placed them under the phone. She raised a hand to wave the money away and then realized the ridiculousness of the act. This was why she had come here, for money; to refuse it would be to deny the nature of their relationship. She wanted to cry but bit her lip instead.

Phil said, "Give no one else your number. This phone is for me only. When it rings, answer. You'll be told when to arrive. Do so and you'll continue in my employ. Otherwise fuck off. Understand?"

She nodded and took hold of the phone and the bills. She understood without being told that it was time for her to leave, that she would leave and come back only when called, that she would leave without his escort or good-bye or even acknowledgment. She left, biting her lip all the way to the street until she realized that it was not holding the flow of tears but was in fact spurring them on.

She stayed for two nights in a room on Roosevelt Island rented to her by a Romanian couple. They ignored her, and she gave them money at the start of every day. On the third day, the phone rang. She answered and heard a woman's voice. It was Mana. "Five this afternoon. See you then?"

"Yes."

In a whisper Mana added, "I'm glad he chose you, dear."

"Thanks."

She spent the day in her room, stared out onto the East

River. A few sailboats passed. The sky over the city echoed with parrot speech: declarations of love, protests, begging, mournful prayers, nursery rhymes, monologues rising and falling as they circled the building. She wondered what new details she'd have to invent about Sara's life and tried to ignore her building panic.

That afternoon, when she entered Phil's lobby, she heard voices above her. At the top floor, she found the door open, Mana speaking to a twenty-something man-child whose hair covered one eye. While obviously years beyond prep school, he dressed in a teenager's school uniform. His one visible eye caught hers. He smiled, and she felt her hands flutter at her sides for something to do, something to grip or squeeze.

Mana turned around and saw her. "You're here early. Good. Always good, remember that. Follow me." Mana walked to a hallway connecting the living room to a cluster of bedrooms. She entered the first, the only one with an open door. White bed linens hung from hooks screwed into ceiling plaster. They separated the room into four semiprivate quarters. Mana led her to the quarter farthest from the door and drew a sheet back to reveal a stool and a clothes rack. There was one outfit on the rack, a teenage girl's school uniform—gray pleated skirt and blue blouse. An emblem was sewn on the right breast: a bird carrying a branch in one claw, a diploma in the other.

"Change into this. If it doesn't fit, let me know and we'll have it tailored." Mana glanced at her watch. "You'd better hurry."

Sara changed quietly and quickly. The uniform fit, and when she turned to look at herself in the mirror, she started at the youth she saw before her. She headed back through the billowing sheets and down the hall. In the dining room, she found Phil, his hair slicked down over his head, seated beside Mana and the young man.

"I'm glad you decided to join us." Phil seemed to look through her, not at her.

"I'm sorry," she said. A lie rose to her lips. "I was talking to Mary on the phone, and she wouldn't let me go."

Phil's face lifted, a smile emerged. Mana cast a warm smile and leaned toward her as she sat down. "Good girl," she whispered, then rose and went to the kitchen. When she returned, she carried large ceramic bowls. One held mashed potatoes with gravy, the other broccoli. She placed them beside Phil, who spooned some of each onto his plate and then passed the bowls to either side. The young man served himself from the broccoli bowl and then set it down in front of him.

Phil said severely, "Joshua, give Sara the bowl. You know how to pass food."

Joshua, hint of a smile fading from his face, lifted the bowl and held it to her. They exchanged bowls and glances. Mana returned from the kitchen again, this time with a platter of sliced turkey. This must be the meal, always and forever. Within fifteen minutes Sara realized she needn't have worried about new lies to tell. Little conversation fell across the table, and most of it repeated what she'd shared in the audition.

Mana sat quietly except to periodically encourage Sara and Joshua to sit up straight. Sara noticed that Mana's eyes always returned to Phil, monitored him, her glances quicker as his mood gradually darkened. Her corrections seemed like a steam valve doomed to fail, the pressure in Phil too great.

He showed little patience with Joshua, whom he chided

endlessly. "You sit like that at school? No wonder your teachers all know you're up to no good. You don't look like you're paying attention."

Joshua rode through it with his eyes on his plate. "Yeah, Pop. Right." Sara couldn't help but think he had the air of an actor not caring for his lines rather than a boy rebelling against the father.

Phil's fingers shook as he watched Joshua roll and unroll a napkin. Sara could practically hear angry words bang against his teeth as he muscled his jaw closed. He put his fork down and leaned back in his chair.

"That's enough for today." He stood, walked to the front door. The latch snapped, and the door banged against the wall; Phil's steps hammered the stairs. Mana and Sara stared at their plates. Joshua, unmoved, stood and left for the changing room, already removing his school jacket.

Mana hissed under her breath, just loud enough for him to hear. "That son of a bitch is going to ruin it for all of us." She pulled a pack of cigarettes from an apron pocket. Sara slowly made her way back to the bedroom, where curtains blew in a breeze from the open window. The sky outside had turned a bruised purple between the buildings. Traffic sounded small and far away.

Sara removed the school uniform on the other side of the sheet from where she heard Joshua changing. She replaced all the items on the metal rack and straightened them, tried to remove creases that had folded themselves into the shirt, the skirt. She wondered if creases would make Phil unhappy, if he would have them cleaned, or if they would call for her dismissal.

She turned, naked except for underwear, to retrieve her clothes and found Joshua standing in a gap between the wall and the white sheet. He smiled at her. He'd changed into a pair of jeans and a dark shirt, his hair falling across his eye. He looked older, but no more comfortable. Sara didn't know where he might look comfortable, wondered if such a place existed. He stared at her body, her face.

"Sorry, sis, couldn't help myself." He laughed. She told herself later that she had been too shocked to cover herself. That her standing before him unashamed had been an accident.

"That's not funny."

"Is where I'm coming from."

She reached for her own clothes and began to dress. He pulled the sheet between them. Through it she could still see his shape and knew he could still see hers. She worked her shirt over her head. Eventually she heard his footfalls cross the room and become distant in the hall.

When she finished dressing, she returned to the dining room. Mana and Joshua were arguing as she counted out money.

"You're going too far," she said. "He's going to end this, and that will be that. Good-bye paycheck."

Joshua recounted the money he had just seen her count and stuffed it, folded in half, into his back pocket. "The old man needs this too bad. Not gonna end it just 'cause I go off script a little."

Mana shook her head, noticed Sara in the doorway. Her face softened to a smile, and she came toward her, arms outstretched for a hug that Sara returned, surprised that she craved it.

"You did wonderful," Mana said. "Next time try to keep him from taking Phil's focus." An accusatory thumb in Joshua's direction. "Maybe between the two of us, we can keep him here and make sure Joshua doesn't ruin it." She leaned in close and whispered into Sara's ear. "Don't pay any attention to him. He's been trying to sabotage this since before I started doing it."

Joshua, already on his way out, called over his shoulder, "You can talk about me when I'm gone. If anyone is interested, I'll be in the bar at the corner." His heavy footfalls were oddly reminiscent of Phil's.

Mana threw her cigarette out a window and said, "Seriously, don't even talk to him. He'll try to get you kicked out or make you want to quit. It's what he does to the Saras."

Sara nodded and followed Mana to the door. As they descended the stairs, Mana paused at one of the landings. "Also, sometimes when you come here, you'll find other apartments open. Never go in them. Just shut the door and go upstairs."

Sara looked up and down the stairs. There were no sounds except for her and Mana's shoes on the steps. "Who lives in them?"

"No one. Phil has things he's sure will be stolen. If he finds doors open, he'll question you, and sometimes he gets paranoid about new actors stealing from him."

Sara nodded, as if this could be normal.

The next two weeks included three performances. Sara was always paid afterward, and always by Mana. The three subsequent dinners were better than the first. Joshua kept to the script and nearly made himself look interested in playing the part of a bored teenager. He occasionally broke to stare at Sara or wink as if they shared a secret. She was careful not to react the first few times. She later found that complaining loudly that he was making faces across the table was better; Phil and Mana could reprimand him for childish behavior, and everyone could pretend he hadn't broken character.

"Pretty clever, aren't you?" he said after the fourth performance. They'd eaten their meal at half past ten in the morning. It was only noon now, and Sara had the rest of the day and her money to do something with.

She said, "If I don't react, you get what you want." She was no longer intimidated. She looked him in the eye until he looked away. She noticed and enjoyed the flush in his cheeks.

"What I want is a drink. How about it? The bar at the corner?"

She pulled the sheet between them and returned to her own clothes. He walked away on the other side. He hadn't tried since the first day to look at her as she changed. She was always acutely aware of where he was and always let him finish dressing before she did and leave first.

She'd collected her money and was on her way out, the sound of her steps bouncing around her in the stairwell, when Phil's voice stopped her. The door on the second-floor landing was ajar. He was crying between words, and she couldn't understand anything but her name, repeated. "Sara," he said over and over again. She stood beside the door and peered inside. Phil's lanky figure moved through a room stacked to the ceiling with junk, boxes crushing one another, broken machinery and tools piled in the corner, bundles of papers and magazines mildewed and black, plastic bags spilling old clothes onto the floor, muting Phil's footsteps as he shuffled through the room. "Sara, Sara, Sara."

She left the building, her own chest heaving. The noontime sunlight blinded her. How would she escape that name she'd been given, the sound of Phil's voice in such horror and pain? Near tears, she looked around and found herself beside Joshua's brown-fronted bar. Through the open door, she saw figures on barstools hold drinks to lips and ignore one another in the dim light. No music, no conversation. She stepped to the doorway and waited for her eyes to adjust.

Before they had, Joshua called to her: "Hey." She followed his voice into the bar.

"I changed my mind," she said. "I could use a drink."

"Know just what you mean."

They sat in the bar and drank until the bartender told them to go. Joshua's arm wrapped around her, his hand moving to places she normally would have protected from even his eyes. She let him steer her downtown, a long, hot walk past Bryant Park and then continuing down Sixth Avenue. They stopped at a bodega for some water. She sobered as they walked, her sweat making her shirt heavy. From the park rose the call of parrots, half-meaningful words squawked into crowds that tossed seeds and dried bread. She wasn't certain she didn't hear them crying "Sara" in anguish.

Sara followed Joshua to his apartment, a walkup trapped between two taller buildings. Joshua climbed the three flights without looking or speaking to her. She wondered if he'd forgotten she followed. The halls were dark. No sounds came from the other doors.

At last he said, "The lights have been iffy." She asked if the building was abandoned. "Not yet," he said with a laugh. As he opened the door to his apartment, some streetlight spilled through and caught the side of his sweat-shined face. Sara reached out and touched his waist, searched the gap between his shirt and jeans to put her hands against the skin of his chest. His ribs stuck out as if he were underfed, and she thought how she had never seen him undressed, only hidden in the too-large school uniform. In the dark she sought out his mouth with her own. As he bent to kiss her, his nose caught the light and his profile for an instant was that of a great bird. She felt at his back, certain that in a moment she would find nude wings branching out from his shoulder blades, that his arms were an illusion.

His bed was a mattress. It sat on the floor beneath a window that was both open and uncovered. The light that came through did little to reveal his home, or him. She felt herself wrapped around him, but she couldn't see him. Her hands slid over the bones of his ribs, his shoulders, his arms. He was too light and frail, she thought. When he came, she thought he might disappear, as if he weren't really there at all but only a memory of someone who used to be there in that space, someone who had vanished long ago.

She woke the next day to find him gone. His apartment was a nest of filth with no furniture, a table of cinder-block legs and a wood-plank top beside the mattress. Clothes covered the floor from doorway to mattress. Behind a blanket curtaining an open closet was a shelf of neatly folded clothes, copies of the same outfit Joshua always wore—jeans and tees, in only two colors, repeated often enough to reduce laundry to an idea.

Her phone vibrated, and she answered it on the fifth ring. Mana's voice at the other end. "I was afraid you wouldn't answer. Get here as soon as possible."

"Already?" Sara searched for a clock in the room. Her head called out every movement as if piano strings rang taut through her skull. She closed her eyes against a splash of nausea and held the floor down with her free hand.

Mana was insistent. "Get here. Right now."

She pulled on last night's clothes. They smelled of spilled drinks and sweat, and she thought with some relief that the school uniform she wore for Phil would be cleaner, possibly even laundered. She made her way north in a bicycle-driven hansom cab, her eyes closed, listening to the birds in the park. She arrived at Phil's building nearly asleep.

Inside, Mana waited in the lobby. "He's upset. The power is out, and he can't get anyone at the diner." The diner around the corner supplied the food they ate during their performances. Sara had never seen the deliveries but had seen the bags in the garbage.

"Has anyone gone around to put the order in?"

Mana shuffled a damp tissue from one hand to the other. "No. I wanted to make sure you both made it here."

Sara walked the two blocks to find the diner's windows dark, a handwritten note on the front door: *Out of business. Thanks for thirty-nine wonderful years.*

Sara stood in front of the diner for a minute. All the neighborhood buildings were dark, some long vacant. Storefront windows with signs advertising hardware, books, and pet supplies were covered with newspaper. The few buildings that showed life were vagrant tenements or hooker-friendly hotels.

Sara returned to the apartment, where she heard a mechanical hum. Mana stood in the living room smoking, and Phil and Joshua sat in the dining room. Joshua wouldn't look Sara in the eye. His bravado was gone, flown away in the night. She heard his heartbeat across the room, high-pitched and fluttering, a fearful animal in a cage, dreaming and dreading escape. Phil's face hung between his hands, his mouth open. The droning mechanical sound came from him.

Sara said, "The restaurant is closed."

Phil's moan peaked and stopped. He dropped his hands and stood up, blind to everyone else, and turned toward the bedroom, away from the actors he'd gathered as a family.

Sara went to the nearest window and looked down onto the street. Traffic lights at the nearest corner were all dark, the street empty. At last a car approached, a yellow cab. It slowed but didn't stop, turned the corner, and drove the wrong way up the street.

She pulled her face from the pane. Beside her, Mana puffed on her cigarette and stared at the wall. Joshua concentrated on his hands. Sara walked past them, followed Phil down the hall. She passed the changing room. The sheets gusted around the open window, swinging over the floor, twisted on themselves. She stood outside the third bedroom and listened through the door. When she felt his sobs through the crystal knob, she almost let go and left the apartment. She knew in that instant that if she did, she would never come back.

She opened the door. Stacks of books and unopened reams of papers sat on a table, along the walls, beneath the windows. Here, as in the downstairs apartment where she'd found him wandering, there were boxes piled high enough to crush themselves. Phil sat at the table, papers spread out before him, copious notes in a cramped, neurotic hand. The breeze created by the door blew pages onto the floor. Phil's frame rocked with heavy sobs. His gray beard was beaded with tears.

She said, "We'd really like you to come out and see us."

His sobs continued. He made no move to betray whether he'd heard her. She stood in the doorway and held the knob, vaguely aware of an unexpected fear of falling out the open window, of hurtling toward the crumbling city. Behind her, Joshua and Mana talked in muted voices, wondering what she was doing and why, what they should do. She ignored them and tried again.

"I really needed to tell you about—" She stopped, unsure of what to say, what lie to promise him without the food and Mana and Joshua. She understood that they couldn't be counted on, that their ability to play roles depended on props and the promise of money. Their being there, playing at family, even a dysfunctional one, was a deception. It was morbidly funny, she thought, that the liar in each of them had found comfort not only in the paycheck but in one another, chewing on terrible food they pretended was edible, a liars' banquet. She ached for the lie, and for the security the lie provided. *They can have the money,* she thought. *I need the lie.*

She said, "Listen, I know that Mom wasn't able to make dinner tonight, but I'd still like to sit down with you and talk. We can talk without eating, right?"

He still didn't face her, but his crying softened. She pulled the door closed again, slowly shut herself out of the room, left Phil on the other side of the door, and returned to the dining room, where Mana and Joshua regarded her with suspicion.

"Is he coming out?" Mana asked.

"I don't know."

"I heard you blame me for the lack of food."

Sara stared at her. She whispered that it was part of the role, that circumstances demanded the improvisation, but Mana didn't care. Sara took her glare in silence. The room was hot despite open windows. She sat at the table, mentally followed a sweat trail from her temples to her cheek and neck, watched the birds through the windows. Joshua had retreated to the other room. She understood now why Mana had warned her about him. But she was beyond his games. Beyond Mana's as well.

An hour later Phil returned to the dining room. The sun had moved on. It was darker without direct light, yet no cooler. He regarded the three actors, his liars' gathering. He took his seat at the head of the table. His hands shook as he looked at Sara. "So you wanted to tell me about something?"

Sara smiled. She was exhausted. Her stomach was empty, and the headache she'd brought with her had snaked down her back and left her sore and stiff. Her mouth was dry, and it was hard to work the words out. "Yes," she lied. "I need to get your permission to join an after-school club."

Mana moaned. "Oh, God." She lit another cigarette.

Phil ignored her. "After-school club? What sort of club?"

Sara's mind turned over. "Theater arts."

Mana waved a hand, her cigarette drawing signals in the air. "Hold on. Before we go much further with this, what are we going to do about food? And will we still be paid the normal rate?"

Phil's eyes darkened. He pointed toward the front door. "Go. I'll send your money."

Mana looked as if she'd been struck. Her head snapped back, and she exhaled a long, stale breath, smoke wisps at the tail end. "Are you kidding me?"

"Go, before I throw you out."

Mana glared at each of them in turn, letting her eyes linger on Sara. Sara tried not to look back but couldn't help herself and met Mana's gaze. Mana gave a half smile. Her eyes had started to water. "I got you this fucking gig, street tramp."

Phil stood and lifted a fist above his head. As tall and thin as he was, his raised fist and voice cracking in anger made Mana step back as he shouted, "Don't you ever talk to her like that."

He had not said "my daughter" but might as well have; everyone in the room heard it in the echo.

Mana stumbled across the living room. When they knew she was gone, Joshua went to the front door and shut it, returned to the table and sat. Phil watched the wall for a minute, then turned back to Sara, tears on his face, and said, "So an after-school club?"

They talked in circles for hours until Phil finally tired of the new game and went to bed. Through the door they could hear him talking to himself and drinking. He cried out at odd times, names Sara didn't know. Joshua sat quietly with her after Phil left the room. Hours later, when Phil was silent and probably sleeping, they watched each other from opposite sides of the room.

She said, "I'm not going anywhere." She had meant in the long term, that she would keep coming back to Phil, that Joshua's attempt to make her feel uncomfortable had failed, but Joshua thought she meant that she would not leave Phil's apartment that evening, and so he left without her, without his money, without a word. After he'd gone, she realized that she had no reason to leave, that the Romanian couple waiting in their apartment for her money didn't need her to return, that they could have what she'd left behind.

In the changing room, she took down the sheets hanging from the ceiling and laid them on the floor, folded one over the other until she made a small, soft pad. After drinking her fill of tap water from the bathroom, she lay on her makeshift bed, and as the sun sank across the river, she watched the window darken to black.

They went out the next day for food. Ten blocks away they found a deli and returned to Phil's apartment with ham and cheese sandwiches, enough for a week. They placed them in the barely cool refrigerator. Sara complained of the lack of furniture, and Phil nodded. "We'll go get some tonight. Okay? I'll call Joshua." She had begun to recognize when he was really there and when he was lost in his fantasy, when he saw her and not some other Sara.

For the first few days of the new scenario, Joshua arrived when called. As it became obvious that the roles had stretched and changed, that conversations were more natural and rooted in reality, Joshua became superfluous. Some days Phil neglected to call Joshua at all, and soon a week had gone by without their seeing him. *I may never see Joshua again,* she thought. And then she thought of Joshua himself, realized he might never *be* Joshua again.

But she was Sara.

Once they settled into a routine, once the apartment was usefully cluttered with tables and chairs, clothes and a hand-cranked washer and decks of cards and candles to fill the evenings, she told Phil she must leave for a bit and would go for hours to window-shop or find the evening's meals, to catch her breath, to escape the clutter of an apartment now exploding with collections grown beyond the confines of the lower apartments. She would return to find Phil passed out, his drinking having crawled from the solitude of his bedroom to the living room with her as witness. In his hand he clutched a strange metal device, silver, with tentacles and a needle. It disappeared during the day, hidden when he woke. She saw it only at night.

One afternoon on her way out, she noticed someone staring at her from under the awning of the dark, abandoned hotel across the alley. At first she didn't recognize that it was Mana.

Mana walked the half block to Sara. Neither wanted to talk, but Mana had come for something, and Sara waited. At last Mana cleared her throat. "You've got him all to yourself, don't you?"

"I'm just trying to—"

"You know Joshua is his son?"

Sara felt herself sink slightly into the cement sidewalk.

Mana said, "If he ever comes back, you can ask him."

"I never asked for you to go. You got yourself fired."

Mana nodded, her jaw set, and again Sara smelled the stale smoke around her. Mana looked up toward the building. "Just don't hurt him."

"I won't," Sara said.

Mana turned and walked away, didn't look back even though Sara stood and watched her until she disappeared at the corner. The street was a silent canyon. Sara imagined Phil waking with nothing to eat or drink and headed uptown to the latest restaurant she'd found with working electricity.

She continued that pattern the day after and the day after and beyond. She found new places for food and then, when the restaurants closed, new places. Some people had begun to farm in the parks, and simple markets formed, competed, merged. The days turned to weeks and soon enough weeks to years, and she and Phil had habits established so that daily routine was as natural as breath. Sara had come to expect that eventually Phil would succumb to his drink, or whatever it was that he suspected might kill him, and that she would have to find yet another new path, and new habits, and someone else to care for. She had thought that until the day I knocked at their door.

Sara finished telling me about Phil. I sat on the bed next to her. I held the tentacled device, and she laid a hand over it. "He has this." She ran a finger along its side. "One like it anyway." She touched the hidden switch again, and the arms slid away from the needle, soundlessly reaching out to hide and reveal the spike. It looked alive, as if it squirmed in her hands, eager to escape, threatening to strike if it had to.

"He would spend hours in his room, making lists, going through junk he brought home," she said, "using this machine to pull little bits of memory to the front, to replay them, trying to live them for the first time again. And he drank. I left him alone, took care of the apartment. Joshua stopped coming at all. I never found out if what Mana said was true. I think it is. Phil never talks about Joshua or Mana. I never ask."

She moved her fingers from the device to my hand. If I asked her any questions, I had a feeling the story would stop, would dry in her throat and catch and make her sick and she'd never tell it again, to me or anyone. I let her talk.

"Eventually Phil's money ran out, or the bank closed or disappeared. He spent a week hanging around the apartment, realizing we had no way to buy anything, and then he stopped using that thing." She pointed at the device. "And then he focused on his collecting. Saving the things of the world." She shrugged. "If he was going to save the world, I had to find some way to get dinner." She forced my fingers from the device, but not to get to the device, to get to my hand. She held it, tight. "There are people with money and memories. I take both and give one back."

She was silent for a long time. Outside my window I saw the fluttering of green-feathered heads where parrots had gathered on the ledge and talked quietly to one another of traffic and stock prices, their chatter comforting. I put the device on the dresser.

"You should get some sleep," I said. "I'll find another room."

She shook her head. "No. I'll go." She stood, and we looked at each other for several moments. Finally she said, "He might wake up and need me."

I nodded, and then we reached for each other and fell as we tangled. I caught us on the edge of the bed, and we lifted ourselves onto it. She pulled herself from me long enough to remove her dress and then straddled me. Her skin tasted of salt, and she smelled of candle smoke. She tugged my shirt and pants from me, and I entered her. Joined together, we stilled, listened to our breath. When I moved again, I felt a desperation I didn't know I could feel. I was blind, though I thought my eyes were open, and at the edge of my climax I gritted my teeth and whispered the name I needed her to have.

I called her "Lily."

It was a name she might have forgotten, or forced herself to not remember. She might never have heard it before. When I said it, she stilled, her body tensed, and she came with a shudder. I heard her sobbing through it and came myself, arched into her and through her. When our shaking stopped, I drew away and looked down at her. Her face was in shadow; even the glint of her eyes was gone, either closed or turned off, I couldn't see. She rolled away from me, pulled herself from the bed, and stepped into the bathroom. She closed the door.

I lay in darkness and listened to water run in the sink, strained to hear more. When she returned, light clung to her damp skin. She padded across the floor, nude from the waist up, her skirt pressed to her with one hand. She looked newly baptized.

"I would stay, but he might wake up. He gets scared."

"I understand. I can come by in the morning."

She smiled. "You should." She leaned forward and kissed me on the lips, then drew back to look me in the eye. "I've helped someone in so much pain, I don't want to do it again. I want someone to help me this time."

I nodded and watched her dress, wondering what I should call her. I regretted that the name I'd carried inside me had leaked out. How badly did I crave her that I toyed with the very things that would kill us both? Reclothed, she returned to the bed and bent to kiss me again. "I'll see you tomorrow."

After she left, I lay back and watched the ceiling flicker from a streetlight that turned on and off at random intervals. It blinked out, and I wondered if it would come back on, and before it could, I fell asleep.

I WORKED FOR most of the next day, trying to let the book-hauling trips to and from Grand Central distract me from the fact that events seemed to be stuck on rails that ran off a cliff. By midafternoon the main concourse had grown so hot that even the painters stopped work. Some climbed from their scaffolds, others slept where they were, high above the floor. I left and walked back to the West Side, back to Lily, for that was how I thought of her now. She was a woman afflicted by baptisms and allowed those around her to arrange them. Phil had provided one and I another. For her sake I hoped she found a way to handle a third.

At first I thought their apartment empty. Despite the open windows, the room smelled of sewage. Nearly too afraid of what I would find, I walked toward retching sounds in the bathroom. Phil was nude, straddling the toilet, a bucket on his lap. Lily held him upright. Both poured sweat. Phil retched into the bucket again, and as he did, the strain forced something out the other end and into the toilet. He moaned and pulled his head from the bucket to gasp lungfuls of air. His eyes rolled in his skull, stared over me, unseeing.

Lily looked up at me with tears and sweat on her face. "Help me."

I stepped forward and grabbed his shoulders. She knelt in the tub, eyes on Phil. He shuddered and nearly fell from my grasp. His skin was cold and wet; his head lolled. Vomit streaked his chest and lap. He retched again, then screamed. At the end the scream turned to words, a jumble of nonsense that made Lily cry openly.

"How long has he been like this?"

She shook hair from her eyes. "All day."

We needed to get liquid into him. "Can you find some ice?"

"I can look."

When she'd gone, I took firmer hold of Phil. He was moaning, but I couldn't tell if he even knew I was there. "I'm going to move you, Phil." He moaned in response. My arms under his, I raised him into a standing hug. I stepped into the tub and brought him down as carefully as I could, although his head still knocked against the edge. He made no sound or movement. I think he was tired of sitting; to rest in the tub might have been a relief. I laid him in the tub, his head to one side. As if he had waited for the moment, he groaned and closed his eyes. His legs were streaked with his thin feces. I dumped the bucket into the toilet, flushed, ran water into the bucket, and dumped it again and again. Then I found a hand towel, wet it with soap, and began to clean Phil. Lily returned with a small bowl filled with crushed ice.

"I'll do that," she said, and held the ice toward me.

"It's okay, I can finish."

Her face grew hard. "Give me the fucking towel."

I handed her the towel. She put the bowl down, and I washed my hands before taking the bowl and sitting near Phil's head to slip slivers of ice between his pale lips. Phil accepted them, his eyes shut. In his fitful sleep, his lips worked and the ice melted, running from them as often as down his throat.

Lily squatted and wiped the towel over him, her face still hard. She let the sink run so that she could wash and wring out the towel with less fuss. She worked for several minutes until he was mostly clean. Her anger at the illness, at him, was palpable and vibrant.

She left the bathroom and came back a minute later with a blanket, which she tucked around him and pillowed under his head. He was silent through her efforts. When she was done, she collapsed to the floor beside me and looked at me with red eyes and a set jaw.

"He's dying," she said.

I thought of lying and telling her he was not, that this was some effect of not drinking or too much drink, that if we could hold him here long enough he'd recover, but I saw in her face her expectation. She waited for the lie, and I wouldn't give it to her. I took her elbow, and we led each other to sit on the nearest bed. She started to cry, and I held her hand. We heard nothing from the bathroom. After a while she checked on him and returned with fresh tears on her face.

I said, "Is there a hospital?"

She shook her head. "No one's been seen in the hospitals for years."

"I can go look for a doctor."

She ran a hand across her face. It had an effect like a magician's wand. Her eyes lifted, and she was steeled. "You can look if you want to. I won't ask you to."

I nodded and stood, unsure what I should do. With the sun setting, Phil asleep in his tub, nothing seemed like the proper response. Nothing felt appropriate. I said, "I'll be back."

Lily didn't answer, but I knew she'd heard.

I can't recall the walk toward the park. My mind was a void. I embraced it. My head was too full of what I knew. I found myself in front of Emma's stand. She was locking handouts and pamphlets into the cupboards at her feet. When she saw me, she smiled.

"If you're here to bring me more phonebooks—" Her smile fell. "What's happened?"

"I need a map that shows all the hospitals in the city."

She started to dig. "Oh, God, oh, God." She knocked her organized piles over and grabbed a stack from a back shelf. She pulled the map open and shoved it toward me. "It's Phil? He's sick?"

I spread the map on the counter. She pointed at a few spots marked with a blue *H*.

"These," she said. "The map is very out of date. Lots of streets have changed. And good luck finding a doctor. Don't remember the last time the hospitals were open."

I folded the map up and thanked her. The sun was already low enough that she stood in deep shadow. Her hand reached out and grasped my wrist. Her skin, thin and pale, felt like rose petals.

"Good luck, honey." Her voice was thick. I walked away,

east, toward the nearest hospital on the map. I don't know if I realized then that it was the one I'd been born in.

I reached the East Side after dark. I stood before the vacant building and looked up at its black windows. Unlike almost any other building I'd seen, this one was completely abandoned—not a single light in a single window, no squatters moving among the rooms. Perhaps there was too much superstition about disease or ghosts of the dead. Whatever it was, the neighborhood gave the building its space. I felt myself cross an invisible barrier at First Avenue, and I stood at the entrance, gazed through the multiple doors into what had been a waiting area.

I didn't bother to enter. There was no one there.

The building across the street, which had once been dorms for medical students, was a wide structure with eight floors and a hundred windows on the front of it, many of them filled with incandescent light. I walked up to it with little hope. In the entrance sat a woman with three small girls hiding behind her. All of them were shoeless and wore simple white dresses, even the mother. They hovered like spirits in the dark.

I raised a hand as I approached. "I need a doctor. A man is very sick."

She shook her head. "None here. Sorry, hon. I haven't seen a doctor in weeks."

"Where was that?"

"One traveled by but didn't stay. She was headed upstate, to family."

I thanked her and left her and her children. They'd grown brave as I'd spoken to their mother and now chased me along the sidewalk to the corner. When I turned and headed west, they stopped and talked to one another in whispers. I didn't look back. I felt an absurd fear that the hospital recognized me.

I returned to Phil's building, the moon now overhead, echoes of the day nipping at me up the stairs. An occasional crash of metal, a cough, a scrape around a corner. I would find Lily and tell her how sorry I was, how I couldn't locate a doctor. I knew I wouldn't leave Phil's apartment to go back to my empty, soulless hotel. I knew the next day I'd go to find her breakfast and lunch, that I'd bring her dinner and sit with her to care for Phil. I knew that we would watch him slowly die.

The next few weeks passed too quickly, even as each day lasted too long to measure. Phil's illness dried up, both ends stopped running out of control, and he retreated from the bathroom to his bedroom. He lay on a pallet stowed in a corner. His desk and papers dominated the room. Lily and I watched him in turns. I stayed during the evening and through the early morning, until just before the sun came up. I would wake midmorning with Lily whispering to Phil's still shape beneath his dirty blankets. What she did during her time away from him, I don't know. For my own part, I had a hard time leaving him. I'd known him only a short while. I had adopted him, it seemed, as much as he might have adopted me.

Most days he didn't know we were there, or if he did, he ignored us. He spoke to invisible people, mumbled stories without beginning or end. He referred to distant memories as if they'd just happened, as if he fell into them again and again, caught in a loop where he answered the same unasked questions. He screamed answers, impotent.

In lucid moments Phil would recognize me and cry.

"It wasn't supposed to go like this," he said. I nodded and agreed. I offered him ice chips hammered from the edges of the rumbling kitchen freezer. He refused them and glared at me as if I didn't, couldn't, understand.

Other times he was more himself, quiet and speculative. He asked questions about my days at the hotel. I explained I was spending most nights in his apartment. I tried to hide the fact I was caring for him, as if he wouldn't know.

"You shouldn't be here watching an old man die. Neither should she." He no longer used any name for Lily. I tried not to as well, lest I confuse him. I think we both recognized that to question either's understanding of her was to question our own.

Sometimes we spoke of his items, his watchbands and eyeglasses, piles stacked on shelves to the ceiling on every floor of the building. "I know they'll come around to collect them," he said of the party guests. "When they do, make sure they only take what I gave them. They can't just take whatever they want."

"I understand," I said. I didn't say that no one would come, that only Emma had inquired after him, but that she was too broken by his illness to visit.

For two days he refused to eat or drink. He wouldn't speak. He lay on his back, eyes on the ceiling. No matter when I looked at him, he was unmoving, staring. Finally, on the second day, well after the sun set, he asked, "What's it like outside?" We had been quiet until that moment in the useless light from flickering streetlamps.

I said, "Same as always. It's getting colder."

He nodded as if this made sense, as if it followed some logic. "I remember when it got cold enough outside that we'd put cans of soda on the sill and they'd be frozen in an hour. Now it only gets cold enough to not sweat to death."

"I can remember Central Park covered in snow."

He laughed, a small gasp followed by coughing. "I know when you're lying."

"Why?"

"Your lips move."

He did his best not to choke when he laughed at his own joke, grasping at breaths, holding tight to them for moments, eyes blinking rapidly. I did all I could, hand on his chest, feeling at the rattle within, poorly hidden sadness in my smile and a dagger of shame at how little I knew of living. I'd gathered information but created nothing, watched so many like Phil turn to dust in graves I celebrated for my witnessing. To know where the cemetery lies tells you nothing of lives. When he was gone, what could I say of him, his era? I was worse than a headstone eroded to blank.

During the days I slept, usually in Lily's room but not with Lily. She either took care of Phil or left the apartment for long periods. I asked her where she went as if she owed me an explanation, as if Phil's crying for her gave me some authority. When she refused to answer, I stopped asking and a mutual silence developed between us.

Occasionally she came to the room while I slept or would call to me when I was in Phil's room watching him sleep. In those rare moments, we would lie together and I would enter her, similar to how it had been the night in my hotel room, but something like a veil drifted between us. I both hated and loved that separation. Some part of Lily was gone, hidden away, so obscured that I worried I might think of her as Sara again. Yet it was also perfect. This didn't seem to be the woman who would arrive at the party; she was evolving into something else, something haunted and fixated. Perhaps I'd done what needed to be done, just by arriving here, by playing through this drama.

Weeks passed. Phil couldn't eat and barely drank. He crunched ice chips, grunting as he did so. He refused to die but talked of nothing else. His voice shrank to silence. His body withered to a husk, and the movement of his skin against itself sounded like dry leaves sliding one over the other. Even his tongue made whispered sounds in his mouth, so that when he moved and talked, it sounded as if a hushed conversation were taking place just out of sight, a conversation about things better not spoken of, things that would become apparent in a minute, or the one after that, after he was gone.

Lily disappeared for longer and longer periods. Some days I didn't see her at all, thought she must have fled, hoped that she would but knew she would return. She always did. Sometimes I found her asleep in her bed, dirty with some work I couldn't guess at, asleep with her face turned to the wall. I could climb into bed behind her, feel the heat of her pooled under the covers and pressing back against me. She smelled of paint and dust, and I wondered if she had become a painter for the library. I could take her and she accepted it without a word, her hands reached around to hold mine against her chest. She would remain silent except for small intakes of air and whispers I couldn't make out. Sometimes I would hear her swear she made no promises to me. The next day I would wake alone.

The weather turned cold and the days dark. Winter passed quietly. I opened the windows and tried to pull fresh air in to Phil. The apartment stank of him. Despite daily sponge baths and my having removed most everything from the room that might smell—sandwiches and fruit squirreled in desk drawers, a potted fern long dead, half-finished glasses of water turned yellow—the room stank of the rot taking place inside him. When not working at Grand Central, I sat in Phil's room going through his papers. In inks too varied to count, on papers of every size and color and age, some brittle with years, some still smelling of the ream they'd fallen from, he'd cataloged everything. Meticulous notes listed how many nuts and bolts he'd found, numbers of hammer heads, still-viable lightbulbs, and even an accounting of those bulbs not viable, by size and wattage, and then those bulbs he had not kept. In the end, without dates or a system to follow, I'd begun to gather the pages according to size of paper, smallest to largest. While I compared the sheet to his life catalog, I spoke aloud to Phil, a running monologue on his system and ideas I had for improving it. I found that he quieted when he heard my voice, or at least I could not hear him and his whispering tongue. I read some pages out loud, wondered at moon phases and weather changes. I convinced myself that he enjoyed the talks, despite the occasional rattled breath and rolling eyes beneath lids.

It was a bright morning in February when his breath changed and the whisper in him grew loud enough to hear. "Sara," he said. "I need to see Sara."

I hadn't seen her for two days. I put the papers on the desk, almost carefully, and left Phil's room. I'd been inside for such a long time that I was shocked to find the rest of the apartment flooded with cold air and light. I'd left the windows open in two rooms, and snow had accumulated on the sills. I heard flakes crunch under my feet as I grabbed a jacket and headed for the stairs. I reached the ground floor but didn't know where to go for Lily. Up and down the street, I saw only a few trails in ankle-deep snow. Most of them crossed the street to the hotel, my hotel, where I hadn't been in weeks. I followed the trail into the hotel. The lobby was dark.

I took the main stairs two at a time to the fifth floor. From the landing I saw nothing in the hallway, only the lights rising and falling with the ebb and flow of power. My room was open. I couldn't remember what I had done with my key, but obviously she had taken it. I could have called out but didn't. Instead I approached cautiously and peered in. Every surface in the room was covered in items I had not missed from Phil's home. They were piled along the dresser and across half the bed, the other half of which was dented into the shape of her sleeping body. Next to the closet sat the video camera on the tripod. The bathroom was dark. A row of six bottles of twelve-year-old scotch sat before the mirror. The metallic squid sat between two of those bottles on the dresser, and the milky fluid that had filled its glassy head was gone. I took the device and squeezed it until I thought it might break. Why hadn't I shattered it before?

A metallic thud drew me to the back stairway, where chains of extension cords wound up the steps. Along the cords hung light fixtures of various shapes and sizes. An ornate brass lamp from the lobby, now without its shade, was tied to the railing half a floor above me, its light shooting straight up the staircase shaft and reflecting from the walls. Cold air gave way to high heat from the lamps; I felt like I was walking up a chimney. I stepped over cords and broken glass. My shadow rolled around me, leaping up the stairs and onto the walls above me. By the time I reached the sixth floor, the light was clear and clean and even. I heard someone above me dragging something metal up the steps.

"Lily?" I called. I'd barely raised my voice, but the name echoed everywhere. The noise stopped, as if she were holding still like a scared animal, as if silence would convince me to leave. I found her at the seventh-floor landing with a metal stepladder and a can of red paint. Her hands seemed blood-dipped and raw. She looked down at me almost with relief.

I said, "What are you doing?"

She shrugged, a casual gesture that the situation didn't warrant. "I'm trying to figure it all out." She looked from me to the wall. Before my eyes could take in the words, I knew what they would say. In front of her was the message "A scar can be trusted." Above her, on the wall of the next turn of stairs, it said, "More than one." Below that the odd command to "Fly east."

Some things would happen despite my efforts, I realized. Perhaps because of my efforts to avoid them they happened the way they were meant to.

"You used this." I held up the empty vial. "You shouldn't have."

She shrugged again. "It was never yours to keep from me."

"What?"

"You're trying to keep me tied to your truth, but you've got no right. You don't know me. I don't need to be saved. And I won't be, if I do this right."

"Do what?"

She pointed at the still-wet words. "It's all mixed up. But I think it will become clear soon enough."

I said, "I can help."

"No you can't." She turned her back to me. "This is mine. Like a kind of poetry that only I can write and understand."

A chill ran up my spine, and I needed to sit on the stairs. Had I really convinced myself that I was only an observer?

"Leave with me," I said. "Let's leave the city and not come back."

She shook her head. "You know I don't do that. I can't. I can't leave Phil." Her eyes scanned her work. "And there's all this to figure out."

I felt the stairs tilt under me. Everything was happening too fast. I'd come here tonight because of Phil, I remembered now. "He's asking for you. He's—"

She waited for me to finish my sentence.

"I think he's almost gone."

She dropped her paintbrush and ran down the stairs.

I listened to her footsteps grow distant and followed slowly. I was dizzy and sick. I was guilty over the relief I'd felt at the thought of Phil's death, that it offered us a way out. If he died, might she leave with me? I pushed that aside. She would need time. I'd been his constant companion for days; she hadn't spoken with him in weeks. Instead of returning to their apartment, I went to the finished room and sat on the bed. In the closet hung my filthy, abused suit.

Any thought that I could control the movement of history drained from me. I was a passenger here. This river flowed only one way, and I could see the cliff's edge, hear the falls roar. I should have crushed the thing into the carpet. Now it was too late. I knew she wouldn't leave, not even if Phil was gone. Not even if she'd shown herself her own death. Not when memories were dripping all around her, tiny puzzles like jewels to be studied and cared for. Me, the great problem solver, I knew nothing other than that bullets waited for both of us.

I followed Lily home. The sun gone, stars battled the streetlamps' flickering. The city embraced its brownout. I crossed the alley and traced the sounds of my footsteps to Phil's apartment. The door stood open. Inside, Lily paced the living room, tracking through melting snow piled under open windows. She stopped at one window, arms tight around her, and rested her head on the pane. Her breath clouded the glass. The cold night air slipped across our feet. Suddenly she was shrieking out the window, calling to Mana and Joshua and Emma, screaming to them as if they were in danger until her words turned to unpronounceable sobs. Leaving her choking back her cries, I slipped on slush through the hall to Phil's room. He lay on his back, face tilted to the ceiling, eyes closed. I leaned over him and put my ear to his mouth so that his cold lips touched my skin. Nothing.

Kneeling over him, I remembered Phil's asking me to watch Lily and realized I wouldn't be leaving the city. I wouldn't leave without her, and she wouldn't leave. I found her on the ground floor tearing apart piles of Phil's newspapers and throwing the pages out the front door. The breeze lifted them and tugged them back and forth in front of the building. I sat on the bottom step, watching her. When she finished with the last paper, she went inside and returned with a box filled with antique glass milk bottles, which she carried to the middle of the street and dropped without care. Before they crashed against the pavement, she had already turned away. I stayed and watched her as she emptied the building of everything but Phil himself. I was certain that she was as untethered as I was, as removed from any guidance or mooring.

OVER THE DAYS that followed Phil's death, Lily emptied the apartment and scrubbed it clean, then repainted. It was, again, as it would be, white. She spoke of it as if she were leaving it soon but never did so. The day after Phil died, she'd brought in the park's ground crew, who had silently gathered Phil in his blankets, wrapped tight as a mummy, and carried him I don't know where. I never asked.

I went back to work, putting in enough hours to earn two sandwiches, which I brought home, As we ate, Lily would say things to test the silence. "It's ham today," she might say. "Nice to have a change."

I agreed. "Don't know where they got it, but it's good."

She would eat the sandwich, and I would take my seat at the window. From here I could see the entire alley and part of the street. If anyone approached the building from the hotel, I could be down the stairs to meet him in moments. I carried a pistol with me, the one I thought of as mine, the one that killed the Drunk. Lily never asked why I watched. She probably had memories that I didn't trust myself, probably surmised I was waiting for my own figure to turn the corner, looking for her. She ate the sandwiches and then returned to the work of painting all the rooms on all the floors of the building. She was nearly halfway up, on the fifth floor, and the only time she left the building was when she needed paint. I accompanied her on these trips out, disguised as her helper.

"You can't carry all those gallons yourself."

She would laugh. "No, of course not."

I kept an eye out for myself as we went from hardware store to hardware store searching for gallons of white paint. No one looked our way.

We ate and talked. If the brownouts turned too dark for reading, we'd follow each other's voice down the hall to the bedroom. We undressed in the dark, apart, meeting at the mattress. Mornings we woke tangled in sheets and each other.

One morning, the windows open for warming breezes, Lily and I stood in the kitchen eating bread she'd gotten from some wandering market near the park, and I asked her what she thought of leaving the city with me.

She laughed. "To go where?"

I didn't know.

"I came to this city to stay," she said. "I'll die here. I've always known that."

"We could go and then come back."

She pursed her lips, almost a smile. "Maybe some other time."

We didn't say anything for a while after that, the sound

of someone hammering giving a metronomic tick through the open windows. I'd begun to suspect that the jumble of memories was untying itself, that she knew more than she pretended.

At last I said, "We could go somewhen else."

As if that were a trigger she had waited to hear pulled, she put down her sparse breakfast and said, "You haven't ever asked me about what I remember."

I considered changing the subject. Instead I said, "You've never asked when I'm from."

"I know what I need to know."

"Which is?"

"We both have layers of lies to spin out for each other. Lies about how things will be okay. We'll do that later. Right now I simply say that you do what you do thinking it's for me. But it's not. You're doing all this for you. I know, selfish."

Our bread sat on the counter. It was rough and tasteless. I wanted to say she was wrong, but the fact that I hesitated made me fear she was right. If she spoke first, it would be the last we'd speak of this. I couldn't let her end it there. I had to.

She ran her hand over her shoulder, across the tattoos that perched there. "Take a walk with me?"

What little faith I had in my altruism evaporated at her words. "Where?" I asked. She wouldn't say, just smiled.

I followed her down Sixth Avenue. It was a warm morning for February, and we stayed on the shaded side of the street. She was always one step ahead of me, no matter my speed. We walked beneath empty office buildings until we reached an entrance with a jury-rigged ramp that reached all the way to the center of the street. Multiple banisters and handles decorated the walls, bolted and screwed into seemingly random locations.

I followed her up the ramp and down a dark hallway toward an open door busy with voices. There were only two people in the room, a naked woman and a man in a wheelchair, tattoos peeking from collar and wrists of his leather jacket. His legs, wrapped in leather, capped in unscuffed work boots, were strapped to the wheelchair's leg rests.

He focused on his work, the humming needles and wiping of blood preoccupying him, seemingly unaffected by the beautiful naked woman under his hands. The strange chatter of voices, repeated and overlapping, muttered from a radio I couldn't see. The tattoo he pressed into her back was an intricate pattern of hooks and chains, styled to appear as if they were woven through her skin. She glanced at us over her shoulder, made no move to cover up or welcome us in.

My eyes darted back and forth, from the woman lying on the table to the tattoo pictures displayed all over the walls to Lily. Her own tattoos snuck around the short sleeves of her shirt. I'd never asked about them. I realized I was probably about to find myself marked in the way I'd been shown I would, given the brand I wore at my end.

We watched for fifteen minutes before the naked woman had had enough. She raised one hand, and without a word the artist stopped. Fresh bandages were laid, tape applied. He cleaned trays and threw away gauze and paper towels while she dressed. They exchanged words, and she bent to hug him. When she left, he grabbed the wheels of his chair with either hand and spun to face Lily. His scowl cracked into a smile easily enough.

"And how are we today?"

Lily hugged him, just as the other woman had. As she did, her shirt lifted and I could see a few of the birds at her waist. She talked to him in a whisper, the unseen voices loud enough to cover her conversation. I looked around for the radio and instead found holes in the ceiling tiles, wooden dowels and bird feeders hanging nearby. Through the gaps in the ceiling, I saw movement, the flutter of green feathers. A gray head with black, beadlike eyes leaned through and stared at me. The man had a nest of parrots living in his ceiling. There was no radio. They secreted to one another, mostly about tattoos and symbols, meanings and menacings that must have been discussed in the tattoo parlor over the years.

Lily came back to me. "Mark will be giving you a gift from me. But you can't see it until it's done."

"What will it be?"

No answer. She knew I already knew. We began to layer our lies in silence. Mark, back turned to us, busied himself with needles and ink. I sat on the edge of the table the woman had just vacated. It was still warm from her body. The room smelled of a mix of rubbing alcohol and bird dander. Mark finished his preparations and smiled at me. It was a hard smile to receive. Hard eyes and white teeth, sharklike. I became acutely aware of the chair he sat in, the needles on the tray beside him, the rustling of feathers above our heads. Murmured secrets.

"She said she wants it on your wrist."

I nodded.

He laughed. It was worse than the smile. "She wants it there. But where do you want it?"

"If she wants it on the wrist, put it on my wrist."

Mark set down the needle. "Listen, I'm not having you come back in two days bitching that the goddamn thing is in the wrong place or doesn't make you feel like she digs you, so when you're sure of where you want it, you come see me. Or not. I don't care either way."

All I could think of was the party, the Body, the way it was promised to me, every bit of it, the ink, the bullet, the painful recoil of a gun in my hand as it shot the Drunk, the smell of copper as Lily bled into her bed.

I said, "Just give me the damn tattoo, whatever she told you to, wherever she told you to, and let me go live what little of my life I give a shit about. Can you do that?"

Mark maneuvered his chair closer to the table and smiled his unpleasant smile. "There you are," he said. "Was that so hard? Sit down on that chair, arm across the table."

Lily, lips trembling, had remained silent through my conversation with Mark. Now, as his needle was about to drop, she said, "Remember, this is a surprise. Don't peek,"

"I can't cover it while I work," Mark said. "So you're just going to have to look somewhere else."

Lily put her hand on my shoulder a moment, enough to let me know she hoped that what was about to happen was what was meant to happen. My own hope lay with hers, but I also saw the Body and his tattooed wrist. I'd ignored that memory for months; I couldn't any longer.

Mark was ready. "Look at me. I want you to think of a time of day, any hour, I don't care which. I want you to whisper that hour into my ear."

Behind me Lily paced like a cat. My mind flashed to all the

times I'd looked at a clock in my life, and I tried to think of any one time that stuck out. In the ceiling above me, a parrot called out numbers, but I couldn't focus on a single one even though I tried. All that came back to me was the time it had been when Lily died, when I looked at my watch and saw that it was nearly nine in the morning. Behind me I could hear her flipping through books and shuffling tattoo photographs in three-ring binders, but the hour she died lit up my head. I wanted the bird in the ceiling to give me another number, but it had stopped talking.

I couldn't make myself say "nine." "You pick," I said to Lily.

Behind me the nervous shuffling stopped. "No, you have to pick."

We could have argued. I could have tried to force her to choose, sat silent until either she gave in or Mark tired of us, of me, but I didn't. I was more than a little sick when I leaned forward and whispered "Nine" into his ear.

Mark nodded, and Lily sat on the chair behind him, under the window. She pulled off her sweater, the tank top beneath seeming to show more parrots than I'd ever seen on her before—impossible given how often I'd seen her naked, yet there they were in an uncountable flock, almost moving with the sounds of the birds above us. I felt hollow inside as I recognized I knew nothing about her. "Just look at me," she said.

"This will hurt," Mark said an instant before jabbing the needle into my arm with a metal buzz. I fought not to flinch and lost. The fire rushed up my arm and blinded me. Each time Mark paused to wipe blood and ink from my skin, I prayed that he was done. I waited for the conversation offered. None came. Lily's eyes were on the street outside, her ears on the ghosts of conversation from the parrots. Above us one parrot sang "Happy Birthday" and another answered with mangled "I love you"s that never quite sounded right, never quite managed to carry the weight of what they ought. The words sounded sadly familiar. I longed for more lies.

When Mark finally finished, I didn't need to look. My grave marker was in my skin, my invitation to the private party at my own convention. Lily stood, came to the table, and peered over Mark's shoulder. I watched her eyes, waited for her smile, some glimmer of approval. Instead she turned away and pulled her sweater on, despite the heat. She reached into her pockets for money I didn't know she had, didn't know anyone still used, and laid the bills out on the table for Mark. I heard her feet pounding down the ramp before I finally looked down at the parrot on my arm. Small, a simple black outline, but clearly a parrot, flying west if my hand was north. I thought of the parrots right above me as "I love you"s warbled in my head.

Mark gave instructions on caring for the wound, instructions I almost committed to memory. The last thing he said was, "She's a question mark, that one."

I gathered myself and headed back to the hotel at my own pace, unsure of what I had done wrong but certain I had done it, had always done it, would do it again.

Anxiety built as March passed, and in the last week I was exhausted but not sleeping, night after night trying to will myself asleep and hearing the pounding of my internal clock. One night, in a growing streak of insomnia, I dragged myself from Lily and our bed and dressed. Out the living-room window, the hotel throbbed with light.

I didn't stagger or trip as I left the building. In the street the rise and fall of light from inside my hotel was bright enough to make me shade my eyes. I crossed the street to the entrance, made my way past the ballroom and through the kitchen. The bulbs and lamps Lily had laid out for her work were buzzing. I clicked off each lamp as I went. At last I reached the walls of graffiti. I stood and looked at the words, allegiances to scars, descriptions of rooms she hadn't yet entered, the command to fly east that she had refused—looked at them once more before I turned off the last lamp.

I was safe in the dark from the words that lined the halls. I wanted to erase all the messages Lily had left for herself, but I couldn't. They stood for so much I didn't know about her, the parts of herself she kept from me. I couldn't erase them, but I could darken them. I gathered lamp cords in my hands and pulled. Below me lamps fell and bulbs broke, the already dark stairs clattered with lamps falling up to me as I yanked them in by their cords. Eventually I pulled the right one, and far below, a plug was pulled from a socket and the remaining lamps blinked out. I'd have pulled the building down if I could.

Broken glass crunched beneath my heels as I descended. At the fifth floor, I stopped and looked down the hall. The door of my room was open, and a box of light lay across the wet carpet in front of it.

When I reached the room, I found it cleaned of almost everything but my suit and the video camera. A typewriter sat in the closet. On the dresser was a folded piece of paper. I hesitated to open it, knowing already what it said. I opened it anyway, saw that it read the same as when I'd found it on the

bar six months ago, when the Brats had offered it to me and
the Drunk had taken it: *"If it's dark, I'm gone."* I put the note
on the bed and ran, splashed down the hall and nearly fell
down the steps. I rushed back to Phil's apartment. My lungs
ached, and my calls bounced back to me from the bare white
walls.

Lily was gone, as she must have known she would be,
remembered she would be, if she woke and saw the hotel
dark, if the collection of lamps she'd left for me to turn off
ever was turned off, if she found me gone long enough to give
her the chance to disappear. The note was her only good-bye.
I sat in the middle of what had been Phil's room and looked
around at the blank spaces, the vacancy of Phil compounded
by hers. I felt like those walls—like I'd been bleach-stained
where she'd touched. I felt an ache in my wrist where the parrot flew west.

I returned to my hotel. My main concern had been to find
out which of me had invited her. I'd carried her invitation
back with me. She'd sent it to herself. The machinery of events
was grinding away, with all the gears lined up for both Lily's
and my deaths. There was only one piece missing, one thing
I hadn't done. Every hope was useless, every effort wasted.
My life had been an illusion of arrogance, a trick I'd fooled
myself with, a deceit that I could step outside of events and
watch history unfold yet remain unaffected. The machinery
of it all was revealed. *Let me be that part,* I thought, a dark and
darkening horizon in my head.

I made the bed and then undressed. I took the suit from the
closet and put it on, then sat on the bed facing the camera. I
scoured the room for a brown paper bag and a ballpoint pen,

found them in a dresser drawer. I wrapped a bottle from the dresser in the bag, twisted the bag around the bottle's neck. How had I thought that staying away was enough to avoid a bad end for Lily and for me? It seemed that some fates were predatory, would leap up and take you if you didn't search every dark corner for them.

I put the bottle underneath the bed. I found one videotape inside the camera and another unopened in a drawer. Lily had brought things here to echo random unexplained memory, but they weren't a mystery to me. I rewound the tape to the beginning and hit "record." I sat on the bed and waited. When I was certain the tape was running, I reached under the bed and began my salute, opening the bag, opening the bottle, and drinking. Whiskey burned my throat—my first drink in months. The sweetness of it surprised me. I didn't recall actually tasting drinks before, only getting them inside me. This was different. I knew that this would be the last drink I'd ever have, that I would likely get sick, that I was toasting my lack of faith in myself, my lack of purpose, the path I'd been on, my failure. It was as if this were my own wake, a farewell from a place I couldn't imagine I'd ever reach or understand. I pulled from memory nods and smiles at the door, cues for my younger self to look at Yellow, to drink, to wonder what came next.

Done drinking my half of the bottle, I drunkenly wrapped bottle and unused videotape in the bag. I remembered then the message that had been on the bag—its meaning still unclear to me—and found a pen on the dresser. I was supposed to write, *"In case of emergency, break glass,"* which was what the bag had said when I'd found it. I wouldn't do it.

My one rebellion against what I knew was coming. I stuck the wrapped bottle far under the bed. A noise in the hallway. I pressed "stop" on the camera and headed to the door, the whiskey swirling around me. I felt particles on my face. Bits of plaster fell from the ceiling, and water trickled down the wall. Here was the growing puddle I would find when I first saw the finished room. Everything was the same. Now the gears were set for the party, and all I had to do was follow the currents.

Only I wouldn't do it. I couldn't. If fate was predatory, then I'd have to challenge it. Let my other selves find the tape and wonder what it was. I wouldn't be there. I would leave. And would take Lily if I could find her, convince her to leave with me. I had to try. If I didn't find her, then, burning knot in my gut, I'd leave without her.

I pulled the door shut and walked down the now-wet hall floor. As I passed the other doors, I wondered what I might have found behind them, if I might have left other items there, other tethers that I might ignore or cling to, other paths I might put myself on simply by imagining they existed.

MY SEARCH FOR her started the next day. I followed the streets east as far as the bridges. She'd sworn to never leave the city, and I believed her, not because she was trustworthy but because I knew it was true of both of us, I felt it in my bones more real than gravity. I searched the riverbed, dry and filled with garbage and abandoned cars, and knew I wouldn't cross over. I turned back and headed north. Days passed. I begged for food or scavenged through boarded-up buildings. I crossed back and forth over the city. To Hell's Kitchen, then east to Central Park, where I wandered up to Harlem and kept going north. When I reached the Cloisters, I turned back. Some streets just tasted wrong, like aluminum on the tongue. I didn't see her anywhere. I searched the Central Park camps, with their rings of barbed wire and patrols. I scanned the line of people with their pillowcases of canned goods in front of the Plaza Hotel, waiting to be interviewed for acceptance into the clans.

"What do you think you would be able to offer a clan?" asked one of the tie-wearing interviewers. He, like the others, sat behind an office desk that had been hauled out onto the sidewalk.

A pert young woman with uneven bangs smiled anxiously. "I'm assertive and good with traps."

The interviewer made notes on a clipboard.

I returned to the eastern edge of the city for no reason other than that it was opposite where we'd been together, and something in the message of "fly east" wouldn't unhook from my thoughts. None of the street crews on the West Side had seen her. Emma claimed she hadn't either, although I thought she might lie.

I walked past the hospital again and found it more dilapidated in the light. Across the street the dorms were buzzing like a hive. The children I'd seen before caught me looking at the many windows and ran out to chat. The oldest teased me that the woman I sought was my "girlfriend," the word stretching out along her wide, wicked, child smile.

"You love her," she purred. I gave the kids some apples that Emily had given me and continued down First Avenue. I walked nearly to the tip of Manhattan. At the foot of the Manhattan Bridge, I considered walking across the East River. I stared across the muddy ground between me and Governors Island. Her promise to not leave the limits of the island repeated inside me. I felt an ache in my body. My back rippled with every step. I needed to rest.

I headed to the subway. I'd been in the tunnels but never seen trains, although others claimed they still ran. The nearest station was City Hall. I passed the agent's booth and jumped a turnstile. On the platform, candles burned in sconces bolted to the support beams. Commuters read books or old newspapers. I picked up some pages myself and read news decades old, thought of the papers that Lily freed after Phil's death. The train that eventually arrived had no headlights, and so it burst from the black tunnel like an eel, its brakes screaming. My heart beat faster, but when the train slowed, I saw that the interior was lit and filled with people.

I stepped into a car nearest the conductor, as if he provided some kind of protection, and examined the other riders. Entire families called the train home. I saw men and women lost in the vague intimacies of life. Five children received reading lessons from a man who seemed father to none of them, a legal pad on his knee as he drew letters, upside down and backward from his perspective. "*Cat,*" he wrote. "*Dog.*" I watched until he wrote "*Train,*" and the children gave knowing smiles to one another.

A blanket lay across several seats, and beneath it moved the shapes of two lovers. I walked past them and those who casually sat near them, reading or sleeping or watching. I found a seat beside a woman with a small electric hot plate attached to a battery. She cooked eggs she sold for a dollar a plate. People lined up and offered their money. She served in order, throwing oil and eggs into a small black pan. She took pity on me and gave me an egg for free. I had no cash and offered her my jacket, but she refused it. In a thick accent, she said, "Be nice to someone else. It all comes back." She said something in a Slavic tongue, smiled, and turned to her next customer. I ate the egg in silence.

At the next stop, a priest stepped on board, and the people

nearest the door shouted at him to leave. Someone from farther down the car shouted back, "Until he hurts someone, he
stays, just like the rest." It might have been the teacher, but it
could have been anyone.

The priest walked among the passengers, speaking of God
and holding a cup for donations. None came. One man told
him, "You'd be better off becoming a carpenter, like Jesus.
Then you'd be productive." The priest ignored him and
quoted a passage from the New Testament.

I returned to Phil and Lily's building, my building. I was
nearly crippled, my back so knotted that standing was difficult. The stairs to the top floor nearly wrenched me apart,
and with every step I recalled seeing Lily carried up them. I
had failed spectacularly in my attempt to save her. She had
disappeared, and I knew that whether I returned to the party
or not, she would be there. My guilt was crippling me.

The next day I regretted having come back to that place.
No one knew I was there. I had little food. I spent hours on
the kitchen floor, lying on my back or my stomach. I crawled
through the apartment on all fours, searching for food.
Instead I found the remains of Phil's hidden stores of alcohol hidden behind cleaning products in the bathroom, in the
lowest kitchen cupboards, and under threadbare blankets in a
closet. I medicated the pain, found that even if the pain didn't
leave, at least I did. I drank myself to a stupor during that day
and the next and wandered in and out of consciousness during the night. Awake, I cursed myself and Lily, Phil, Emma,
whoever passed through memory. When I sobered enough to
look out the window at the hotel, sunlight blurring its windows, I would wonder what day it was for an instant and then

turn to the next bottle. I relived Phil's death. I talked to ghosts and memories. I waited for suns to rise and set.

When at last I ran out of Phil's remaining stash, I filled the bottles with water and watched light filter through them, ran my fingers through the rainbows they cast on the floor. I waited for daylight to break through and catch them in new ways. I drank the bottles during the evening, telling myself over and over that there was more I could have done, nothing else I could have done. My ears were filled with my own circling babble, and just before I fell asleep, I heard words slip from me that made the pain in my back crackle like electricity.

"It was her choice to go," I said. Then I fell asleep.

The following morning the pain was gone. I woke and turned to my side and didn't shudder or moan. I lay still for several minutes, sure the pain would creep up and take me again, certain it waited for me to think it gone in order to injure me more when it returned. When it didn't, I sat up and looked around the room. It was dark, and the sky outside the windows rolled with heavy clouds. Thunder shook the bottles on the sill.

Rain splattered against the bottles, ran from the sill down the cracked plaster wall, and pooled on the wooden floor. The puddle was growing, gathering bits of plaster debris, dust, small pieces of paper that floated across the top like water bugs. The water followed the unseen contours of the floorboards, the paths dictated by grain and wear, toward the center of the room, jogged sideways twice, and then formed a pool beside my mattress. If the rain continued, I knew that the mattress would be ruined. For the first time in days, I stood. I found the tentacled device, no milky fluid or smell of memory around it. It was as if someone had cleaned it. I took it back to the mattress, lay down, and held the device to my chest.

Outside, the storm continued, the sky so dark it was impossible to say if it was day or night. Streetlamps and neighborhoods blinked on and off in the distance. Nearby, lightning lit the streets. I followed the odor of food down the hallway to the living room and found a milk crate with three Styrofoam containers inside. I opened the top one and found a turkey dinner with potatoes and broccoli. I opened the other two and found two more of the same. Had Lily taken some odd kind of pity on me, or had Mana or Josh come to make peace with Phil? I put two in the refrigerator; the third I ate with my bare hands. When I was done, I left the container on the floor and carried the device back to bed. No longer bogged down by my stomach, I knew what I wanted: to see if the device worked. I wanted to see Lily again, even if only in memory, and this twisted thing might give me that. But I was still afraid to find out. I curled my hands around it and held it under my pillow.

Rain hammered the buildings, and I lay listening to its work. I could imagine the years of dirt that washed away down the drains of the city, the dust taken from the air. It tasted cleaner. I ate the other two meals when I became hungry and then wondered at who had brought them. The empty containers floated around the living room on top of the half inch of water that covered the apartment floor. It ran under the front door, spilled over the steps, and rained down the stairwell. My mattress squished beneath me.

Another day or night and I woke to more smells. I followed them to the living room and this time found a plate wrapped in foil. Under the foil, held firm by coagulating gravy, were nine Swedish meatballs. I walked to the window, looked across the alley, and saw lights glare from the first and second floors of the hotel. My party was tonight. I saw one of myselves run through the rain to the front entrance. The Elder, I was sure, who had brought this food. In a flash of lightning, I caught another scurrying along the side of the building, a Youngster, probably one of the first, maybe even the Inventor. I left the plate on the sill, and rain mixed with the gravy.

Lily would be there tonight. If I could have convinced her to leave with me, then the deaths would be avoided. Six months hadn't been enough. A year would be. I'd go further back. I'd try again.

I found my suit in the closet and my three guns. I'd been wearing clothes that belonged to Phil, so going back in them, meeting Lily and Phil a full year earlier, while wearing his clothes would lead to unwanted questions. A year earlier, or more. Two, three? And no memory device; she'd never steal her memories back from me. I changed into the suit and then weighed what to do with the guns. They anchored me to the spot as I debated. If they weren't present in the present, if I took them further back and got rid of them, if I also took Phil's gun from a year earlier, then the Suit's events might change so dramatically that the shooting would never occur. I'd never come back here, and I might not know what events would come, but at least the deaths might be avoided.

At the front door of the building, I watched the hotel pop in and out of sight as lightning flashed, the scramble of the guest-hosts arriving. I couldn't go back, but I had to go back. It had to come to this, to my return. I wasn't going to attend the party. I was going to get back to the roof, to my raft, and then I'd be gone from my Elders and Youngsters for good. I'd save myself from myself, and Lily as well. To do this meant hiding in plain sight. I'd have to act like I belonged so that I could disappear. And in a flash of lightning, I knew how to do it. In that flash I saw my reflection in the door glass. In that reflection I saw the Drunk.

I had lost weight, gained gray and a beard. My eyes were dark, my hair long and unruly. I was sober but didn't look it. I was the Drunk. I was the one who would kill Lily. I wasn't a drunk. I wouldn't kill Lily. No one would want me there. No one would talk to me. I could walk through the lobby and to the stairs, reach the roof, and be gone. But I needed to be cautious. Taking the guns with me to the past was one step. The second was keeping them from working. I took the guns from my pocket and emptied the bullets, dropped them to the floor of the lobby. They clicked around my feet, spun away into the dark. I repocketed one gun, stowed the others in my waistband, hidden under my jacket, and stepped into the storm.

I ran across the alleyway through the rain, getting drenched, and went in through the side entrance. An Elder, head wrapped in a plastic shower cap, jacket soaked through to his shirt, swore as he wiped rainwater from his sleeves. Two Youngsters, both near the Inventor's age, laughed at the Elder with the sad recognition in their eyes that they would, one day, literally be him. Their high-pitched giggles seemed forced. One of them looked up at me, and I realized he would later become the Nose.

"Oho." he called. "The life of the party has arrived."

I felt the weight of my jacket, the water running down my back. I played my part. "Is the bar open?"

Both boys laughed. Had I really been so self-centered and judgmental? I had. *I am,* I thought. "Not yet," he said. "They're waiting for you."

I longed to scare them away. I realized I had all the ammunition I needed. "You know, it's not too many years before you become me." Their laughter stopped.

I headed for the main stairs. They were rotten and dangerous, and I'd avoided them for years, but this time I toed past soft steps and railings that were only casually attached. I'd hoped to reach the penthouse on them, but on the landing between five and six lay the rubble of what had been the stairs from six to seven. Broken windows leaked. Water slid over splintered wood. A gap too wide to jump yawned before me. I left the stairwell and walked down the empty sixth-floor hallway. The lights were out, and I followed the wall with one hand. I heard whispers, soft-edged words, secrets in the dark. I stopped and held my breath. Parrots, I thought, or the echoes of my own progress. Or, I wondered, was I talking to myself?

I navigated from memory. Just a few paces past the last room, I found the intersection and the door to the rear stairs. It was dark, as it had been for the Suit on his descent from the penthouse. I'd have to hurry to avoid crossing his path. I counted steps as I ran, my chest burning and legs shaking as I reached the penthouse. I continued up to the roof, the last flight ending at the heavy door. I threw my weight against it, the alarm blaring above me, and exited the building onto a roof empty except for an inch-deep puddle and slanting sheets of rain.

No matter how long I stayed on the roof, it would still be empty. My raft was gone. I gasped for air, still winded from the climb, and swore at myself. Had I mentioned to Seventy where I'd put the raft? How had they found it? Why move it?

"They want me here," I told no one. "They need me here." I could almost picture Seventy sending Screwdriver up here, one more task for Screwdriver to carry out. Another roll of thunder and I took hold of the door handle, but a thought froze me and I couldn't open the door. I was still tethered to an Elder. For someone downstairs my struggles were memory. I cursed myself. I plagued myself.

My arm worked at last, and I yanked the door open. The alarm blasted again, a stuttered bleat as it malfunctioned, and I recalled the alarm at the elevator's descent that I'd heard as the Suit. He'd go to the stairs soon. I rushed down the steps. I expected to find them dark and deserted, but I heard voices again. I fought to keep my breathing quiet and even. Footsteps in the dark below me. I strained to hear voices through thunder. Before I reached the tenth-floor landing, the voices stopped. I reached for the handrail but found a hand instead.

"You're late. Get downstairs and act normal." The voice was mine and older, but I couldn't tell how much.

"Late for what?"

The hand against my chest. "Just go downstairs. It's already started."

I reached into my pocket, possibly to get a gun, I don't know. I withdrew my hand from the pocket and felt something fall and hit the floor between us.

The Voice repeated himself. "Go. Now." Before whichever me this was realized who I was, I turned and descended, unseeing but somehow at a step-leaping pace. I'd gone three floors when my voice called from above me.

"Hello?" That would be the Suit, I recalled, the elevator now misbehaving. I realized I'd dropped my timepiece.

I reached the second floor. No one there. I'd expected the muttering group, the conspiracy. I heard nothing, saw no one. The elevator button was lit. Before I could consider what it meant, I heard the grind of metal on metal. A rush of air smelling of oil and rot spilled from the elevator shaft. The floor beneath me shook a little until at last the elevator's fall stopped and I heard the chatter of cables striking one another. The button stayed lit. I knew what waited inside. I ran down the hall into the nearest open room, closed the door save for a crack. In moments voices came into the hall. They spoke clearly, not whispering.

"It's here all right," said one much like my own.

"Of course it is," said another, older. Probably Seventy, I realized. "As you knew it would be."

"As we all knew." Another voice, younger than Seventy. Something hard in its edge made me think it was Screwdriver. "Move out of the way. I'll get it open."

I heard metal being worked at, the snapping of forced latches.

The oldest voice said, "Put him right there, on his side."

The youngest said, "He still looks peaceful. He cleaned up well."

Seventy's old voice rattled toward me, as if he were looking in my direction. "He always will. Now, where is he?"

"It's a longer walk down than you'd think."

I opened the door a crack and looked at them—Yellow, Seventy, and Screwdriver—as they waited for the Suit to arrive. I tried to remember how long I'd stayed upstairs, how long it had taken me to come down. Where would Lily be right now? Could I find her? For an endless minute, I wondered if I'd become untethered from the Suit, if I'd already changed something and he might never arrive and start the search for the killer. At last his footfalls echoed from of the stairway.

Seventy looked at the others. "Don't forget, I do the talking."

I remembered their conversation as it unwound. I remembered it as I remembered so many of the events of the evening, from multiple viewpoints and deepening understanding. I didn't need to hear them tell the Suit that someone in the building had killed Sober in order to know it wasn't true. As the Suit I'd killed the Drunk. Had they cleaned the corpse and planted it here? The dead man was me a few hours from now, at the evening's end. Seventy's lies rolled out as I listened from the door. If I was untethered from them, they wouldn't remember I was there. I worried that I was still tethered to one or more of them. They'd tricked me before. They could trick me again. None of them moved toward the door, none of them looked at it. Was I that good a liar?

They knew I would shoot Lily. They knew I wasn't a team player. They were toying with my death, their own survival, and Lily's life. I cursed them for taking my raft. They were running this for something, some benefit. I couldn't see what. I could only clumsily chase after it, like a blind and wounded animal. I would look for Lily. Maybe I could get her out of the building. She would enter the ballroom. I'd look for her there.

I forced a window open, and rain fell in. I spotted the fire escape ten feet to my left and climbed out to it. I looked up. Hours from now Lily and the Suit would break the top loose, letting it crash into the alley. I lowered the escape ladder and climbed down, soaked from wet to wetter. Lightning lit my way to the side entrance again. I made sure to stagger in and fell without meaning to. Some Elders reached out to me to help me up, hesitant to touch me. I avoided eye contact.

I slurred out a thank-you, made a show of brushing visible and invisible dirt from my pants and jacket. They stood back, let me shuffle past into the lobby. I bumped more than a few selves as I ran. I noted that some cleared away before I arrived and remembered doing so myself. The Drunk's run through the lobby was a favorite memory, and at the last moment I recalled what made it so memorable—the leap over the dessert cart. A Youngster saw me coming and stepped aside to reveal a rusting cart loaded with a punch bowl and pastries. By that time I was already airborne. The tip of my foot knocked a brownie from a plate, but otherwise I cleared the cart easily. I landed and ran on without stopping to accept the roar of applause. I was haunted by and haunting my past.

I bumbled along the wall, shoving chairs aside and receiving an odd mix of annoyed glares and averted eyes. The Youngsters hated me, which I could understand, as I was their unpleasant-smelling future. No one wants to think his future stinks or, worse, deserves to stink. What confused me were the responses of the Elders. I had imagined at first that there must be embarrassment behind the Elders' lack of concern for the Drunk, but what I felt wasn't embarrassment. It was impatience. They shook their heads and whispered.

I reached the bar and passed by to go through the door where Lily would enter. Beyond it was the empty hallway and several locked doors. I scouted from one end to the other, even as far as the deserted kitchen, but saw no signs of her. I hadn't had a drink for a long time and didn't want one, but I needed to appear to be both drunk and sloppy. I returned to the bar and took a seat. One of the Bar Brats leaned toward me, sweet vermouth on his breath.

He scrunched up his nose when I said, "Pour me a whiskey. Something cheap."

"Cheap?"

"I want to get drunk, but I don't want to enjoy it."

When he set the drink in front of me, I stared at him until he looked away. I poured it onto my sleeves and the front of my jacket. I poured some into my hand and wiped it in my hair.

The Bar Brats assaulted one another with seltzer bottles and unpeeled bananas, the elder two especially harsh toward the youngest, who didn't yet know the order of punch lines. I tapped my knuckles against the bar for their attention, pointed at my mostly empty glass, and turned it over to indicate I needed more. A small bit of whiskey spilled from the glass and pooled. The youngest Brat pointed at the puddle. "Uh-oh," he said, voice mockingly grave. "Liquor spill."

I soaked it up with my sleeve. "Don't you mean 'Lick her spiel'?" I immediately regretted having provided him with his terrible joke.

His face cracked, and he laughed.

I would stay here, I decided. Lily would arrive, and I'd try to speak with her. Behind me rose whispers; I turned around.

The Suit entered the ballroom.

I cursed myself for not thinking this through. I was right where the Drunk was supposed to be.

The Entrance took place. I understood his distracted eyes better than even he could. He'd just seen the Body. He'd just been given the task of stopping a killing that had already occurred. I lost track of myself and took a sip of the drink, which was meant to be a prop. Grimacing as he approached, I turned it into a horrible grin and greeted him with a wave. He looked through me, unseeing, and ordered his drink. I watched him through strands of my too-long hair, trying to seem harmless and praying I smelled of alcohol and filth. Disrespect was my camouflage.

Yellow joined the Suit at the bar. I watched condensation fall from their glasses and wondered after Lily. Images of her arrival unwound in my head, and I was stunned at my recall, despite how much the Suit was drinking. She would arrive shortly after Yellow went to fix the skipping record. I looked over my shoulder and saw a group of Elders arguing over a pile of phonograph records, each with a different remembrance of the music's order. I wondered which, if any of them, was tethered to me. I took Lily's farewell note from my pocket, read and reread it. *"If it's dark, I'm gone."* She was desperate to leave behind everything she'd been, and that also meant me. I knew too much. She didn't want to be saved. Well, he was just the man to not do it.

Behind me the Fifth Dimension skipped. Repeated suggestions to fly away in a balloon, their panic palpable, filled the room. Yellow stepped over to do whatever it was the Elders did with the record player. As he passed, he tried hard not to look at me but couldn't help himself; I saw the same Elder glare, the disappointed expectation I received from the others. After he walked by, I slid two seats closer to the Suit.

I took my glass with me and laid my hand over the mouth, then laid my head down as if on a pillow, as I'd seen Phil do, and as I'd seen myself do six months ago. The Suit pretended not to see me. I remembered pretending. I said, "Not enough women at this thing."

Gears sometimes turn when we least hope they will. I'd never worked to maintain conversations; as I grew older, I'd trusted that I would say what had been said. This was not a play. I'd learned no lines. But now I wondered how I could free myself enough to keep things from unraveling as I'd remembered them if I couldn't even keep myself from delivering a script. At least I'd left my worst props behind, the bullets in another building, harmless. I should have thrown them into the sewer months earlier.

Suit laughed at my observation. "I guess that's the truth."

I pitied his discomfort. I hated his judgment. "You have no idea what's coming."

"Do you?"

"Yes and no." If I weren't going to change my lines, I should at least remember my character. I slurred my speech, rolled my eyes. I pointed at the bottle of twelve-year-old scotch that was just within reach. "You'll want to refill the flask."

I recalled his biting comment before he said it. "You would know." I felt his remorse at saying it.

I closed my eyes as he poured the whiskey. The dark behind my eyes reminded me of those nights when Lily would return and lie with me, take me into her, my arms around her sides, hands looking for cool spots along her ribs, waist, hips. "Wake me when she gets here."

"What? Who?"

I heard the door beside the bar open and couldn't help myself—I looked up to see Lily. Beautiful in the tight red dress—I never did find out where she got it. It hugged her figure and revealed just enough of the long tattoo I wished I could forget she had. It made her, for only a moment, someone I didn't know. Brown hair fell around her face; green eyes ignored the room.

The Suit poured whiskey over his arm and the bar.

The Brats leaped forward. "Liquor spill, liquor spill." The youngest shouted, "Lick her spiel." His eyes on mine, smile crumbling when he realized I wouldn't return amusement at my own joke.

The Suit put the bottle down and leaned back as the Brats swiped white towels at the spill, making a wet situation worse when the bottle tipped. One Brat caught it against his wrist. They squeezed the towels into tumblers, prepared to drink the fresh-squeezed whiskey themselves. The Suit could only watch Lily. I remembered his confusion: She flashed like a beacon, yet no one else saw her. I looked over my shoulder and realized how wrong that was. The Elders were already conspiring. They casually walked to block the Youngsters' tables, kept them from viewing Lily. Some carried phonograph albums and chose that moment to hold them up before Youngster noses. At the card tables, games suddenly grew loud and boisterous, arguments erupted to draw eyes and ears. Youngsters always loved to watch Elders fighting among themselves. Now

I saw that the Elders only pretended to argue. The conspiracy began long ago.

Middle Brat held out the folded note to the Suit. It dripped inky whiskey. "Is this yours?"

The Suit took it and read the message. "No," he said. He set it afloat in a puddle of liquor.

I reached for it, trying to fail at acting casual. The Drunk was awkward before, he'd be awkward now. "Must be mine." I pocketed it.

Events were lining up too well. Seventy escorted Lily to the table beyond the bar. He pointedly did not look at either the Suit or me. I laughed at the list of things he must have to remember, all the details of his times here that he must re-create. Then I remembered my own list, details I had to undo. I had multiple guns. I had to get rid of them, hide them somewhere in an upstairs room. I left the bar knowing that the Suit wouldn't notice or care.

I left the ballroom and spotted a group of familiar faces in the crowd of me. The Pilaf Brothers. My nose was about to not be broken. At a spot where I could witness the nonchange of my face structure, I leaned against the wall, then squatted down against it. Others walked around me with only a moment's glance. The line at the bathroom grew by one when Savior joined. The Pilaf Brothers muttered and munched on rice. They stared in my direction conspicuously. This was all a plan, I thought. One placed his plate on the floor and looked back at me with a grim smile. I prepared for the event, the mix of trip and recovery that demonstrated untethering, but at that moment a pair of legs stepped in front of me. It was Yellow.

"Can we talk?" His face flickered with panic.

I still didn't like him and took some consolation in the fact that we were untethered. "I suppose."

"You know what's happening here. You realize what you have to do."

"What's that?" I asked.

He was flushed, sweating heavily in his yellow sweater.

"You look hot. Take off the sweater."

"Fuck the sweater." He grabbed my arm and pulled me from my squat, tried to yank me down the hall. I pulled back, peered over his shoulder. There I was, on my way to not breaking my nose.

I whispered, "What the fuck's your problem?"

Yellow leaned in so that only I could hear him. I could smell whiskey on his breath. Lots of it. I was impressed that it didn't show more. He didn't stagger, nor did his words slur when he said, "You were supposed to plant the fucking gun."

He looked me in the eye, blinking rapidly. I was locked in place. My arm felt cold in his grip. "What do you know about the gun?"

"You're monkeying around with my timeline. Fuck things up and we lose what little control we have. Stick to what you remember. Do what should happen."

"Where did you move my raft?"

His teeth bared. "I have no idea what you're talking about."

We appraised each other for a moment before Screwdriver appeared.

Screwdriver grabbed Yellow's arm and twisted it to force him to release me. He shrugged at me, almost like an apology, then pulled Yellow close and said something into his ear. Screwdriver cautiously patted at my jacket and found the unused revolver, yanked it free of my waistband, and handed it to Yellow who nodded several times and moved off through the crowd.

Screwdriver said to me, "Keep doing what you're doing. We have no doubt you'll figure this out."

"The gun is no good," I said. "It doesn't have any bullets."

"No, I collected them off the lobby floor. I already put them under the table."

I tried to breathe but couldn't. So I was tethered to Screwdriver? He knew where to find them? "Why would you do that?"

As if to answer my question, he raised his head and yelled out to no one and everyone, an affected slur mushing the words, "I told you I could barely remember it." After, he stepped away, as if embarrassed, eyes on me, all but pointing. I looked to the restroom doors and saw Savior, Nose, and the Suit begin their swirl of nasal investigation. It was that moment that the untethering began. It was in that moment that I'd broken free and trouble had leaked in. That moment was the reason I was going to die in a couple hours. Screwdriver had slipped off. I turned to walk away from the stares.

Young eyes followed me through the hall, but once I had reached the lobby, only the Elders watched me. In the ballroom I found Seventy walking toward the table Lily sat at, a drink in both hands, cane hanging over his arm near a crooked elbow. He sat, and they smiled at each other. I stopped. I couldn't recall when I'd last spoken to Lily. I was jealous of his being with her. Details of the room fell away, sounds muffled. I reached out to tap Seventy's shoulder.

He turned and looked up at me with a grin. "Yes? How are things going?"

"What are you doing?"

"You're drunk, and you smell like the saloon spittoon."

I leaned over, my eyes on Lily, waiting for her to break her pleasant visitor smile and reveal she knew me. Maybe she didn't know. Maybe we all looked alike to her. "I'm not drunk. I'm trying to stop this thing from happening, but you're actively working toward it. And you lied about what's going on."

Seventy's smile faltered. "What do you mean?"

"How did Screwdriver know what to yell? I thought you all were untethered."

Seventy screwed up his face. "We are, but that doesn't change some facts. For example, I should think it would be clear that he knew what to yell because he was always the one to yell it. Not you."

Questions about the raft floated in my head, but somehow I kept my mouth shut. Was it possible he didn't know that Screwdriver knew something only I knew?

I looked from him to Lily, whose smile was gone. She knew who I was. I reached out and touched her hand, the same one held by Seventy. For a few moments, we made a sandwich of her fingers, Seventy and I. She didn't pull away, but her muscles tensed. I said, "You're on the wrong side of this. You should get out now."

She shook her head. "This is my place. I remember it this way."

I laughed. "Have you remembered how this ends?" When she wouldn't respond, I said, "Shit. Just go out that door. Please."

Now she did pull her hand away. "I know what I'm doing."

To Seventy I said, "You're not as in control of this as you imagine."

No smile. They were all for the Suit, apparently. "Who among us is." Not a question.

I reached into my pocket and found the two revolvers I still had. I stood and turned, and my eyes fell on the Inventor. He was leaning back in his chair with a group of Youngsters, who watched the Suit skulk across the room to the bar again, their envy and impatience obvious. They thought him everything they longed to be, even as they recognized that from him it was all downhill to me. I marched across the room, and behind me I heard Lily tell Seventy, "Here's where he does something stupid."

I stood across from the Inventor until he looked up. Everyone at the table had youth's arrogance, each assuming their own brilliance beyond their years. The Inventor was the youngest, but the others treated him with deference, since without him they wouldn't be there. They hadn't yet remembered that his arrogance was rooted in fear and self-loathing, hadn't yet seen through their own dark cores to that hard truth. I hated and marveled at them.

When the Inventor finally looked up at me, he said, "How will I get that scar?" His companions laughed. Of course there could be no answer, if I followed the rules. It had been my habit to test this rule and laugh at the Elders' reaction.

I reached up and found the line on my temple, which he'd delivered to me six months earlier, which he would deliver to the Suit later that night. "Come with me and I'll tell you."

The table fell silent. He said, "Seriously? What about the fourth rule?"

"Fuck the rules."

The Youngsters looked at the Inventor, and he looked at me. I was unorthodox, feared and exciting. They all exchanged glances. Those older than the Inventor understood that this hadn't happened previously. They weren't as drunk as the Bar Brats, and they leaned in to whisper with one another about my deviation from the understood timeline. A few quivering fingers combed figures in the water rings on the table. I felt a little dizzy. Although I was already untethered from them, I realized with some flips of my stomach that I had just untethered them from one another, and not in a minor way. My conspiracy cut them loose. I could almost see each of them— they looked at one another as at strangers—with the streams of their thoughts and fears pouring out ahead of them, in similar currents but each one unique, slightly apart, arrogant, and paranoid enough to think himself the prime mover, the source of the current. I recognized that need, though I no longer felt it myself.

The Inventor lacked their frames of reference. Untethered but unaware, he said, "Okay." His voice cracked, and I realized, perhaps again, perhaps for the first time, how young he was, barely out of rude dreams. He was a baby. I looked at his face, my own, and wondered who he was. I called on a child to vanquish men.

To the others at the table, I said, "Stay close. He'll be back, and he'll need you. God help him, you're the only friends he has." The others, slightly older than the Inventor, seemed even more naïve. I wondered at myself then. Was I either better or worse off than any of them?

I steered the Inventor around the corner toward the hallway

full of our future and past chatter, forced passage, belches, farts, rude jokes, odors, inhibitions, fears, taunts, and terrors. I leaned in close to his ear and whispered. "There's something going on."

His eyes were large, his lips lifted in a conspirator's smile. "What?"

"Elders," I said.

The smile dropped. "You're an Elder."

My eyes glazed, and I lost focus for a moment. *What am I doing?* I thought. "You realize that's all relative. Next year you'll be your own Elder."

"I guess."

"Elders—*my* Elders, if that's how you have to think of it— are up to something. There's a woman—"

"Someone brought a woman?"

I smelled hormones. "Forget the woman. She's not important. What's important is who she's with. An Elder, the eldest of us. Old man. Tweed suit. He walks with a cane."

"And a woman."

I took hold of his arm and squeezed. "She's not the key here. The old man is. You understand. Tell me yes." I tightened my grip.

He winced. "Yes."

"She's just a flag waving you to him. You find him, when he's alone, not with her, and you take him to someplace upstairs."

His eyes darkened as he tried to imagine an upstairs that hadn't fallen downstairs.

I said, "Trust me. There are places. Fourth floor you'll find lots of empty rooms. Take him to one and keep him there. Have some of the others help you if you have to. Nothing too harsh. He's an old man. He's who you will be. Treat him as you would want to be treated." I instantly regretted those words. I knew it meant poor treatment at best.

"What if he won't come?"

"Convince him. You started this whole show. He'll listen to you. He's just you, after all."

"He'll know I'm lying. He'll remember."

"He won't. You're not on the same timeline. Part of the reason he's up to something."

He blinked rapidly in confusion, and I realized I look ridiculous when confused. "What?" he said. "What's he doing that's so—"

"Just trust me, right? Now remember: only him. Not the woman. No one else. Anyone asks where he is or why you took him, no answer. Keep him there until dawn." I released my grip. The boy would do as I asked. "Are we agreed?"

"Yes, all right. But at the end you tell me what all this was about."

"At the end, if you can do this, I'll tell you everything." Because if he could, it wouldn't matter any longer if he knew.

The Inventor skulked into the ballroom to gather his future conspirators. If only they took Seventy upstairs and kept him there, this plot might fall apart. If the plot fell apart, perhaps Lily would survive.

In the alley at the hotel's back entrance, Phil's building, dark windows yawning, stood over me. Dirty rain stung my face. I felt I might never be dry again. Steel drums half filled with refuse lined the wall. I pulled out the gun I'd taken from the Drunk, the one responsible for shooting Lily. I wrapped the gun in some newspaper and buried it under the garbage in one can. I pictured the bullets skidding across the tile floor of the neighboring building's lobby. I wished I'd kept them, if only so Screwdriver hadn't gotten them. I'd keep the final gun as a warning to others. If I needed to wave a useless weapon, I would. Yellow would have planted the gun by now. I'd need to get under the table before the Suit. Efforts to maintain events was idiocy. Seventy and Screwdriver were maintenance. I would be avoidance.

I entered the lobby for the third time, dripped on the carpet, smiled grandly at Elders who muttered about me under their breath.

"I'm gonna be sick," I whispered with gusto into the crowd, and found an easy path to the buffet table. For a moment I feared that the gun would be gone, that the evening was slipping away too fast. As I knelt down, I landed in the arms of Yellow and another Elder I'd not seen yet.

Yellow took a tight grip, his fingers squishing filthy rainwater from my jacket. "Poor old boy," he muttered, eyes on the rivulets running down my temples. "Under the weather?"

They pulled me off my feet and took hold of my arms, Yellow's fingers jabbed deep in my armpit. I heard a pop in my back as they twisted, and I grunted in pain. They moved us quickly through the halls toward the restrooms. The crowds of Youngsters were gone, and Elders watched them drag me through halls despite my calls for help. Yelling was unnecessary and my calls perfunctory. The fact that they all watched and did nothing meant they never would.

"Help," I said to one, voice calm despite my pain. "I think I'm being kidnapped." He turned away, and Yellow dug his fingers deeper. "Careful," I warned. "We're ticklish."

In the restroom an empty stall waited, and we entered as a trio. Stall door slammed, footsteps as others left, and the bathroom door clicked shut. Accomplice let go, but Yellow threw me down. I fell forward hard against the toilet, striking my side, losing my breath. When I looked back at Yellow and his Accomplice, they glowered at me. I tried to stand. Yellow shoved me against the toilet, and I sat down.

"You thought I wouldn't watch for you?" Yellow held a fist in my face. If the sweater were any less dapper, he might have been threatening. "Quit getting in the way. Do as you're supposed to."

My side was killing me, and I worked to force a breath into my lungs. "What?"

Accomplice nudged Yellow. "Is he serious? Shouldn't he have been upstairs by now?"

Yellow shook his head. "The Suit goes upstairs soon. This one disappears for a while. That's what we're trying to prevent." He leaned in on me. "Look. We're all on the wrong side of this death, and it's got to be straightened out."

Now I did feel sick. "Why?"

"The shooting. Because of the shooting."

"I'm working on it."

"No you're not. The Suit is. You're the shooter."

I looked at them both. I shifted, and we all heard my gun knock against the toilet-paper dispenser. I said, "I'm the shooter?" Did he mean I'd shot the Drunk or that I would shoot Lily? Which was more important to him?

Accomplice touched my shoulder. "Look, trust us. This all works out."

Yellow shook a fist at Accomplice. "The hell it will. He keeps getting in the way. I shouldn't have had to put the gun under the table."

"You know that everything will work out."

The bathroom door squeaked.

Both Yellow and Accomplice put a finger to their lips. Yellow called over the stall door, "We're almost done in here. Two more minutes."

"No, I don't think so."

They stared at me, and Yellow said, "It's him."

Accomplice nodded. "I'm really sorry I can't be of more help." Both Yellow and I looked at him. "All I want is to get on the right side of the shooting."

Yellow said, "What the fuck are you talking about?"

The end of a screwdriver appeared in the gap between stall door and frame and flipped up the latch. The stall door opened, and Screwdriver grabbed Yellow by the collar and yanked him out. Accomplice put his hands up and smiled at me. "Good luck. You're doing fine."

Accomplice turned, and I leaned around him to see Screwdriver punch Yellow in the jaw. Yellow fell into the gap between two sinks and slid to the floor. Blood on his chin, splattered on tile; he moaned. Accomplice kept his hands in the air and stepped out of the stall past Screwdriver. To Yellow he said, "Again, sorry I couldn't be more help."

Screwdriver pointed at the door. Accomplice left.

Screwdriver joined me in the stall, shut the door, and looked down at me. "How you doing?"

I sat on the toilet and considered the question. My side was feeling better but still ached.

"That should feel better soon. It'll look worse than it feels."

I lifted my jacket and shirt. The skin was already turning a deep purple.

"You'll be fine." He didn't wait for me to respond. "You get the mood. There's a general—"

"Impatience."

"Impatience. Yes. Give me the gun."

His hand hung before me, empty. I said, "Why move my raft?"

"I didn't." His smile said he knew more. He wouldn't say what. "I've got to make sure you're ready for what comes next. Give me the gun."

Gun lifted from my pocket, I handed it to him. As I did so, his eyes locked on something. At first I thought it was the gun, but as I drew my hand away, he reached out and grabbed my wrist. He pulled the sleeve back and turned my hand over, stared at the tattoo I'd gotten from Lily.

"Is there a problem?" I could see the same tattoo on his arm, just as I'd seen it on the Body, just as I imagined Seventy had it and Yellow and everyone in between.

Screwdriver's eyes locked on mine. "He said you were tethered."

"Who?"

"The old man." I imagined he meant Seventy. "He said you and I were tethered."

I didn't know what to say.

Screwdriver turned his own wrist so that it was parallel to mine. We stood beside each other, arm resting against arm, each of us looking down at our tattoos.

Our parrots faced in opposite directions. If our hands were north, then my parrot flew west, his east.

Screwdriver, voice shaking, "He said you weren't tethered to the Body, but you are. What does that mean?"

"You and I *aren't* tethered."

"What does *that* mean?"

I said nothing. He pulled back and stepped partway out of the stall. I could see his mind trying to realign around this new information. Long moments of listening to water drip in from leaks behind the sinks, the toilets, in the wall. "What has he been telling you?" I asked at last.

He watched dirt stains on the floor, Yellow's blood drying on the tile, our face in the mirror. "Nothing. Nothing. It's too late. I've got to stick to the plan."

"I've learned that our planning doesn't account for shit."

He laughed and looked back at me. "It's all I've got."

"If you're finding that things are moving off the track, you can make your own choices. You don't have to listen to the old man. We can still change things."

He continued to hold my gun in his hand, bounced its weight up and down, looked at his own tattoo. He shook his head, an internal debate I was losing. "No. No, there's too much to be done for you to go around fucking everything up. This will still work out. You're doing fine. And I'm sorry."

"For?"

He swung his fist, gun handle out, in one smooth upward arc, struck me once on my right temple, and I was out.

I REMEMBER BEING in line behind the Pilaf Brothers. I remember seeing the way they suspiciously glanced at one another, how fixated they were on an Elder I couldn't see from where I stood. I remember the plates on the floor and the ugly pattern of the rug, the worn spots where jute backing was black as soot, the sounds of chanting through the bathroom door. I remember thinking that when the one who would break his nose would leave the bathroom, he'd trip on those plates, and how simple it would be to fix it, and I remember thinking that not one Elder, not a single one, ever offered him any patience or thoughts or help, not because it was the right thing, and not because it followed a rule, but because doing so had been easier than facing the truth: that our brilliance was a failure. Our failure was in not trying. I remember hating every Elder and thinking, *to hell with the rule.*

I remember moving the plate aside, if only to spare myself that sliver of suffering.

I WOKE ON the bathroom floor, my head pressed against the cold porcelain of the toilet bowl. There was an oozing gash across my temple, and a dull throb rolled down my head and neck. Overhead, the lights rose and fell with my breath. After a minute I found arms and legs, sat up, then stood. The bathroom empty, Yellow's blood dried under the sinks. I checked myself in the mirror. I was filthy, still damp, and now mottled with bathroom-floor grime. My pocket was heavy with familiarity. With a sinking feeling, I took the pistol out of my pocket and looked at it carefully. It was loaded with one bullet. Screwdriver's commitment to follow the set path. I could follow that path, too, but in my own way.

I returned to the stall, emptied the bullets, and dropped them in the toilet. I flushed, but they just spun at the bottom of the bowl. Another flush and again they refused to go down. I took long strips of toilet paper and wadded them into balls and dropped them into the bowl, hoping some traction would force them down. Instead the toilet plugged and overflowed, rusty water spilling over onto the tiles. I stood above the toilet, watching the water rise, trying to think clearly. Then I closed and latched the stall door and lay down in the cold puddle to crawl out from underneath the door, sloshing water across the floor with my belly. When I stood, dripping, I realized that not only had I locked the bullets in the stall, I'd left the gun behind, too, on the toilet tank. I left it.

The few Elders in the mostly empty hall gave me looks but left me alone. Apparently, seeing Screwdriver beat up Yellow was enough to convince them to let me take my course.

The ballroom already echoed with preparations for the films. I wondered where all the Youngsters could be. The Inventor might have gotten hold of Seventy. I'd told him to hold him upstairs, so I'd look there. At the main stairs, I lost track of which floor I was on and climbed until I thought to stop and look around. The fifth floor perhaps, maybe the sixth. I ignored the rubble and entered the hallway, unsure of where to go or what to do. Excited chatter echoed in a room several doors away, like birds trapped under a blanket. As I walked down the hall, I caught the sound of a child crying, then a crash. A woman screamed a curse. Preteens and children erupted from the door ahead of me, poured into the hallway, knocked me backward, flowed around and over me. I worked to hold my ground. Some glanced at me over their shoulders, then followed the shrieks of the children to the stairwell at the end of the hall, disappeared into its darkness.

In the room they'd come running out of, I found the Inventor and a single wailing six-year-old. On the floor lay the Suit, unconscious, in a position that illustrated his—dare I say my—understanding of the evening's events: arms locked in a near shrug. Lily knelt beside him. I wanted to reach out to take her hand, to pull her up like pulling a flower from the ground, take her from the hotel, away from the swirling torrent. I knew she wouldn't come.

Across the room the child sobbed. His face curled out around his open mouth; snot and tears coursed over his face, dripped from his chin, wet the collar of his pale blue shirt. I started toward him, tried to imagine what his terror meant to the Inventor's perceptions, how he must remember the moment. I wasn't tethered to any of them and could remember nothing of the children's time in the hotel, but the Inventor might. I wondered if he had already untethered himself from the children or if he'd been wiser than I was. I looked over to him, curious if he showed any concern or compassion toward his own youthful suffering, but I couldn't see, too distracted by the gun he held.

"What the hell are you doing with that?"

The Inventor looked down at it and studied its weight. "I found it."

"Bullshit."

His eyes left the gun and glanced around the room. Even in the dark, I could see his skin flush. "Someone gave it to me?"

In this light, flushed as well with indignation and shame, gun bloody from the pistol-whipping he'd given the Suit's temple, I thought of him as a guilty child. Couldn't he have been more curious? I wondered. Had the world held so little for him? He was the one who began all this, who traveled where no one else might have been able to, ever, and yet he had nothing to show for it but an embarrassed face and a mis-used weapon. Whichever of me had given him the gun, I was to blame for this child's corruption.

I reached into my own pocket and felt the emptiness there. "Which one gave it to you?" I didn't ask "who" because I knew "who."

The six-year-old gasped for air. The Suit shifted but remained unconscious.

From the door came the answer: "I did." The Nose walked in, robes wrapped tight around him, and stood beside me, not wasting a glance at the bleeding Suit or Lily. "I gave it, but not to him. It's been passed forward."

My heart stopped. I felt the pulse of the timepiece in my pocket, like a fluttering bird. "You pulled it from the trash?"

"Yes."

"Why?"

The Nose shrugged. "I watched you go outside and hide it. It couldn't have been for no good reason. I figured if it was worth you hiding, it was worth my taking."

"And you gave it to—"

"Pimples."

"Who?"

"Us at sixteen." He smiled, unrepentant. "Told him to hang on to it, that it might be needed at some point. I told him where to find the raft, how to come here. Figured we'd need to outnumber the Elders. I think he's the one who started going back further, bringing the children." Six had finally stopped screaming. He pressed himself into the corner, happy to be ignored.

I opened a window, hung my head outside, and listened to

the rain hit the building and the sidewalk below. "You brought the children here?"

The Inventor coughed before answering. A delaying habit I worked hard to avoid. "Not on purpose. The Elders are up to something. You said so yourself. But then I realized it wasn't really the Elders. Not all of them." He waved the gun toward the Suit. "It was him, mainly. I realized that instead of trying to figure out what the old man was up to, we'd better figure out what Suit was up to."

"I told you to leave the woman out of this," I said to the Inventor.

The Nose answered. "I realized that you weren't telling me everything you knew. You're with the Elders."

"I'm not with anyone, you shit."

"Prove it."

The three of us stood at the points of a shadowy triangle, the Suit and Lily at the center. Six sat on the floor, arms wrapped around knees. I looked at the Inventor and then the Nose. His handsome robes now seemed only costume, as cheap and threadbare as my own.

"So after you pulled the gun from the trash, did you ever get bullets for it?"

Eyes bounced back and forth. Six took in everything. Tethers unraveled furiously.

I asked Six, "Did they give you a loaded gun?"

He shook his head.

I felt a thud in my chest. Until that moment I didn't realize I'd held my breath.

The Nose said, "We're younger than all of you. As long as none of you found out it wasn't loaded, what's the harm?"

Lily laughed at that, and we all looked at her. To me she said, "See? Selfish."

I thought back to myself last year, when I was Suit, almost ready to pull the trigger on my younger, armed selves. I hadn't done it. I wouldn't do it. And if I could figure out this mess and get Lily out of the building, I would take the gun with me. Everything could reknit itself into whatever scarred shape it might need to take, and I wouldn't return.

"Show me your gun," I said. Nose and Inventor exchanged glances, and I raised my voice. "I don't care who, but one of you give me the fucking gun."

The Inventor stepped forward, palm up, gun presented like a gift. I took it and stepped to the window to see it in the streetlight. I touched the sides and worked the mechanism. It was rusted and sticky with old dirt and grease.

Turning the gun in the light, I imagined what I would have done with it at six, seven, eight, twelve. In between trips I would have taken it out, played with it, held it, pretended it protected me from hordes of who-knew-whats, of things unseen but known, of older men not yet nicknamed. Played with and dreamed of, broken and rusted from lack of care and misuse, it would never fire again.

I threw it back toward the Inventor. It hammered the floor and echoed in the hall.

"You children should get downstairs. They'll be starting the movies soon." No one moved.

I joined Lily where she crouched. Something in her eyes said she wouldn't take my hand, so I didn't offer. I leaned down, my face close to hers, and I breathed her in, just a little. Her hands stroked Suit's blood-wet hair. I told myself I'd get over it. I suddenly felt my beard in a way I hadn't before. I wasn't that man on the floor. I exhaled a bit of Lily when I asked, "What will you tell him? Assuming you both survive."

She gave a look that made me think of a sealed crypt. "Nothing."

Her answer surprised me. "Why?"

"When people know things about you, it takes a part of you away. I'm tired of being picked apart."

That was when I knew why she chose the man beside her, the one who was free of the time and knowledge that tied me to her, the one who hadn't been marked with the bird flying in the wrong fucking direction. The fact that he knew nothing of her made him attractive; the fact that he held no preconceptions or beliefs about her made her choose him over me. He could still be pricked in the right way, bleed the way she wanted him to. I had facts. I had knowledge. I'd seen her surroundings, and I had lain in them with her. She felt burdened by my knowledge. She felt pressure to perform in an expected way; she felt trapped in a current of circumstances. But with the Suit, none of that existed. He was new. He might never know.

She understood the equation: Him plus her equaled me. She ignored me as a solution. She cared only for the problem. She knelt beside him, hands on his bleeding head, his hair between her fingers, and I groaned as I watched.

"Then don't tell him shit. For his sake." I suddenly saw both of them clearly, as if a switch turned on lights throughout the room. I said, "I mean ever. Don't ever tell him a thing. Because the moment you do, you'll start trying to kill him a little bit at a time."

She refused to meet my eye. Her voice fell out in a whisper. I no longer knew or cared whether Nose and Inventor stood behind me, whether she was whispering to hide it from them or from some part of herself, but I heard every click of her tongue on her teeth when she said, "We both know I don't have a lot of time left."

I stood up and took an absurd inventory of my pockets. Empty. "Nothing has to play out the way we remember it," I said finally. It was as close to a good-bye as I would ever have with the woman called Lily.

I DECIDED TO leave the hotel, alone. Nothing would matter once I left. If I simply disappeared and didn't return, there would be no shooting. Lily would live.

I cut through the ballroom on my way to the back exit. It was dark and littered with chairs. On the wall played images from the accidental video, the steps to Lily's apartment, the shadows cast by me and Screwdriver as he carried her home, her blood splattering on dusty steps. Despite the chilled air, I broke into a sweat. My head hurt more than it had moments earlier, pulse tapping behind my eyes. I wanted to look away, but that was hard, too.

Most of the Elders I passed watched the flashing wall, alert and attentive, hands on knees, fingers worrying along pant seams. One or two cried, tried to keep it quiet, failed, cried anyway. There was no consoling, no hands on backs, no kind words. They were too like me to find and offer consolation in any way except mutual suffering. I walked through the scattered selves, drew attention as I passed. It would have taken effort not to notice the suddenly steeled eyes that followed me. Had something changed from my last time through here, or would they pretend to sleep when the Suit passed?

Seventy sat near the projector, turned slightly away from me but aware of my approach. Had I really thought the Inventor could lure him upstairs? I'd unleashed my own problems yet again. I sat next to him. We stared at the wall for a few minutes. Above us the video played to the end and Seventy hit a button on the remote, the tape rewound, still playing, pulling everything backward at a slightly-too-fast pace. The gentle bounces of the camera became harsh shaking, a panic as the point of view was no longer that of the pursuer but the pursued.

I said, "How many times do you show it to them?"

"Oh, I lost count. It's all they care about."

On the wall the staggering figure holding the woman lurched backward down the stairs.

"I prefer the film this way," Seventy, all nostalgic, whispered. "Easier to take, knowing that she's gaining life as it goes on, rather than losing it." He never had quite the same expression as the other Elders. Understanding and secrets floated behind his eyes, words I knew he wouldn't share. What event had changed the quality of him, I couldn't imagine. I wondered exactly how tethered he was to the others that he alone could treat me well. No, not well. Respectfully.

"I'm leaving the hotel."

"I know you'll try." Eyes on the wall, shuddered lights reflected back at me, my silhouette at the center, inside what would be my own pupils.

"Maybe you didn't hear me?"

At last his face turned toward me. "No. I heard. Just not going to happen's the problem. Others won't let you."

"The Youngsters—"

"Not Youngsters I'm talking about. You've got to be a bit more self-aware, pun intended. These fellas haven't been too happy with you ever since you put on that suit." His hand stayed on the remote, fingers on buttons, waited for the video's start, waited to press the action forward again. But in that hand I saw muscles twitch. He tried, with effort, to force calm into his limbs. How much of that was just elderly tremors? I wondered. How much was what I feared, that he was no more in control of events than I was, that the Elders were as much a mob as the Youngsters? He forced a casual smile to his lips. "You've been under the gun yourself. Will be again if you try to leave. And I heard that your raft is missing."

"I'll just go find one of the Youngsters' rafts."

"That would mean leaving the hotel. And that's not happening."

For an instant I couldn't help myself, looked up at the wall, saw only Screwdriver's shadow, distorted by Lily's hanging arm and hair. I looked away, saw dark eyes shine in my direction, the video playing in each one. Elders watched me watch them.

"You told me the Youngsters were the threat."

"They were and are. But right now you've got to move forward with your mind on who you'll be, not who you were."

Seventy leaned back in his chair. He was done with talk. The rows of heads turned away from me to watch their film. I edged close to the wall and made for the hallway, aware that some of them must have watched me leave. I rushed to the front doors and looked through the glass to the street. Elders waited, hands in pockets, eyes locked through the dirty glass on mine. I gave an absurd wave, and they returned one, smiles on their faces too genuine.

Testing them was pointless. I'm sure more would show up if I tried. I was tired of everything. Something told me to hide in the finished room. Up the main stairs, I heard only dripping water. The Youngsters' hunt for the Suit and Lily must have taken them upstairs by now. Possibly as far as the dumbwaiter. I found myself on the fifth floor, in front of that door unlike the others. Clean and cared for. My door, open. I sat on the bed under the burning lights and looked at the mess the Suit had left. The bed was rumpled, the video equipment still warm. I checked the bottle under the bed and found it nearly empty, as I knew I would. I finished what remained. Beside it was the brown paper bag. Written on it was the message in my handwriting—"*In case of emergency, break glass*"—the message that I hadn't written. My hands shook as I read it.

The bathroom sparkled with splashed water. I added to the puddles, washed my face, my neck. Suddenly I was desperate to wash away the filth of the Drunk and stripped to the waist. I looked at the reflection in the mirror, watched water drip from long whiskers, run down my neck and onto my chest. My cheek glowed red with Screwdriver's punch. My hair hung in greasy ropes to either side of my face. I had never seen myself this filthy before. I washed myself again, stripped naked, scrubbed at myself with wet hands. I looked around the bathroom and found no soap but a pile of scratchy towels. I wet one in the sink, ran it over myself again and again, turned it gray on one side and switched to the other side, then another towel. Standing before my reflection, cold, tired, bruised, I couldn't care what might have happened before. I held a strand of my long hair in my hand and pulled at it, felt the grease it left on my fingertips. I remembered the shooting, the hooded eyes of the Drunk, the angry whispered words condemning whomever they lit upon. Perhaps me, perhaps Lily. No one. Who did I blame for this? I pushed back my hair and looked at my face, my eyes. Red and puffy, they blamed no one. The Suit needed that, to see my eyes, to recognize I wasn't a threat.

The liquor bottle smashed easily in the tub, curtain drawn, reduced to a handful of large shards. I picked up the largest shard and turned it in my hand until I found the best angle, careful to avoid cutting myself. I ran water and went to work with the glass blade. Handfuls of hair fell away, shaved with a minimum of skin cut free. The water ran. Hair clogged the drain, the bowl began to fill. I worked blind on the back of my scalp, yelped when I nicked myself, brought my hand back covered in blood, ignored it and cut more hair. I felt with oversensitive fingers for hair too long to be called stubble and worked the glass edge at it. At last the uneven shave was done. My scalp ran red in some places, but not for long, I imagined. I looked nothing like the Body. His beard wasn't on my face. If I died, I couldn't be him.

I hoped I'd miss the gathering upstairs but knew I wouldn't no matter what I did. Still naked, I climbed into bed and fell into a dream where I managed to bury the gun in the soil behind my childhood home and walk away, certain that no one saw, no one knew. I don't know how long I slept, but I woke to the sound of water splashing on the bathroom tile. I hadn't turned off the hair-clogged sink. It had overflowed, and an inch of water covered the carpet. I stood in it, watched the ripples move to the periphery and return. On the bathroom counter was the gun, the one I'd left on the toilet tank downstairs. Seeing it made me feel sick, but not surprised. Someone was placing all the necessary pieces together for a bloodletting. I felt sympathy then for Screwdriver, working so hard to do what he thought right, putting pieces into place that would lead to someone's bleeding to death on the penthouse floor, and as I felt sympathy for him, I felt a little of it melt into me as well.

I dressed and pocketed the gun. The suit, still wet from rain and sliding under the bathroom stall's door, stank like I'd already died in it. I put it on anyway, ill at its odor, its clammy grip. I stood at the door and pretended I wouldn't go upstairs, pretended that the Elders weren't outside the door at that moment, ready to put the gun in my hand and make me shoot myself or take that bullet as the Drunk had before.

I went upstairs.

GRAFFITI SCARRED THE stairwell walls. I saw only the mistakes, the partial handprints that speckled the plaster and handrail, small disks like blood on the steps, bubbles of latex dried to permanent teardrops at the bottoms of letters. In a way the messages revealed that Lily was trying to control the evening. Her need to escape, to save herself, was proving to be her failure.

Someone, or some*ones,* was running ahead of me in the stairwell. I didn't worry if they saw or heard me. I hadn't planned on chasing them. I hated the idea of catching up, because that scenario ended one of two ways. I wasn't going to kill tonight. That left me with the other end of that pointed, shit-covered stick. I focused on my stinging scalp, the cuts that speckled it like Emily's new constellations. I wouldn't be the dark, harried Drunk they expected. Perhaps that was all it would take.

They clattered up the steps. I knew it was me. I knew it was Lily. She was tired, her head spinning from her graffiti, her death visions coming fast, I'm sure, as she recalled her memories of the chase, the shooting, her own death in the home she'd grown to hate.

I pulled my gun from my pocket. It was loaded—Screwdriver again. His job was to ensure that all the elements came together. He was good at his job. I'd ditched the bullets at the bottom of the toilet, yet here they were, fished out. Was I locked on the path? I opened the chambers and removed the bullets. Nothing was set. Being untethered must prove that, I thought. I still drew the sharp end of the stick but could make sure that Lily didn't join me on it. I left the bullets on the steps. This gun, at least, couldn't kill her. I imagined that the Elders expected me to kill the Suit, to untether all of us older than him on this side of the Body, and they must have trusted that I wasn't tethered to them. Kill the Suit and whatever happened to me wouldn't affect them. But I wouldn't do that, I wouldn't give them the Body they needed, and I could no longer *be* the Body they needed. If it meant the end of the Elders, I can't say I felt all that much need to defend them and their behavior.

Above me the suite door slammed shut. Locks chattered.

I turned to the servants' entrance that would lead into the suite's kitchen. It remained painted shut. I could hear someone moving on the other side, the Suit, trying to find some way out. I heard his footsteps fade back out to the living room. Something drew my eye up. On the doorframe rested a screwdriver. I pulled it down, worked it into the gap between frame and door, a gap barely there, filled with white paint.

As dark as the stairwell should have been, I felt full of light. I felt my stomach rising, my heart skipping beats. I worked the screwdriver along the seam, split the paint, levered back and forth, heard wood creak, yanked at the door and felt it give, then give again. I tugged once more, and it released me into the kitchen with a loud crack. Beyond the doorway to the light-filled living room, I heard whispered warnings. I looked at my hand. Between one moment and the next, I'd somehow lost the screwdriver and replaced it with the gun.

A window hung open, and a breeze blew the door shut with an authoritative bang. I put the gun down, rubbed my hands over my ravaged scalp, felt my fingertips slicken with blood. I thought for a moment to run water, clean myself, make myself less threatening. As if I had the ability to hurt anyone here any longer. The man who'd fired the shots that killed Lily really had died, even before he—I—stepped into the room. I was no closer to shooting the Suit or Lily than the six-year-old I'd watched cry with his rusted relic gun.

The Suit's gun clicked.

I placed mine on the counter. As different from the Drunk as I could be in that moment, head shaved, unarmed, I stepped into the room, hands up. *Fuck the Elders,* I thought. Fuck their need to be on the other side of the death. If my death meant nothing more than a claim to innocence, innocence I hadn't had since I'd built the machine, then I could live, and die, with that. If I failed now, it was only because of the laziness and guilt of my life up to this point. I stepped out knowing only that I could hurt no one other than myself.

Suit and Lily clung to each other beside the open window. The words I'd heard the Drunk mutter rose in my throat, rumbled at the back of my tongue, but I choked them down. I realized that they had been meant as a warning but were far too poorly chosen. Last words should do more than invite demise.

I looked at Lily and said, "I'm so sorry. For everything. For bringing you here. You should go. Both of you. Go away, don't come back. Go. Shoot me if you need to, but go."

The Suit narrowed his eyes, unsure what I meant, hand shaking, gun getting the worst of it. I imagined the trigger fairly close to release. Lily put a hand up and placed it on top of the gun, wrapped it round the Suit's hand, lowered it toward the floor. The gun that had gone off in my hand six months ago was lowered, unfired. I realized I was wet with sweat and breathing fast. Both Lily and Suit watched me, then, realizing I really was as I looked, ill and harmless, came to help.

I repeated my suggestion. "Go. Both of you. Get out of here."

Suit, eyes older than I would have remembered them as being, laughed. "Where to?"

To Lily I said, "Phil's place."

Suit stared at me. "Who the fuck is Phil?"

"He was her father," I lied.

Lily nodded. She took Suit's hand, tried to pull him with her. He stayed rooted, watched my face. His eyes held themselves on my temple. Hand to it, I felt for what fixed him, and found my scar.

"We're tethered," he said.

"We were."

His eyes narrowed, returned to mine, his own hand to his still-raw wound, "You have my scar."

"Of course I do."

Lily tugged at his hand again, and this time he followed. They disappeared through the doorway. Footfalls called to me for a minute, faded, turned to echo. Behind me someone muttered, "Tether, tether." A parrot at the open window, head tilted to one side, blinked at me hopefully. "Tether."

Long after they were gone, I sat in a sheet-covered chair, eyes on the eastern horizon, blinking away stars in my vision that refused to disappear. I thought of things I could have said to both of them, but him especially. Advice rolled around in my head, but it was for no one except me. He would live with her as I had, but not as I had. She was not the woman I'd found. She was another, no better, no worse, different, and in control of what she would be to him. I wondered if he would ever know of her what I knew of her, her past, the woman she had tried to leave behind and reinvent, if that part of her would be shared with him or anyone, or if she would become someone else entirely, carrying around the vision of a death that was once her own but was now some other woman's, no more than a dream. How long before she convinced herself it was just hallucination or fantasy? I wondered. How long before she could forget that it had been memory and that I was real, too? That getting past me, away from me, was to leave part of herself? I laughed at myself then, at my last attempt to cling to vanity. She had the Suit, she would either keep or lose him. She would not miss me. She would be fine.

Heavy, slow footsteps broke my reverie. "You've been up here a long time." It was Seventy, cane tapping at the chair's legs. Fingers touched my shoulder, by accident at first, searching for support, but they lingered, and I realized he was trying to console me.

"Nothing to go down for. You won't find them. They've left."

"I know. Watched them leave. Climbed down a section of the fire escape that hasn't fallen yet. Never will forget how I hurt myself back then in that rush. I was certain we were being chased."

He sat in another chair, turned his face to watch me, sunlight brilliant. The light brought out his age, the spots across his forehead, the wrinkles I hadn't seen in the horrible and inconsistent lighting downstairs. He tried to smile, turned his head again, and as he did, I spotted the line above the temple, pale as paper, thin. He shared my scar.

My hands shook. "We were tethered."

Face too calm, too at peace, he said, "Until you shot the Drunk, yes. I never did that. But then you kept it from happening a second time. You let us go."

I couldn't speak. He'd never shot the Drunk. He'd gotten away. He'd done everything that I had just helped the Suit do. Our eyes stayed on each other until he looked away and said, "Yes. I'm tethered to him."

"And the others?"

"Some of the others." I wondered which. Yellow at least.

I held my hands together, laced fingers, covered, flexed them. Somewhere under my skin ran blood. I felt for the pulse of it in my own hands. I was cold, as if inanimate.

I said, "You needed to make sure you got her."

"I can't tell you what happened, you know that."

"But you did. You made sure you got her."

The others had been as used as I'd been, untethered from me and him, tricked by promises he knew to be untrue, details he hadn't lived. I squeezed my hands again and felt bone and blood. I hadn't his memory; none of us did but him. In that moment I realized he'd lived a life with Lily, however long it lasted, decades perhaps, and that he'd only ever come back to the hotel to ensure that his life would take place.

He said, "You'll help me now. You'll have to grow your beard back a bit. You'll lure the Suit to the penthouse, and then you can help make sure everything happens as it's supposed to."

"I won't be Screwdriver."

He laughed. "Is that what you called him?"

He'd said this to me before. Did he really not remember? Something had changed.

His eyes were too merry.

"Were you happy with her?" I asked.

"You know I can't—"

"You never knew her. Not like I did." I didn't have proof, yet I was certain. His eyes darkened and knuckles tightened around the cane. "I know it," I said. "I forgive you. But you'll never know what I know. You'll never know her like I did."

He looked out the window. I could tell he tried to unhear me.

I said, "Did she ever tell you her real name?"

His eyes darted to me, just barely, but enough for me to know he'd never known that Lily wasn't her truth. I'd opened a seal he'd never known existed.

I stood and cataloged the room, looked for some kind of comfort. There was nothing for me. I left Seventy behind with his lifetime of memories and questions he'd never thought to ask, about what he'd missed, what I knew, what lurked in the gaps that I knew Lily had left in him. I left the room and chased Lily's and Suit's echoes to the ground floor.

Without a body there had been no need for any of the others to stay. Elders were gone. The convention over, all that remained were the empty food tables and litter. I wondered if another visit in another year would prove to have corrected everything, as no body existed now, if there was no longer any mystery to solve, or if I might find myself able to watch everything from outside. It was a question I considered for less than a moment, for I knew I wouldn't ever revisit. The convention, if it existed in this new circumstance, would take place with the Elders and Youngsters who'd been before, but not me. I wasn't tethered to them and wouldn't reconnect. I would go and find something for myself, separate from them. Alone and in the world, as I should always have been.

I remembered that I had no raft. To return and ask Seventy where it might be wasn't an option. Instead I simply left the hotel, walked down the street.

I walked past Lily's building. I couldn't go there. She and Suit most likely watched me from her windows. I wouldn't look up, wouldn't give the impression I even thought of doing so. I buried my hands in my pockets, and though I couldn't think where to go, I walked on.

The sun rose behind the buildings ahead of me as I walked toward Bryant Park. The crews had been hard at work in recent weeks, and trees stood ten yards apart down the center of Sixth Avenue. Broken asphalt chunks made improvised planters. The trunks and what little soil filled the holes was wet with water from someone—local tenants, probably—reaching out to make something, even something bound to die, grow. Emma's stand was dark and locked, as was her coffee-shop home. Perhaps I intended to wait for her, perhaps not. I don't know anymore. Years make this part fuzzy, despite the clarity of the earlier events. I do know I sat on the bench by her kiosk. I sat and stared at the ground, sidewalk cracks, and parrot droppings. In the road, pedestrians with purpose navigated through tourists with none. Someone sat beside me. Long moments passed—or didn't, I didn't care—before I allowed myself to wonder why he stared. I turned and saw my face, the face I have now, old, lined, filled with the effort I'd avoided all my life, and I blinked only once to be sure the face was real.

Older than I imagined possible, he had outpaced Seventy by some years. His face cracked, teeth showed me a smile I hadn't seen much of lately, if ever.

"You'll be looking for a raft, then." Pleasant voice, not as old as I thought it might be, light in the eyes; maybe life covered that face, not years.

I nodded. "Yeah. I have no idea where—"

"Up on top of the library."

I turned and glanced over at the old gray building. "Okay, thanks." Gratitude rose in me until I realized he must have hidden it from me.

"I knew you'd be fine." He stretched out his legs, flexed until something popped. "You'd be fine and she would live." At his wrist, a little westward-headed parrot echoed my own. I was tired and couldn't figure why something in this felt like swallowing a glass shard.

I ran a hand over my head, forgetting that my hair was gone, that cuts decorated my scalp. I caught one and winced

at the pain. He mirrored me, ran his hand over his own bar-
ren scalp—bare from age, not from shearing. "Your haircut
tells me you got my message."

The brown bag. I nodded. "How'd you get in there?"

"That's been my room for a long time. I know that hotel
like you know that hotel. Not hard getting in and out. You
know that." I did. I wondered if I really could make it my
home as he had.

I stood. "Will you be okay?"

He laughed. "Have been for a long time."

I looked up at the sky just as the sun slipped behind a cloud,
slipped back out. "When do I go?"

"I don't need to tell you that, do I?"

"No."

He watched me a moment. "You'll be fine, you know. Get a
job. Meet people. You will meet people."

I nodded. "What about the convention rules? You've just
told me my future."

"Fuck the rules."

Sun fell on his face. He seemed brighter than the light.

"So how can I destroy the raft?"

"When you go back, arrive over the river. You'll have to
swim like hell, but that thing sinks like a rock." This all made
such lovely sense. What was it that cut inside my head?

Behind us an awkward voice muttered, "Rock, rock." A
group of parrots eyed us with curiosity.

He pulled a bag of sunflower seeds from his pocket and
began to throw them one at a time to the birds, who talked
to one another about the heat, about the hazards of driving,
about things that mattered only if the world worked.

My feet burned to move, and I said, "I'll be going, then."

"Yes. You should. Good luck."

Before I thought it, I said, "Did I just . . . fail?"

He lowered his chin to his chest and took a deep breath. "I don't know."

I raised a hand in a good-bye he didn't acknowledge. The library sat beyond the park's yard. I was going to go there, do as he suggested. As he'd made sure I would know.

I stayed where I was. "You had no right."

Seeds fell from his now-still hand. "What?"

"You kept me there, when I might just have left it all behind. If I'd left—"

"If you'd left, there's no guarantee she would have lived."

"You had no right."

His hand shook, and I recognized in his face the shock of what I'd just done. He'd remembered the moment differently. I'd untethered from even him. I left him to feed his muttering birds.

I headed for the library, wondered if Emily would be inside to let me in, to let me climb to the roof, or if I'd have to break in. I would have liked to say good-bye to her. As I approached the back of the building, I realized I was embracing ignorance. The old man had expected I would go to a moment when I could spend decades waiting for the party to arrive. Instead I could return to the point I would have been at had I lived my life chronologically. My return could reintroduce me to life in a way I hadn't lived, had feared. I thought of the clock at Grand Central and wondered if my life would end up leading me there to redesign it, or had that been an act of the man feeding birds in the park? I guessed I would find out.

I climbed the steps and began to hammer on the old doors, hoping Emily would answer, and wondering if I might recognize her as a young woman someday, if I returned to the library steps some half century earlier. Could I sit and wait and recognize her, call to her by name and introduce myself as a man she knew briefly, once? Or Emma? Or Phil?

I knocked, knowing that I would find a place weighed in my favor just by there being one person willing to help me more than I'd ever been willing to help myself. I had no idea what was on the horizon. The future vibrated with uncertainty. I had failed. I had ignorance. I had hope.

ACKNOWLEDGMENTS

In no particular order, thank you to: All of my family, my parents, my brother by blood Matthew, Stephanie, Aidan, Sue; Janet and all of FinePrint; Bronwen, Juliet, Meredith and all of Soho Press; my brothers by ink Jeff and Dan, and everyone who takes the time to put up with me in any capacity. And to my readers: Any effort I put into this work falls short of the honor you bestow by reading it. Thank you.